“Y[illegible] in here.”

“I am.”

“Why?”

“You’ll run away,” Jack said.

“I won’t. I told you that I’d live up to my father’s agreement. Dammit, I’m going to marry John! What more do you want?”

Even his hourly reminder that Laura Lee belonged to John failed to curtail Jack’s lustful thoughts. “You’re lucky you’re going to marry John. With me, you’d be the mother of half-a-dozen children. I’d take you to bed morning, noon and night.”

Laura Lee lifted her foot and came down hard with her heel on Jack’s instep. “Scoundrel!”

She didn’t know the reason behind the peculiar sensations he caused low in her belly, but she knew intuitively that she wasn’t the only one who’d felt them.

Finally, she worked up the courage to ask, “What’s happening between you and me?”

“Nothing.” he said in a strangled voice. “You’re going to be my sister-in-law.”

Dear Reader,

Once again, let us take you on an unexpected journey into a past you might not have thought of exploring before. In *Tilly and the Tiger*, bestselling author Marianne Willman begins her tale in Jamaica, then follows her characters to the mysterious, ruin-filled jungles of the Yucatán. Adventure and danger go hand in hand with love as dashing Tiger Flynn courts the only woman fit to be his match. For Matilda "Tilly" Templeton, Tiger is a riddle, but one she can't help falling in love with, so she's more than happy to find out that her dangerous, enigmatic tiger *can* be tamed.

Jo Ann Algermissen has developed a strong following as a writer of contemporary romances. Now, in *Golden Bird*, she works her storytelling magic on the past, as well. This is a down-to-earth story of a Louisiana belle who finds love—and laughter—in the arms of a rugged Texas rancher. You won't want to miss a moment of their delightful tale.

Next month, the excitement continues with new books by Kristin James and Erin Yorke, and there's more to come after that. Pick up a Harlequin Historical—the past has never been so romantic.

Yours,
Leslie Wainger
Senior Editor and Editorial Coordinator

Harlequin Books

TORONTO • NEW YORK • LONDON
AMSTERDAM • PARIS • SYDNEY • HAMBURG
STOCKHOLM • ATHENS • TOKYO • MILAN

Harlequin Historical first edition October 1990

ISBN 0-373-28656-2

Printed in the U.S.A.

JO ANN ALGERMISSEN

is the author of numerous contemporary romances that she has written under both her own name and a romanticized version of her maiden name, Anna Hudson. With *Golden Bird*, Jo Ann brings to her first historical the same energy and humor that have made her contemporaries so popular. Jo Ann lives near the Atlantic Ocean, where she spends hours daydreaming to her heart's content. She remembers that as a youngster, she always had the comment "daydreams in class" written on every report card. But she also follows the writer's creed: write what you know about. After twenty-five years of marriage, she feels she has experienced love—how it is, how it can be and how it ought to be.

Chapter One

Blytheville, Louisiana, 1867

As the minute hand of the clock above the door at the Blytheville Citizens Bank inched toward three o'clock, Laura Lee Shannon's eyes moved nervously from the door to the cash drawer to her drawstring purse. She wanted to reach through the ornate metal bars of the teller's cage and push the hour hand backward. Each hushed ticking sound of the clock was like a hammer striking, driving in the nails that would seal her fate. Hope shriveled in her heart with each passing sweep of the second hand.

In less than ten minutes she would be the sister of Blytheville's largest landholder, a bank robber or the banker's mistress.

Come on, Tad, she silently chanted, come on. Get the money order at the telegraph station and bring it here. We'll go to the tax collector's office together. Come on, Tad!

Sheets of wind-driven rain splattered on the window-panes, distorting Laura Lee's view. Lightning cracked, casting an eerie light on the deserted street. It had been raining for two weeks solid.

"'Tain't fit for man nor beast out there," Bill Carpenter commented as he tallied up a column of figures in his ledger. He shut the leatherbound book, removed a cashbox from a drawer and placed one on top of the other. "Worst spring storms I've seen since the beginning of the war. Telegraph lines still down?"

Laura Lee nodded. "They were at noon. Tad's waiting there, just in case they've been fixed."

Nothing, she silently fumed, would fix the breached contract between the Shannon and Wynthrop families if the payment didn't arrive!

She'd done her best to uphold her father's prewar agreement to manage both the Shannon and Wynthrop plantations while Jacob Wynthrop and his two sons took a work detail to Texas, bought land and grew crops to help supply the Confederacy. Last year, when she'd received the letter informing her that Jacob had died of yellow fever, just as her own mother had, John Wynthrop had offered to shoulder the tax burden on both plantations.

In return, he'd politely requested her hand in marriage, pointing out that the Wynthrop-Shannon agreement had listed such a marriage as one of its requirements. Reluctantly she'd agreed, but she'd stipulated that Blythewood Plantation had to be fully recovered and ready for Tad to manage. She figured whatever mild affection John felt for her would dwindle into nothingness over the space of several years. The vague memories she had of John were being obliterated by the ticking of the bank's clock.

"Damned shame, that's what it is," Bill muttered under his breath, so as not to be heard by Luke Reynolds, the bank's owner. He swiped at his bushy mustache with his forefinger, then pushed his wire-framed glasses up on the bridge of his nose. Automatically his hand trailed over the empty sleeve where his left arm should have been. Concern overlaid his voice as he whispered, "When Betsy Mae Reynolds was here telling here telling her husband about the folks who'd refused her invitation to his fancy birthday party tonight, I overheard Reynolds tell Betsy Mae that nobody would dare to slight her socially once she's the new mistress of Blythewood. He promised her she'd be the town's leading lady."

It would take more than Blythewood to make Betsy Mae a lady, Laura Lee thought uncharitably. Luke Reynolds's wife had traded her good looks, her flirty smiles and God only knew what else to get her greedy hands on his money. As the daughter of an overseer, Betsy Mae knew she couldn't climb the social ladder, so she'd tried to buy it.

To Laura Lee's way of thinking, Betsy Mae had sold her soul to a direct descendant of the devil. Luke Reynolds wasn't content with having a gorgeous wife. His heavy-lidded eyes followed Laura Lee's every move. He never lost an opportunity to innocently brush up against her. His double entendres had Laura Lee's fingers itching to slap his face. Shame and humiliation were the price Betsy Mae had paid for each rung she'd attained on the social ladder.

"He watches you when you aren't looking," Bill added. "Everybody knows about the pact the Wynthrop and the Shannon families made before the war—but maybe you should've set your bonnet for Reynolds. He's here. He'd have married you."

"I'd eat dirt first!"

"Shh!"

"Copperheads don't have ears," Laura Lee said disdainfully, though wisely she kept her voice down. Luke Reynolds could have been the last available man south of the Mason-Dixon line and she would still have chosen to die a spinster rather than marry him. Like other Rebels, she considered the Southerners who'd helped the Yanks win the war lower than a snake's belly, even more treacherous than the copperheads they were named for.

"He hears everything." To prove his point, Bill jingled two coins in his pocket.

A voice boomed from the back office. "Two minutes till closing. Mr. Carpenter, I'll check your daily records now."

Bill's shaggy eyebrow raised a notch, silently making his point.

Laura Lee chewed nervously on her lower lip. The minute hand had reached its zenith. Bill was inside Luke's office before she reached for her purse. The feel of hard metal beneath the flimsy fabric comforted her. She knew she could shoot a snake; she wondered if she could drill a hole in the two-legged variety of copperhead.

Laura Lee dreaded the thought of having to ask Luke for a loan. She knew what he'd really want for collateral, and it was the last thing she'd be willing to forfeit—her honor. She'd shoot the snake before she'd stoop to crawling under a rock with him.

She rubbed the short barrel of the pistol in her purse to bolster her courage. What she actually had planned for Luke was worse than a quick bullet through the heart. She was going to hit him hard where it hurt the most, right smack-dab in his pride. Just as he had hit every other Southerner.

Like McKenzie's Raiders, she'd hit and run.

Unable to stand still any longer, she poked one hand through the drawstrings of her purse and walked to the front door. Rain was pouring in a steady stream off the shingle roof and into the muddy street. A cloud of vapor condensed on the windowpane beneath her nose. Her blue eyes widened when she spotted Tad across the street, running pell-mell down the board sidewalk. Wind and water plastered his jacket against his ten-year-old body. With a flying leap, he jumped over the miniature stream that twisted along the edge of the street. Mississippi gumbo sucked at his boots as he pumped his legs, lifting his knees waist-high.

Too impatient to wait, Laura Lee slipped quietly out the door. Her brother saw her and cupped his hands around his mouth, yelling, "The lines are still down!"

Laura Lee motioned for him to keep coming. She had little choice left. One way or another, by fair means or foul, she had to get money to the tax office. She'd need Tad's help.

"Damn you, Jacob Bradford Wynthrop," she muttered. "Your sons owed us that money!"

She watched as her younger brother hopped, skipped and jumped until he reached the porch where she stood. His brown woolen cap sat askew on a mop of curly light blond ringlets. Fist clenched, he stomped twice to knock the mud from his boots.

Were the droplets of moisture running down his cheeks rain or tears? Laura Lee wondered. She heard him sniffle, saw him swipe the backs of his hands over his eyes. Laura Lee's heart swelled in her chest, aching for Tad.

She hated to implicate Tad in what she was being forced to do, but she couldn't accomplish the deed by herself.

"What are we gonna do?" Tad asked.

"I'll get the money," Laura Lee assured him, wrapping her arm around his shoulder and giving him a sisterly squeeze. "Have I ever let you down?"

Tad buried his nose in the folds of her skirt and hugged her waist. She could feel his fingers wadding the cotton fabric of her skirt. His voice cracked with emotion as he asked, "You gonna rob the bank?"

"No!" Laura Lee said promptly. She struggled to make a reassuring laugh, but fear and tension trapped the sound of mirth in her throat. "I'll just borrow the money from Mr. Reynolds. Remember how father used to float down to New Orleans and see the banker when he needed to borrow money?"

"Yeah, but the bankers father knew went busted during the war!"

She bent her knees, crouching until their blue eyes met. His were older than hers had been at the same age. She straightened his cap, wishing that their money problems could be set to rights as easily.

"Don't worry, sweetheart. I'll take care of the money. I have something very, very special that I want you to do. Remember my telling you that it's Mr. Reynolds's birthday today?"

Tad nodded.

"He's going to be in a generous frame of mind when he sees the cake I baked last night."

"You baked that cake for him?" Tad squinted at her skeptically. "Do I get to come to the party?"

Unable to look her brother in the eye and give voice to a lie, she nodded. Glancing over her shoulder to make certain no one could hear her, she cupped her hand over Tad's ear and whispered instructions to him.

"Gee whillikers, Laura Lee." Tad stepped back and put his hands on his hips. His cap slipped to the back of his head as he watched his sister straighten. "Do I have to go there? Betsy Mae always pinches my cheek and pats me on the head like I'm a pet squirrel."

Laura Lee hated implicating her brother, but she couldn't be in two places at once. "Won't you do that for me? Please? Then come right back here to get the money. Okay, sweetheart?"

"I don't wanna go, but I guess I'll have to," he said reluctantly.

Laura Lee tweaked the tip of his pug nose. It never failed to bring a smile to his lips. "How'd you like to ride out to Blythewood later this afternoon?"

"Really? In the rain? You mean it?" The automatic smile she'd coaxed from him turned into one of genuine delight. "Oh, gosh, Laura Lee, you're the bestest sister in the whole wide world!"

Tad was about to bestow another enthusiastic embrace on her when the bank door opened and Bill Carpenter urgently motioned for her to get back inside. Laura Lee grinned, knowing Tad thought he was too old to be seen hugging his sister, and made a shooing motion with her hands.

"He's waiting for you in his office," Bill said as he awkwardly pulled his coat collar high on his neck while at the same time holding his broad-brimmed hat with his one hand. "The wires still down?"

"Yeah. Nothing from Texas arrived."

Bill pulled the brim of his hat low on his forehead to hide the red tide of frustration that stained his cheeks. She heard his feet shuffle on the wooden boards. She knew that he was silently castigating himself. Like thousands of other war heroes who'd fought for the Cause and returned home maimed, Bill felt dispirited, frustrated, damned helpless. He couldn't protect his own womenfolk, much less defend her. She touched three fingers to his tightly compressed lips and shook her head.

"Blythewood belongs to the Shannon family," she said. Summoning up a brave front to hide her anxiety, she smiled and winked.

Bill took her hand and brushed his mustache over the back of her fingers in a salute. "Miss Shannon, if courage could be tallied up in the bank's ledger book, you'd be a rich young lady."

"Not courage," Laura Lee told him with a cocky grin. "Just plain ol' ornery cussedness."

A small smile tilted the corner of Bill's mouth as he squared his shoulders, reopened the door and doffed his hat. "Give 'em sweet hell, lady."

Head held high, Laura Lee sashayed into the bank as though she were its main depositor. Luke Reynolds was exactly where she'd expected him to be—leaning against the doorjamb of his office, with one leg crossed over the other at the ankle, one thumb hooked arrogantly in the watch pocket of his satin brocade vest. Some of the townswomen thought he was handsome, but Laura Lee couldn't see his dark good looks through the red haze of antagonism she felt toward him.

"Quittin' early to celebrate my birthday, Miss Laura Lee?" he asked, mocking her soft Louisiana accent and pointing to the purse dangling from her wrist.

Be as sweet and sugary as thick molasses syrup, she reminded herself, smiling. She was close enough that she could see the dark pupils of his eyes widen when she said, "No, sir. I have a business arrangement to discuss with you."

His low, husky chuckle made the hairs rise on the nape of her neck. Goose bumps peppered her forearms, but she wouldn't give Luke the satisfaction of seeing her chafe her wrists.

"The high-and-mighty Laura Lee Shannon going to beg for a loan?"

She ignored the remark, moving behind the counter to gather her ledger and cashbox. He wasn't the only person in the bank who could tease and torment. The weight of the pistol hidden in her purse dragged against her leg.

His brown eyes simmered, lingering on her lips, lowering to the hand-crocheted lace edging the collar of her dress before dropping down the tiny buttons, one by one. His large hands reached lazily toward her. "I'll take those."

She outflanked his open arms by stepping sideways through the door, letting the hem of her dress just brush the toes of his polished boots. She was close enough to hear him inhale. She braced herself for the feel of his fingers biting into her shoulders to detain her.

"I'm a patient man, Miss Laura Lee. Very patient. Wouldn't you say I've waited a long time to have you come to me for a favor?"

She plunked the book and the box on his desk, grinding her back molars to keep from telling him what a despicable louse he was. He underestimated her if he thought she was going to beg. She'd die first.

Spinning on one foot, she fluttered her long eyelashes to conceal her hatred and replied, "Why, Mr. Reynolds..."

"Luke."

"Ah, yes... Luke." Calling him by his first name was a minor concession, she decided. She had to at least give the appearance of having had a change of heart.

Laughing aloud, he closed the gap between them, stopping short just before the lapels of his coat touched the front of her dress. "What happened, Laura Lee?" he prompted softly. "Did your fiancé in Texas forget you?"

"Fiancé?" she repeated, somewhat surprised that he knew of the marriage plans. Like the other carpetbaggers, Luke was a relative newcomer to Blytheville. She wondered how he'd gotten wind of the Wynthrop-Shannon agreement.

"Um-hmm." His head dipped to within scant inches of the long, silky curls that framed her heart-shaped face. "Your hair smells of lavender soap."

She started to edge away, but he rolled a lock of her hair around his finger.

"People who need money are eager to talk, to share family secrets. I know everything that goes on in this town," he said. His thumb centered under the slight cleft in her chin, lifting it. "I'm most anxious to learn your secrets."

Laura Lee didn't realize that she'd been holding her breath until black specks started to float in front of her eyes. Blood pounded in her ears. Damn his hide!

His knowledge of her private business knocked her seductive routine off balance. She'd practiced flaunting herself and taunting him in front of the beveled glass mirror in her bedroom. Glib phrases designed to promise everything while giving nothing were lodged in her throat, trapping her breath in her lungs. Having Luke Reynolds's hands on her body petrified her. She'd miscalculated her strengths.

Her lips yielded under the light pressure of his thumb. Air hissed between her teeth, over the back of his hand, stirring the short, dark hairs. She stood frozen as his mouth lowered, closer and closer.

She hiccuped. Loudly.

He paused. His face stayed suspended over hers momentarily, then continued its descent.

She hiccuped again. Louder this time. Clamping one hand over her mouth, she mumbled, "Excuse me."

Her carefully laid plan was rapidly going awry. One more blasted hiccup and he'd be tossing her out the front door on her ears. She struggled valiantly to recover her composure, not realizing that he'd circled his desk and seated himself until she heard his leather chair squeak.

"Will you loan me the money?" she blurted out.

Luke propped his feet up on his desk, folded his hands behind his head and grinned. "I doubt it."

He was baiting her and she knew it. Her hatred of him intensified. He held the whip, and he was going to make her dance to his tune. Slowly she inched the drawstring of her purse between her fingers.

"You're no gentleman, Luke Reynolds."

"And you're no lady, Miss Laura Lee, despite your hoity-toity airs." Luke lifted the lid on his humidor and extracted a cigar. "You don't mind if I smoke, do you?"

"And if I did?"

"Honey, one of the first lessons you're going to have to learn if you're going to get greenbacks from a man is to put his pleasure before your own." He opened his desk drawer, pulled out a stack of money and a box of matches and tossed them on the desktop. "Light my cigar."

It would have given Laura Lee the greatest of pleasure to whip her gun out of her purse, blow the end off his cigar, grab the money and run. But instead of reacting impulsively to his command, she lazily walked around the edge of the desk, picked up the box and withdrew a wooden match. She raked her thumbnail over the red tip the way her father always had. Instantly the match flamed.

As she looked down her nose at Luke, she realized how smart she'd been not to brandish her weapon. The hand she'd thought was in his lap was actually in the second drawer of the desk. He must have expected her to do something rash.

"Should I sing 'Happy Birthday to You'?"

One dark eyebrow rose as he licked the tip of his cigar, eyed Laura Lee's breasts and countered, "Should I make a wish?"

She made one. She wished she could drop the flaming match on the crotch of his pants. She'd be doing every woman in Blytheville a favor.

"Yes. But don't tell," she said coyly, "or it won't come true."

Luke blew out the match without lighting his cigar. He rose lithely, picked the money up off his desk and dangled it between his fingers. "Boys make wishes. Men buy what they want. I want to own you."

He deftly grasped her wrist and turned her hand palm upward. He slapped two bundles of twenty-dollar bills in her hand.

"Isn't that illegal since Lincoln's emancipation proclamation?" she asked dryly. "I thought that was why you helped the Union, to end slavery."

"I helped myself." He grinned in that cocksure fashion of his, slowly circling Laura Lee, as though he were appraising her. "You've got a sassy mouth, Laura Lee, but you'll learn to curb your tongue. Do you know why?"

Clutching the money she so desperately needed, she shook her head mutely. She didn't want to antagonize him further. Only the hope that he'd pay for each insult he spoke kept her from giving him the sharp side of her tongue. She'd have her revenge later.

"Because tonight you're going to convince the whole town that you've fallen madly in love with me. At the surprise birthday party Betsy Mae is having in my honor you're going to fawn all over me. Of course, for Betsy Mae's sake, I'll pretend to spurn your affections."

Laura Lee realized that if she appeared to agree too easily it would arouse Luke's suspicions. He had expected her pride to keep her from begging for money; he would also expect her to plead for her honor. Demanding that she declare herself openly was his way of publicly humiliating her.

Lowering her eyes, she whispered, a hint of defiance in her voice, "And if I don't?"

"Anyone who double-crosses Luke Reynolds doesn't live long enough to spend the money or brag about it. I get what I pay for, my dear."

Oh, you'll be paid in full, Mr. Reynolds, she thought, worrying her lower lip with her teeth. She reached up and touched his face, pouting sadly, "You're *sooo* handsome, but you know I'd rather die than have everyone pointing their fingers at me and whispering behind my back. Couldn't we compromise?"

"I'm listening."

"Well, uh . . . couldn't you come to my place here in town?"

"And sneak up the back stairs?" He shook his head. "No. Betsy Mae never notices what I do, but I won't have the town laughing at me, thinking you have the upper hand in our affair."

"But . . . I'd be waiting for you . . . eagerly." His jaw hardened beneath her fingers. She gave a drawn-out sigh. "You could come to the front door, I suppose."

"This afternoon?"

Laura Lee nodded and bit the inside of her lip hard to get a convincing tear to slide down her cheek. She dabbed at her eyes and sniffed when the tear failed to appear.

"I'll take the money to the tax office. Then you can come to the house." Giving him a sad little smile, she turned, saying, "Happy birthday . . . Luke."

With as much grace as haste would allow, she gathered her cloak and her parasol from the peg on the back of the office door. The sound of Luke's laughter followed her as she hurried through the lobby and out the door.

Tad was waiting, hunkered down beside the entrance to the bank. "You got it!"

"Did you do what I told you to do?"

"Yeah. She's probably already at the house."

"Good boy. You take this to the tax collector's office, then run home fast as you can. Don't forget to get a receipt." A triumphant smile curved her Cupid's-bow lips.

Luke Reynolds could whistle the "Battle Hymn of the Republic" until he was blue in the face, but the tightfisted tax collector wouldn't refund the money. "Hurry!"

Laura Lee snapped open her parasol. A gust of wind whistled through the stretched fabric, threatening to jerk it from her slender hands. She gripped it tightly and shifted it until the spine rested on her shoulder, then turned in the direction opposite to that her brother had taken. She raised her skirts circumspectly to keep them from sweeping on the muddy boards, then lengthened her walk from ladylike steps to a long-legged stride.

Silently she congratulated herself on tricking Luke Reynolds into believing she was a simpering, brainless Southern belle who had to resort to the oldest profession to make her way in a man's world. She'd show him. No one degraded a Shannon without suffering the consequences.

Her mind was racing faster than her high-buttoned shoes, and her heart was pounding wildly. She focused her attention on what she planned to say to Betsy Mae. She wouldn't allow herself to think about anything but getting the money and getting revenge. A natural mathematician, she intuitively knew the consequences of combining an equal amount of positive and negative numbers: the sum total was zero. That was what she would personally end up with: nothing. But she'd saved Tad's birthright for him. Blythewood was safe for another year.

Laura Lee turned at Jackson Street. She darted agilely over the row of single planks placed end-to-end that started where the boardwalk ended. Narrow two-story town houses with deep verandas sat back from the oak-lined street. Automatically she turned at the sagging knee-high picket fence that edged the Shannon property. In a carefree time that now seemed long past, she would have ignored the fat raindrops dancing on her parasol and jumped back and forth over the whitewashed fence.

Her leather soles scraped against the worn steps as she took them two at a time. She'd become accustomed to the warped steps, the cracked paint on the windows and the door, the make-do repairs to the roof. Basic needs took priority. She had to juggle her household budget nimbly just to meet them. Many of the other once-proud owners of neighboring sugar and indigo plantations had made ends meet by selling their second homes, but she had had to keep two places. The ten-mile ride from Blytheville to Blythewood along the river road was too much to make every day, even when the weather was agreeable.

Slightly breathless, Laura Lee paused on the porch, setting her open parasol next to the railing. Betsy Mae had evidently taken the liberty of waltzing right in, for the door was partially open and tracks of mud disappeared into the front hall. Justifiably indignant, Laura Lee inhaled deeply, puffing out her chest. The woman had the social graces of an alley cat!

"Laura Lee? Is that you?" The high-pitched, girlish giggle punctuating the questions grated on Laura Lee's tense nerves. Her guest had made herself at home on the blue velvet settee in the parlor. "Land sakes, girl, I nearly popped my corset strings when your sweet little brother delivered your message. Imagine! You baking a cake in honor of my husband! I just *love* surprises."

Laura Lee deposited her cloak in the curved banister that led upstairs. She pasted a congenial smile on her face. "It's the least I could do to show my appreciation. Would you mind joining me in the kitchen for a cup of tea?"

"I thought—" Betsy Mae's eyes swept around the parlor and landed on the brass servant's bell. Her brow puckered in disappointment. "Oh, well, I guess it would spoil the surprise if I was sitting here when Luke arrived. We won't be able to stay long, anyway. Everybody who's anybody is coming to our house shortly. Luke expects you to come."

Nodding, Laura Lee momentarily viewed the room through her guest's eyes. The furnishings were neat but worn. The lace drapes her mother had imported from France had yellowed with age and neglect. Sunlight had faded the handmade carpet from its original rich royal blue to various mottled hues. Her father had emptied the sideboard of the family silver and donated it to support the Cause. Only the precious china serving bowls that her mother had painted, which were displayed in a fruitwood cabinet, retained their true color.

Genteel poverty. God, she hated how Betsy Mae lifted her nose and sniffed, as though the odor of mildew permeated the air. It didn't, but there was no longer the fragrance of beeswax and lemon oil lavishly applied by servants.

"I can't wait for you to see how the Tarrington place sparkles," Betsy Mae said enthusiastically, referring to her house. The carpetbaggers could buy the old family homes, but the properties retained the names of their original owners. She gestured toward the dining room as they passed by. "I bought a gilded crystal chandelier for the dining room. And I had gold braid sewn on the cuffs of the servant's uniforms. It's just beautiful."

Laura Lee rolled her tongue in her cheek as she imagined how Betsy Mae's glittering additions must clash with the Tarrington's tasteful furnishings. "It's been ages since I've been there," she said.

"You wouldn't recognize it. Luke says everything looks as shiny as newly minted pennies." Betsy Mae twirled around and clapped her hands together when she saw the flattish cake Laura Lee had prepared. A thick candle planted in the cake's center listed to one side. It compared unfavorably to the towering confection her own cook had prepared. Luke would compare the two houses and the two cakes, and this time he wouldn't tell her to copy Miss Blythewood Manor's style and grace.

Gloating inwardly, she prattled on. "I can't wait till Luke gets here. What a...nice...little cake. You must have baked it yourself. I know how awful it is to have to do without the finest ingredients. Money does make a difference, doesn't it? I just hated being poor."

A pound of rat poison was the only missing ingredient in the cake, Laura Lee mused, ducking her head to conceal the animosity that she knew must be gleaming in her eyes. "There are worse things than being poor," she retorted, unable to control her tongue completely. Her pockets might be empty, but her pride was still intact.

Betsy Mae fanned her long lashes faster than a hummingbird's wings and giggled. "I can't think of any."

You will, Laura Lee thought, smarting from Betsy Mae's stinging remarks, and from her fake sympathy. She lit the solitary candle. "When I shout 'Surprise,' you carry the cake into the parlor and sing 'Happy Birthday.'"

"Oh, I hear him coming up the steps." Excited, Betsy Mae flapped her hands and bounced on her toes as she pushed Laura Lee toward the kitchen door, telling her, "Don't dawdle. He expects a servant to have the door open before his hand touches the doorknob."

"You stay here," Laura Lee said, closing the kitchen door.

She schooled her trembling lips into a charming smile. Her stomach twisted, but she summoned up all her reserves of poise and good breeding. She needed them if she was to get through the next few minutes.

When she flung open the door, her blue eyes went round with surprise, her face drained of color except for twin flags of embarrassment high on her cheeks and her chin dropped. Luke Reynolds wasn't a man who wasted time. He stood there with his brocade vest unbuttoned, clutching his silk tie in one hand and tugging at the buttons on his shirt.

It was a good thing she hadn't made him wait at the door, Laura Lee thought. Ten seconds longer and he'd have been standing there in his birthday suit!

Luke's cocky grin inverted into a scowl. "You're dressed."

Observant, Laura Lee thought, woodenly gesturing for him to come inside. She didn't trust her voice or her tongue. Did he think she was so eager to keep her end of the bargain that she'd come to the door undressed?

"We can't dally. I'm expected at home." He shrugged out of his coat and concentrated on ridding himself of his shirt. "Damned starched shirts," he muttered under his breath.

Backing away from him, sneaking a glance over her shoulder to make certain the kitchen door was still closed, Laura Lee stammered in a hushed voice, "I c-c-can't undress here!"

"Why not? You get a loan from some other man, too? You expecting more company?" He chuckled at his little joke, then added, "I'll buy their notes."

Laura Lee swallowed hard to keep from disgracing herself. He'd peeled off his shirt and tossed it on the Chippendale chair her father had had shipped from up north by special order. Automatically her arm stiffened between them, and her hand raised. This wasn't what she'd planned!

Her idea of letting Betsy Mae catch him in a compromising situation didn't extend to her finding him buck naked in the front hallway. She'd thought Luke would rush upstairs, undress and climb into her bed while she made an excuse to dally downstairs for a moment. She'd planned on sending Betsy Mae upstairs while she escaped out the front door!

The muscles in his arm bulged as his fingers worked beneath his fly. From beneath his hooded eyes he sent an unmistakable message: Your clothes are next.

She wouldn't be able to stop him from ripping her clothes off. He was stronger, and he was determined to collect the first payment on her loan. Panic clamored in her veins.

Her mouth opened wide, her throat worked, she bellowed, *"Surprise!"*

Chapter Two

Luke's pants hit the floor just as Betsy Mae arrived, heralded by the first notes of "Happy Birthday to You." When she saw her husband's state of undress, the chirping notes were strangled by an audible gasp of outrage.

Run, Laura Lee thought desperately. But where? Her eyes searched in vain for an escape route. Luke was blocking the front door, and Betsy Mae stood between her and the back door.

Laura Lee hiked her skirt above her knees and made a wild dash for the staircase. She felt the air whistle by her ear as Luke grabbed for her, but he was hobbled by his britches, which were down around his ankles. He missed her arm, tripped and fell face first on the hardwood floor.

His grunt of pain mingled with the squeals of rage that punctuated the string of foul names his wife was hurling at him. "You lousy bastard! You have the nerve... to call me... a slut... you son of a bitch! Cad! Worm!"

With each profanity she banged him on the head with the bottom of the cake pan. The pitiful cake Laura Lee had baked exploded. Every time she whacked him, the chunks of cake flew higher into the air, until crumbs covered them both like yellow snowflakes. Dodging blows, scrambling to get to his feet, shouting obscenities of his own, Luke vainly tried to protect his head and grab his irate wife's plummeting arms.

Laura Lee hesitated at the top of the stairs. She would have burst out laughing at Luke's plight if she hadn't been so damned scared.

Revenge! God, it was sweet! But she knew that its sweet flavor would sour once Luke managed to get control of his wife and pulled up his pants.

"Psssst! Hey, sis!" Tad was crouched on the landing with his head poked between two banisters. His eyes were dancing merrily. "Some surprise party!"

Laura Lee grabbed Tad by the collar of his jacket, hauled him to his feet and ran down the hall toward the back of the house, towing him behind her. "We've got to get out of here!"

Tad's legs, which weren't hampered by a long skirt, were faster than his sister's. He raced into his bedroom and hiked the window open. "I figured you were in some kinda trouble when you gave me the money," he panted. "I saddled up Foxfire. Can you make it down the oak tree while I get Captain Bligh?"

"No, Tad! We've got to get out of here! You can sneak back into town tomorrow and get the parrot."

Tad ducked, and snatched his sleeve from her hand. Then he shot her a mutinous look and dashed from the room.

"Go! Hurry!" Over the sound of her labored breathing and Tad's footsteps she could still hear the commotion going on downstairs. She'd had no idea Betsy Mae had such a violent temper.

She stuck her head through the open window and gulped. The raindrops pelting the side of her face drew her attention to the hazardous, slippery trek she'd be making down the tree trunk. She'd never make it in a dress.

Quick as a flash of lightning, she stripped down to her chemise and her pantaloons. She yanked one of Tad's shirts and a pair of his trousers out of his dresser drawer and held them up to her waist. She'd almost stopped growing at his age. Maybe she could squeeze into them. Anything was better than a dress.

Hopping from one foot to the other, she tried to pull them on over her pantaloons but failed. The wide bands of cotton lace bunched in the crotch midway up her thighs. Tad might return at any moment, so modesty kept her from untying the drawstring of her pantaloons. She dropped the trousers. She recklessly ripped off the handstitched layers, one row after another, until she saw her knees. Then she jerked the britches over her hips.

Tad said not a word when he saw what she'd done. He reached behind the door and removed his extra jacket from the peg. She couldn't run back downstairs to get her cloak.

Captain Bligh wasn't as polite. A piercing wolf whistle followed by a raucous squawk joined the tumult coming from below. "Pretty girl! Pretty girl!"

"Hush, Captain," Tad said. The parrot's wicked vocabulary was an unending source of delight to him, but he didn't have time to mess with him now. He quickly wrapped a shirt around his cage. "No naughty comments!"

"Bad bird! Bad bird!" came from beneath the cover.

Laura Lee sucked in her stomach unnecessarily and buttoned Tad's britches at her waist. A sixteen-inch waist and tiny feet were the trademark of a Southern lady; Laura Lee had both.

"They've stopped screaming," she said, cocking her head to one side. "Oh, Lord, he's going to come after us. We've got to get out of here . . . out of Blytheville!"

Tad led the way; she followed, mimicking his every move. For the life of her, Laura Lee wouldn't be able to explain to anyone how she managed to clamber down the limbs and trunk of the tree without landing on the gnarled roots like a sack of potatoes. The scratches and scrapes on her hands, forearms and shins would attest to her clumsiness. What seemed like hours of strenuous torture was actually less than two minutes.

Her feet on solid ground, Laura Lee mumbled a prayer of thanksgiving as she fled with Tad to the dilapidated stable at the rear of the property.

Where are they? she wondered frantically, glancing over her shoulder. She fully expected to see Luke lunge into the barn at any moment, spittle frothing from his mouth, crazy with anger. She had doubted the sincerity of the threat he'd made at the bank, but after the abuse he'd suffered from his loving wife he would want to strangle her with his bare hands.

"Stop shaking, sis! Put your foot in the stirrup, grab hold of the saddle horn and swing up there."

Laura Lee was oblivious of her chattering teeth, of the uncontrollable tremors coursing through her body. Her knees weren't cooperating, and neither were her trembling hands. Mindlessly she obeyed her young brother.

Foxfire sensed her fear and shifted beneath her weight, but she clung tightly to the saddle horn until she was hunched upright in the saddle. The fingers of her right hand curled around the reins that Tad thrust at her along with the bird cage.

"Hurry, Tad!"

Tad jumped from the railing onto Foxfire's rump. He circled his sister's waist with his arms, swung his boots straight out from the sides of his horse, then clamped them together with all his might. Foxfire was unaccustomed to being expected to do more than amble along, so this sudden demand startled him. Still, like the old cavalry horse he was, he took the bit between his teeth, lowered his ears and charged from the barn.

"Whoooeee!" Tad's Rebel yell split the air. His arms squeezed tighter, and he hung on for dear life.

"Damn you to hell!" Luke shouted from the front porch. "I'll get you for this!"

The sound of his voice snapped Laura out of the paralyzing fear that had gripped her. They weren't free yet. Luke was running toward the open gate at the end of the path leading from the stable to the road.

"He's blocking the gate!" Tad squealed. "He'll cut us off before we reach the road!"

Luke waved his arms; his fists were clenched. "Whoa, horse! Whoa, you swaybacked son of a bitch!"

"Cutthroat! Stick 'em up, mister! The ship is sinking!" Captain Bligh squawked, batting his clipped wings against his cage as he fell off his perch.

"Hang on, Tad," Laura Lee screamed. She felt his young arms tighten fractionally.

She jerked the leather reins to the right, and Foxfire swerved toward the pocket fence. He lost his footing momentarily in the slippery mud but regained his balance.

"Tad, we're going over—"

They landed safely on the other side of the fence before she finished issuing her warning to her brother.

"Whoooeee!" both Shannons chorused as they galloped down the river road in the direction of Blythewood.

"Take a good look, Betsy Mae," Luke said, his eyes firing blank rounds at the backs of the bobbing figures on the horse. "There goes a woman in trouble. Big trouble. She'll wish she'd never made a fool of Luke Reynolds!"

* * *

A couple of miles from the plantation, Laura Lee slowed Foxfire to a slow walk. Her pleasure at having triumphed over Luke, Betsy Mae and the tax collector had ebbed. She silently mulled over the consequences of her actions as Tad clung sleepily to her.

Up until the very last minute she'd counted on the Wynthrop family helping her. Jacob B. Wynthrop and his two sons had broken the pact between the two families. Because of that, she'd known that staying in town or living at Blythewood would be impossible.

And now she'd broken the law.

There was no doubt in her mind that Luke Reynolds would accuse her of having robbed his bank. She hadn't signed an IOU, and she'd had a gun in her purse. He had probably been as aware of her gun as she had of his.

"I'll pay every penny back," she vowed, uncertain exactly how she'd accomplish that feat.

For some unknown reason, her single source of income had abruptly ended. The Wynthrops owed her, but collecting from them was another matter. They were in Texas; she was here in Louisiana. It had never occurred to her father that there would be a problem. He had made a gentleman's agreement with a friend.

"Friends! Hmph!" she snorted. "Gentleman's agreement—double hmph!"

She'd done her best to keep her father's word of honor. No one in his right mind could blame her for the damned Yankees burning down the mansion at Heavenly Acres. She'd tried to stop them, but they'd been like a swarm of blue locusts with flaming tongues. They'd destroyed the house first, then burned the fields, where sparse crops had been planted and finally the barns, where she'd stored their meager food supplies. To this day she bore the scars of that night on her soul.

Laura Lee rubbed her fists into her eyes to keep the memories from eating away at her. Salty tears seeped past her knuckles and spilled on the leather reins.

"Stop it," she told herself. "You survived. Their land survived. Stones and mortar can be replaced. If the Wynthrops cared as much as you did, they'd have come back right after the war ended."

They don't care, she thought. She cared; Tad cared. And Brandy, her cousin, who had joined them at Blythewood after the fall of Atlanta . . . she cared, too. They were the only people on God's green earth who gave a damn about the Shannon land or the Wynthrop land.

And now, she moaned silently, you've exiled yourself from the land and the people you love. You sure as hell can't stick around hoping Luke will forgive you. And you can't help anyone, yourself included, from behind prison bars.

Running was the only answer.

"Did you say something, sis?" Tad asked in a sleepy voice.

"Just thinking out loud."

Tad yawned. "Guess I fell asleep, huh?"

"I guess."

"Want me to hang on to Captain Bligh's cage?"

"He isn't fussing or cussing. We'd better leave well enough alone."

"Mmm . . . 'kay." Tad rubbed his cheek affectionately in the hollow between her shoulder blades. "Sis."

"Ummm?"

"What are we gonna do? Are we gonna hide out at Blythewood?"

She shook her head. "Don't worry, Tad. Mr. Reynolds doesn't know you helped me. He won't be after you."

"He was mighty mad." His face puckered into a childish frown. "He'll be coming after you, won't he?"

"That's a risk I had to take."

"He'll be as mad as when he caught me splattin' mud balls up against the side of the bank, won't he?"

"Sort of." Only worse, she added silently.

"He made me wash 'em off. What's he gonna make you do?"

"I'm not going to stick around long enough to find out," she replied evasively.

"We're leaving Blythewood?"

Laura Lee heard the catch in his voice. Blythewood was the only secure thing in this child's life. "You're staying. I'm leaving."

"But—"

"No buts, Tad. I've already thought through what I'd do if worse came to worst. Luke's birthday party at his house will keep him busy tonight. That'll give me a head start. By morning I'll be long gone. When he arrives at Blythewood you can tell him I've gone to visit relatives in New York."

"New York? We don't have relatives up north, do we?"

"No."

She'd actually considered heading north to a big city to find anonymity, but she'd kept herself from making a rash decision. In true banking fashion, she'd drawn an imaginary tally sheet inside her head the day she'd decided to trick Luke. She'd listed three cities—New Orleans, New York and Austin—with debits and credits beneath each city. To make certain the direction she chose was logical, she had gone over her options methodically.

"Oh, I know what you're doing," Tad said, grinning. "It's like the time we played hide-and-seek and you walked backward into the barn. When I followed your footprints I thought you'd headed away from the barn, but you were in the loft, giggling while you watched me. You aren't goin' north. You're goin' south."

She nodded. "You'll have to pretend you don't want to tell him anything."

"Sort of like a Confederate spy caught by the Yanks?" Tad asked, instantly warming to the idea of helping his sister escape. "I have to make him squeeze it out of me."

"Don't make him squeeze too hard. I don't want you hurt."

"Don't worry about me, sis. I'll blubber and act real scared. Where are you going?"

"I thought about New Orleans. I could probably get a job working in the bank where Father did business. But it's too close. Once Mr. Reynolds figures out that you've thrown him off the track, that's the first place he'll send someone looking for me."

The implicit threat in Luke's statement that he always got what he paid for confirmed his earlier thoughts. Luke would have Wanted posters in every bank and sheriff's office within a hundred miles of the Mississippi. One step inside a bank and she'd be arrested.

"If we weren't so mad at the Wynthrops, you could go to Texas and live on their ranch," Tad said.

Tad had reached the same conclusion she'd come to when she'd made her mental tally. Giving him credit to take the sting out of his being left behind, Laura Lee said, "That's a good idea, Tad. Texas is the logical choice."

He pondered the idea for several seconds. "I don't know, sis. To my way of thinkin', the Wynthrops deserve a tongue-lashing for not sending the money like they promised. We're in this trouble 'cause of them."

"But I'd be safe there."

"Yeah, but that's a long, long way from home."

"I'll be back," she promised. Circumstances had forced her to commit a crime that necessitated leaving Blythewood, but she had to think of her imposed exile as temporary. If she didn't, she'd go crazy. "I'll be back."

"I'm going with you." His fingers burrowed into the folds of the jacket she wore. "You aren't going without me."

"You can't tag along this time." She felt his nose bob up and down in the center of her back. Parting would be difficult for both of them. She'd practically raised him since their mother's death. "Who'd look after Blythewood if we both left?"

"The land isn't going anywhere. Who's going to look after you if I'm not there to protect you?"

"My gun is in my purse. Nothing will happen to me."

Tad snorted contemptuously. "Fat lot of good it did you the last time you were in trouble."

"Shush!" Laura Lee said. Remembering what had happened the night Heavenly Acres had burned would bring on a series of nightmares for them both.

"I won't shush! That bluebelly was gonna hurt you. Me and my knife saved you."

Laura Lee tried to block out the memory, but her imagination filled in the blanks with long-remembered sights and sounds. She could smell the Yankee's foul breath on her face, could feel his dirty hands squeezing her breasts while his forearm blocked her windpipe. Bright red blotches swam behind her eyelids. Blood. Hot, sticky blood, dripping from her assailant onto her face and throat. A howl of pain and rage, curses, then air pouring into her lungs as he lunged toward his small attacker. She heard Tad's high-pitched scream and the sickening thud of a small body thrown against the parlor wall. The sound of heavy boots running, staggering out the door, across the porch.

"You'd be dead or worse if I hadn't heard the scuffle and come running with my pigsticker."

"Hush, Tad." Laura Lee shivered. "We aren't going to discuss what happened that day. You're staying at Blythewood with your cousin Brady. That's final. Don't argue."

"But, sis..." he said plaintively, "you can't leave me. Don't you see? Everybody leaves me, and nobody comes back. Something will happen and you'll die, too!"

Laura Lee couldn't refute his logic. His father and his brother had ridden off, never to return. She did the only thing she could do—she appealed to his family pride.

"Blythewood needs you. You're the last Shannon male. It's your responsibility to take care of your property."

"No! I'm going with you." His defiant shout echoed through the rows of live oaks leading up to Blythewood. Foxfire's pace quickened as they came closer to the stable. "You can't make me stay here!"

Feigning anger at his rebelliousness, Laura Lee raised her voice and said, "You stay here or I'll have you picking switches and visiting every woodshed between here and Austin, Thaddeus Alexander Shannon. I robbed a bank to save your birthright. Had I known Blythewood meant so little to you, I wouldn't have bothered!"

Tad sulked for a few seconds. Then, his voice quavering, he said, "Promise you'll be careful and you won't let anything happen to you?"

"I promise." Laura Lee knew such things were beyond her control, but she had to reassure Tad. "You give me your word of honor that you'll stay here and protect Blythewood and Brandy. Your cousin will need you."

Solemnly Tad replied, "You have my word, Laura Lee. I won't let anything happen to Brandy or Blythewood." He added a phrase under his breath.

"What was that you muttered at the end?"

"Nothing."

"Tad, I heard what you said. You won't die of boredom with me gone."

"It's gonna be just plain old tiresome around here without you stirring things up a mite." A slow grin replaced his pout. "I wish I coulda had one of those new photographs of Mr. Reynolds with his pants around his ankles and Mrs. Reynolds banging him over the head with the birthday cake. I could make a fortune selling them."

Laura Lee gave Foxfire full rein, and her laughter joined her brother's as they galloped up to the front steps of Blythewood Manor. Tad slipped off Foxfire and relieved his sister of Captain Bligh.

"You run inside and explain what's happened to Brandy while I take care of Foxfire," she shouted as she rounded the corner of the house, heading for the stable. Stroking Foxfire's coarse mane, she leaned forward. He nickered softly. "You're earning your keep tonight, aren't you, old girl?"

Inside the vacant ten-stall stable, she dismounted and began unsaddling Foxfire. The familiar smells of hay, oats and leather teased her nose. At Tad's age she'd spent most of her time here, much to her mother's dismay. No ladylike embroidery or candlemaking or dressmaking for Laura Lee Shannon. Her mother had halfheartedly chastised her, but the minute she'd be out of her mother's sight she'd be headed for the barn. Although their ten prize horses had been donated to the Confederacy years before, she still loved the place and the memories it evoked.

"There you go, fella," she crooned, leading Foxfire into his stall. "You deserve an extra scoop for clearing that picket fence, don't you?"

After she'd fed, brushed and curried Foxfire, she sprinted to the kitchen door. Brandy was waiting for her with a dry towel in her hand.

"That's some disguise you're wearing," she said dryly, giving Laura Lee's appearance a disapproving once-over. "If it weren't for the lace hanging below your trousers and your long hair I'd have sworn you were Beau."

The mention of her older brother's name caused a band of pain to tighten around her heart. She'd never get used to the idea of Beau's not returning from the war.

Fluffing her hair until it was nearly dry, Laura Lee followed her nose across the kitchen to the black iron kettle on the potbellied stove. Luckily, Brandy had been able to duplicate the recipes in the family cookbook when she'd been unable to decipher them successfully. Sniffing appreciatively, Laura Lee asked, "Where is Tad?"

"In his room, changing into dry clothes. You'd better do the same, or you'll come down with the ague."

"Did Tad tell you what happened?"

Laura Lee didn't have to turn around to know that a scowl of disapproval marred her cousin's brow. She sighed and ladled hot soup into a bowl, knowing she was about to get a lecture on proper decorum for a lady.

Brandy and Laura Lee were opposites in appearance and attitude. Seldom was there an auburn hair out of place on Brandy's head; Laura Lee's wavy blond hair defied hairpins. Brandy could look most men in the eye; Laura Lee could walk under most men's raised arms. Brandy's fashionable hourglass figure contrasted with Laura Lee's petite, willowy form.

Their mothers, who were sisters, had agreed that Brandy's vivid coloring suited Laura Lee's disposition—hotheaded, unpredictable, with a tendency to be a mischievous hoyden. Blond Laura Lee, the image of a Southern belle, should have been charming, sweet and subdued. She could be when it suited her, but Brandy was a perfect lady without any effort. And yet, perhaps because of their temperamental differences, the two women got along famously—except when Laura Lee exceeded the boundaries of good taste with her pranks.

"Yes, he did." Brandy's mouth thinned into a prim line. "Couldn't you have borrowed the money without... without..."

"The surprise party?" Grinning, her blue eyes dancing merrily, Laura Lee said airily, "Nope. I'd sell my soul for Tad and Blythewood, but I won't share a bed with a copperhead."

Brandy gasped at her cousin's outspokenness. Her brown eyes seemed to double in size. "Tad didn't tell me that was what Mr. Reynolds wanted as collateral."

"Tad doesn't know. He'd want to get out the dueling pistols and shoot Reynolds. You'll have to keep a sharp eye on him after I leave. I had to coerce him into staying here."

Brandy nodded. "He said you got the money."

"Um-hmm. The land is safe for another year."

"I do wish the Wynthrops had wired the funds." Brandy looked at her cousin with genuine regret in her eyes. She knew what it was like to lose a home. She'd lost everything she had during the siege of Atlanta, including her family. "Tad told me you think Mr. Reynolds will press criminal charges against you. How are you going to get out of this scrape?"

"I can't talk my way out of this one," Laura Lee replied simply. "The birthday party Betsy Mae planned for him is probably the only thing keeping him in town tonight. I've got to be long gone by daybreak." She sipped the soup, recalling what Brandy had said when she'd first entered the kitchen. "But you may have solved a major problem I was struggling with on the ride home."

"Me?"

"Inadvertently, I assure you." She pointed at Tad's too-short trousers. "You saved Beau's old clothing, didn't you?"

Brandy put a restraining hand on Laura Lee's elbow. "You aren't leaving this house dressed in Beau's clothes. It's—it's indecent for a woman to wear men's pants."

"It's functional. Expedient. Practical. Aren't those the respectable traits you harp on?" Winking at her cousin, who had opened her mouth to protest, she added, "It's your idea, so it must be respectable."

"You're insane, Laura Lee Shannon. You couldn't fool a blind man by dressing up like a boy."

Laura Lee turned her back on Brandy's objections and walked over to the window. "It's getting dark. Lordy, I wish it would stop this infernal raining. I'll need Beau's greatcoat, as well as two or three pairs of britches and a couple of shirts." Spinning around, she asked, "Do you want to find Beau's clothes while I eat, or do I have to hunt for them and leave without eating?"

Predictably, Brandy tilted her nose toward the ceiling, flounced the hem of her skirt and walked sedately to the staircase. She was past the age where she felt she could stomp her foot. "I should let you starve! You're... incorrigible!"

Nodding in agreement and grinning, Laura Lee straddled the seat of the kitchen chair the way she'd seen Tad sit. Men's clothing did give a person a certain amount of unrestricted freedom that petticoats and bustles prevented.

She consumed her soup as she thought about her disguise. If she was dressed as a man, many of the problems of traveling alone would be overcome. A man traveling alone was less likely to be stared at or bothered than a woman.

Reflexively her hand moved to her curly hair. A slouch hat pinned up high on her head would cover it. Brandy would require smelling salts if Laura Lee dared to go so far as to shear off her hair.

Glancing down at her chest, she wondered how she'd disguise that portion of her anatomy. Compared to Brandy, she was nearly flat-chested, but her small waist and hips accentuated her apple-sized breasts. The thought of binding them was repugnant to her. Well, she'd face that problem when the weather cleared and became seasonally warm. For now Beau's clothing should hide her gender adequately.

Tad entered the kitchen with his handtooled saddlebags slung over one shoulder. His sister's unladylike perch on the chair went unnoticed. He opened his hand and extended it to Laura Lee. A lady's gold wedding band, a garnet ring and a man's diamond pinkie ring lay on his palm—all that remained of the Shannon family jewels. When they'd hidden them under the floorboards in the attic they'd solemnly vowed never to part with them.

"You're gonna need these."

"I can't take them." Laura Lee bit her lip to keep sentimental tears from brimming over. Her voice caught in her throat as she said, "They're yours."

He took her hand, pried open her curled fingers and emptied his hand into hers. Before she could drop the rings on the table, he wound his arms around her neck. "Don't be stubborn, sis. You risked your life to save Blythewood for me. Take them. Sell them."

"All right, Tad," she said, though she knew she'd starve to death before she parted with them. Her arms closed around him, and her head dropped to his too-thin shoulder. Her heart ached for him.

Oh, God, she silently prayed, *take care of him for me. Please, please, watch over him.*

She blinked rapidly to hold back her tears. She couldn't let her little brother see her cry. She had to be strong. The Wynthrops had left her without a choice. She had to go; he had to stay.

Getting a slender grip on her emotions, she put her hands on Tad's shoulders and unwound his arms. "You're a Shannon. Make me proud while I'm gone, you hear?"

Tad nodded, turning his head so that his sister wouldn't see him wipe the childish tears from his cheeks. "I will, sis."

Over his shoulder Laura Lee saw that Brandy had returned. She mouthed, "I won't let anything happen to him."

Nodding and rising from her seat, Laura Lee squeezed Tad's shoulder and said, "Let's see what Brandy found for me to wear."

"You're gonna wear Beau's clothes?" Tad asked, shooting a bewildered glance from the neatly folded stack of clothes in Brandy's arms to his sister's face.

"Brandy's idea," Laura Lee told him, covering the tense moment with a weak attempt at humor.

"I did wonder how you were going to fit your clothes in the saddlebags," Tad admitted, grinning. He gave his sister a sharp look. His clothes were tight in the wrong places. Her ankles showed. Tad felt a blush crimson his cheeks, and his smile faded. "You can't wear those."

Striding to Brandy's side, Laura Lee sorted through the stacks and selected nutmeg-brown cotton trousers, a logan-green shirt and a leather belt. She took the gray greatcoat

Brandy had crooked over her arm. Wordlessly she strode into the big pantry and closed the door.

Swiftly she disrobed. She didn't dare linger. "Tad, saddle up Foxfire, would you?" she called. "Be sure you use a dry saddle blanket."

She heard the back door open, then slam shut.

"He'll never learn the art of closing a door without rattling the windows," Brandy complained without malice. "Do you need help?"

"Underclothes."

Brandy poked a pair of slightly moth-eaten drawstring underthings through the door of her cousin's makeshift dressing room. "I'll pack the saddlebags," she said.

Scant minutes later, Laura Lee stepped out and pivoted on one foot, as though she were wearing a taffeta ball gown. "Well?" she asked.

"They're—" Speechlessness plagued Brandy. Her cousin looked like a young boy who'd been dressed from a rag-bag—as, in fact, she had.

"Scandalous?" Self-consciously Laura Lee smoothed the gathered fabric she'd cinched under the belt with her hands. She didn't need a looking glass to know that her appearance had changed radically, and for the better. Tad's clothes had been skintight on her, accentuating her femininity, but Beau's were baggy. Her rounded hips vanished beneath the fabric. His shirt ballooned at the waist where she'd tucked it in. She felt certain only a discerning eye would notice the gentle swell of her breasts. "Hardly."

"They'll do, I suppose," Brandy allowed, hating the way Laura Lee had corkscrewed her damp hair into a knot on her head. Reaching to her own nape, she extracted several hairpins. The string her cousin had used would never hold; the weight of her hair had already caused the knot of hair to droop precariously to one side. She moved beside her cousin, motioned for her to bend forward and planted the pins snugly in strategic places. "Those should help."

Hairpins were as precious to Brandy as the Shannon rings were to Laura Lee, but before Laura Lee could murmur her thanks she hugged her, hard. "Don't you dare thank me. You've given me a roof over my head and food in my stomach and put up with my persnicketiness. What are a few hairpins in comparison?"

"But I'll lose them."

Brandy smiled sadly. "Yes, you probably will."

Unspoken words of love and gratitude hung between them like stars on a clear summers' night.

"You'd better go. Don't worry about Tad or the house. I'll take care of them. You take care of yourself. Let us hear from you the minute you get settled."

"I'm going to Texas by way of New Orleans. I'm not going to allow the Wynthrops to welch on their end of the bargain. Soon as I get what they owe us I'll come home. Reynolds should have cooled down by then."

Imitating a man's ambling stride, she sauntered over to the kitchen table, where Brandy had placed Tad's saddle-bags beside her purse. The incongruity of the two items side by side made her grin as she unbuckled one leather bag and shoved her dainty purse inside it.

"Keep an eye out for Foxfire tomorrow morning," Laura Lee said, thinking of last-minute details. "You'll know I'm safely aboard a boat going downriver when he gets here."

Both of them knew that if the rain continued the river would be flooded, too treacherous for a boat to navigate.

"If Foxfire doesn't show up, send Tad down to the river to fetch him. In the meantime, I'll stop at the Clairmonts' and make arrangements for a horse. I don't want you all stranded here without transportation."

"Stop worrying. We'll manage," Brandy assured her.

The heavy shower had slowed to a gray drizzle by the time Laura Lee swung on her coat, set her hat on her head, tugged the brim low on her forehead and stepped out onto the back porch, just as Tad trotted Foxfire out of the stable. She had to leave quickly, she decided, or the three of them would be huddled together on the porch, still saying one last goodbye, come daybreak.

Tad swung down from the saddle and held the reins for her. She hugged him one more time, then mounted Foxfire.

"See you," she cried, waving to Brandy. The reins in her hands, she swatted the horse on the rump with the flat of her hand. "Save your Confederate money!" she called over her shoulder. "The South will rise again!"

Chapter Three

The huge oak trees that bordered Blythewood's lane sheltered Laura Lee from the wind and rain, but once she turned south on the river road her protection from the elements was sporadic. Windswept rain stung her face. She hunched over Foxfire's neck, her greatcoat billowing behind her, flapping like the Stars and Bars at a cavalry charge. Foxfire's hoove splattered muddy water on her boots and legs.

In the total darkness Laura Lee had to concentrate to keep to the winding road. She cocked her head to one side when she heard hoofbeats coming from the other direction. Only one other person that she could think of would have cause to be out on this wretched night—Luke Reynolds!

She sawed at the reins to slow her pace, then shortened one rein to veer off the road. Foxfire responded nimbly until he stumbled in a deep mudhole. Lightning forked overhead, and the crash of thunder that followed spooked them both. Foxfire reared in fright, and Laura Lee's heart clamored in her chest. She grabbed for the saddle horn and pulled her feet out of the stirrups in preparation for a nasty fall.

She screamed in fright when she felt a strong arm snake around her waist and pull her from the saddle.

Foxfire pawed the air with his hooves, eyes rolling.

"Let go! My horse will get hurt!" Certain that Luke had caught up with her, Laura lee flailed her arms and kicked in all directions.

His grip held, biting into her flesh.

"Damn you! Let go!"

Her teeth snapped together on his upper arm. Instantly he released her. She fell through the darkness, landing on all fours. Her knees and elbows buckled, and she pitched facedown into a churning mud puddle.

She was scared witless. Her reflexes took command. Her hands and feet clawed from one puddle to the next in an effort to escape. She coughed and sputtered from having breathed a considerable portion of mud, knowing that her only chance of salvation lay in getting to Foxfire, remounting and making good her escape.

"Whoa, Foxfire," she gasped, in a voice that was little more than a whisper. He whinnied and raced back toward Blythewood. She shook her fist at the horse's raised tail. "Come back here, you son of a horse's patoot!"

A deep, throaty chuckle punctured her panic.

Her head snapped up angrily. Miraculously, her hat remained squashed on her head as she grabbed hold of a gnarled tree root and levered herself to her feet. She swiped grit from her eyes and mouth on her sleeve and spit indelicately to clear the foul-tasting mud off her tongue.

She'd kill him! How dare he laugh at her while she was drowning in a river of mud!

"You runnin', boy?"

Laura Lee's fingers separated and gave her her first clear look at the man astride the horse. It wasn't Luke! The man's features were hidden by the brim of his hat, but she knew she'd recognize Luke Reynolds's hateful voice if it were coming from the other side of the moon.

The stranger's voice boomed again. "Hey! Did you bite your tongue off? I asked you if you're a runaway."

Her hands moved to her hips. She didn't owe this man an explanation. Besides, he was too damn close to the truth for comfort. She *was* running, and she didn't want him to know it.

"Get out of my way," she muttered, stomping past him.

The stranger backed his horse up until he loomed over her. The creak of wet leather warned her that he'd shifted his weight toward her. She dodged and twisted, but his fingers caught the collar of her coat.

"Son, I figure you owe me at least an apology for biting my arm clean down to the bone."

Seemingly without effort, he lifted her until her toes were barely touching the ground. Lightning split the darkness. She caught a glimpse of a blond mustache. Big. Strong. Dangerous, she thought. She knew now how a puppy felt when it was caught by the nape of the neck in its mother's jaws. This stranger could defeat her physically without straining himself.

"Sorry."

Her voice held not a trace of regret. Why should she apologize? He'd started this by grabbing her, and his action had cost her transportation to the river. She'd sustained one loss. She couldn't afford to waste time standing in this downpour jawing with a stranger.

He released his hold on her collar. "Where are you headed, son?"

His calling her "son" skewered her raw nerves. "I ain't your son," she told him, careful to keep her voice low-pitched and her words ungrammatical. Young boys who were full of springs oats always cussed. She added, "You mind your own darned business and let me tend to mine."

"Did that sassy mouth of yours ever earn you a trip to the woodshed to get your butt whipped? If it didn't, it should have. You're surly as hell."

Shooting him a murderous glance for the hint of amusement she heard in his voice, she pulled her hat down over her ears and started walking. Surly, huh? she fumed. For two cents she'd teach him the meaning of the word *surly*! But she couldn't waste any more precious time. She had to get rid of him!

"Nobody asked you for your opinion, stranger," she said.

He turned his horse until it blocked the narrow road. "Just answer one question, kid, and then you can march straight to hell and I won't stop you. Do the Shannons still live down this road?"

A whisper of fear crawled over her flesh. She glared up at him. What did he want? She had to know. Protective instincts for Tad and Brandy made her break the hostile silence.

"Who's asking?"

"Name's J. B. Wynthrop. What's yours?"

"Liar." She twisted out of reach when he leaned toward her. "Anybody from these parts would recognize a Wynthrop when they saw one."

Her recollections of Jacob and his son John were hazy, but neither of them had had a blond mustache. Both men had had hair as dark as their eyes. The younger son, Jack Wynthrop, had been sent north to a military academy when she'd been younger than Tad was now. She couldn't recall what he'd looked like, but it stood to reason he'd look like his father and brother.

"You're mighty short on Southern hospitality," the stranger said, dismounting from his horse. "No snot-nosed brat is going to call me a liar. You take it back and apologize. Now!"

Laura Lee sidestepped around him. Next to her petite frame, he was a giant of a man. His voice was soft, but beneath the deceptive calmness she could detect tempered steel.

"Keep your hands to yourself," she said bravely, trying to fend off the hand that was reaching for her arm.

"Get a civil tongue in your head, boy. I asked your name and I'm going to get it."

His determination clashed with her stubbornness.

"Luke," she snapped, giving him the name uppermost in her mind. "You got my name. Why don't you just get on down the road and leave me alone. Ain't you done me enough harm? You ran me down, unseated me from my horse, nearly trampled me to death, and now you're pestering me with questions. What are you gonna do next? Bloody my nose? You're nothing but a big, overgrown bully!"

"Bully?" he repeated disgustedly. "I'll bet your old man packed your saddlebags and threw you out of the house. You little rapscallion! Don't you realize I saved you from falling off your horse? Why don't you just answer my questions before I show you how a real bully acts!"

"You gonna leave me be if I do?"

He nodded.

She pointed in the direction he'd been heading and said gruffly, "Last I heard, the Shannons moved into Blytheville. I seem to recollect somebody mentioning something at the general store about them joining relatives in . . . Atlanta. Or was it Nashville? Hell, mister, half the plantation owners around here have been booted off their land by the tax collector. How am I supposed to know where they went?"

She scrutinized his face, watching for his reaction. If he was a Wynthrop, as he claimed to be, casually mentioning the tax debts should elicit some observable response.

Nothing, she noted. Not so much as a hair of his mustache twitched. He'd lied, as she'd suspected. Well, she'd thrown him off the track, she thought smugly. He'd ride right by the lane leading to Blythewood. By the time he made it into town and snooped around she'd have found some means of getting a message to Brandy. If he thought *she* was ill-mannered, he'd be convinced the Shannons weren't to be messed with when Brandy greeted him with a loaded six-shooter pointed straight at his lying teeth!

Another thought occurred to her. Could this stranger be someone Reynolds had hired? The telegraph wires could have been repaired. Reynolds undoubtedly had unsavory friends outside Blytheville that he could contact. If the stranger was in cahoots with the banker, the only thing that had saved her was her disguise.

"Thanks, Luke." He started to put his foot in the stirrup, but then he stopped. He felt mean and low-down for leaving a kid stranded in a rainstorm. "One favor deserves another. Come on, kid, climb up behind me and I'll help you round up your horse."

Before she could reject his offer, his long arm snagged her around the waist. She felt herself being lifted as though she weighed no more than a goosefeather pillow. Her hat slipped backward, precariously close to falling off and revealing the crown of blond curls bunched beneath it.

"You ain't takin' me nowhere, stranger! My horse is back at the barn by now. I ain't goin' back there. Never!"

"I'm a mite stronger than you." He chuckled, wrapped his arm around her rump and swung her behind him. He made a clucking sound with his tongue. His mount turned and headed back in the direction she'd come from—back toward Blythewood.

Twisting suddenly, she slammed the heel of her boot into the stranger's knee and gouged her sharp elbow into his belly. The sound of the wind hissing from his mouth was music to her ears.

When he freed her, she was ready. She landed on her feet in a crouched position and bolted into the woods beside the road. Within seconds the darkness would swallow her completely. Unless he was a blond-headed Indian tracker, he'd be unable to follow her.

Wet leaves slapped her in the face; she blocked them with one folded arm, holding the other straight in front of her. He couldn't see her, but she couldn't see where she was going, either.

Disoriented, she zigzagged between trees. Since he thought she was a boy, he wouldn't have any qualms about beating her to a bloody pulp if he caught up with her.

Half crazy with fear, she stopped for a second to get her bearings. The rain had slowed to a drizzle, but huge droplets dripped from the branches overhead. Glancing upward, she silently begged the clouds to part and let the moon shine through. She jumped a foot when she heard the sound of twigs and limbs snapping coming from directly behind her.

Lost! With that damn man hunting her down. Cat and mouse must have been his favorite childhood game! She'd never surrender, she vowed silently, straining her eyes to see through the tangle of undergrowth around her.

Off to her right she spied a narrow trail. A deer path, she surmised. She moved toward it as quietly as possible. She'd tagged along with Beau once or twice when he'd gone hunting, and she knew that most paths animals made eventually led to water. If she stayed on this path, it should take her to the river.

"All you...have...to do," she gasped, "...is stick...to the path."

She was unaccustomed to running, and her calves were beginning to ache. She tripped over a root and fell. Her lungs felt as though they'd caught fire, and her throat was dry. She swiped the moisture on her face across her lips with the back of her hand. She had to keep moving; she dared not stop to rest.

She realized as she staggered to her feet that her having found the path was like a double-edged sword that cut both ways. On the one hand, the path made traveling easier for her, but on the other it also made it easier for the stranger's horse. She could hear him steadily closing the gap between them.

That knowledge sent a wild spurt of power to her legs. She'd loped several hundred yards before she realized she'd broken out of the forest. The tree trunks were evenly spaced. Spanish moss, not leaves, brushed against her upheld arm.

She charged up the open space between the oaks, glancing over her shoulder. He was back there. He'd seen her, she was sure of it.

"Leave me alone...." she tried to call to the man who was relentlessly pursuing her, but she'd lost her voice along with her sense of direction. Her head swung around again. In the distance a beam of light peeped through the darkness. "Help! Help me!"

And then she started to giggle hysterically as she realized where her blind flight had taken her. The cat didn't have to catch the mouse; he'd chased her back to her own hideyhole! The last thing Laura Lee saw before she collapsed into an hysterical heap was Blythewood, with Brandy standing in the brightly lit doorway. She'd led the imposter straight to his destination.

For the first time in her nineteen years, she fainted.

"She's coming around."

Blurred faces swam in front of Laura Lee's eyes: Tad, Brandy...and a blond-haired, black-eyed stranger. Instinctively she squirmed against the arms that were holding her against what felt like a stone wall.

"He's a hellion," J.B. grumbled, stalking across the hardwood floor to the davenport. "Ma'am, if you're the one who whaled the stuffing out of him, I can't blame you. He bit me, kicked me and elbowed me in the—"

He stopped in midsentence when Laura Lee's hat finally fell off. A waterfall of blond ringlets cascaded over his sleeve. He dropped his burden none too gently on the couch.

"Well, I'll be damned. He's a she!"

"What'd you do to her?" Tad demanded, hostility bristling like porcupine quills in his voice.

"I'll get the smelling salts," Brandy said, more concerned about her semiconscious cousin than about the interplay taking place between the young master of Blythewood and the belligerent stranger.

J.B. rocked back on his heels, both admiration and irritation causing his tanned complexion to turn slightly pink. He'd sailed the stormy Gulf and ridden hundreds of miles on horseback to have a slip of a girl best him?

A Comanche Indian was civilized compared to her. This mud-caked "boy" was the sweet Southern belle he'd agreed to bring back to Texas to marry John? For a second he sincerely doubted his brother's sanity.

He could understand his father making an agreement with a longtime friend that meant abandoning the Wynthrop's comfortable plantation and going west. The two men had a common cause—supporting the Confederacy. He could understand that nostalgia caused John to insist on continuing to support Heavenly Acres financially. But understanding why his brother was obsessed with making Laura Lee Shannon his wife was beyond his comprehension.

"Nothing," he muttered. Doffing his Stetson, he introduced himself. "J. B. Wynthrop... at your service."

Brandy nudged the intruder aside and sank to her knees beside Laura Lee. Unbuttoning the greatcoat, she glared up at J.B. "One of you help me get these wet clothes off her."

"Don't you touch my sister," Tad warned J.B., doubling his fists. "The Wynthrops aren't welcome on Shannon property."

Moaning, Laura Lee fought the waves of black swirls that were making her helpless against the hands touching her. Her eyelids fluttered open, then closed when hair the color of noon sunshine blinded her. She swatted weakly at Brandy's fingers.

"You're home, Laura Lee," Brandy crooned closer to her cousin's ear as she swept her hair back from her face. Impatiently she snapped at Tad and J. B. Wynthrop, "You two can square off at each other later. This is your fault, mister. The least you can do is help repair the damage you've done. Lift her shoulders while I get this wet coat off of her."

Two termagants and a disrespectful smart-aleck kid, J.B. thought, but he bent over and hoisted his brother's fiancée into a sitting position.

"No!" Laura Lee cried, swinging her hand at her tormentor's face without making contact. She heard a seam rip and fought harder, but to no avail. The blond giant had the strength of ten men.

Brandy uncorked the vial of smelling salts and placed it under her nose. "There, there, dear. Don't fuss. We aren't going to let anyone hurt you. Just let us get those wet clothes off of you."

Shaking her head from side to side to rid herself of the foul odor, Laura Lee sat bolt upright, eyes wide open. The dark smudges of mud beneath her incredibly long lashes accentuated their brilliant blue coloring. Her hair tumbled around her shoulders.

J.B. felt as though she'd landed another punch in his gut. How could he have mistaken her for a runaway boy? Her heart-shaped face, and the sensual pout of her lower lip, should have clued him in to her disguise. The boys at the Red Satin Garter Saloon would really laugh when they heard this one.

Cringing away from the masculine hands that had pinned her arms to her sides with her coat, Laura Lee dug her heels into the cushion and attempted to scoot her bottom to the end of the davenport.

"Slap her," J.B. suggested to Brandy. He'd never intentionally struck a woman, and, tempted though he was, he couldn't hurt Laura Lee. "She's hysterical."

"You hit her and I'll blow your head off." Tad snatched the six-shooter from J.B.'s low-slung holster and cocked the hammer. "I mean it, Mister Whoever-you-are!"

"Give me that gun before you shoot somebody," Brandy snapped.

The sight of her brother pointing a loaded pistol at a man's face startled Laura Lee out of her state of shock. He'd shoot to protect her; he'd stabbed a man for the same reason. She swung her trouser-clad legs off the cushions and shrugged her shoulders to remove the coat.

She silently held her grubby hand out to her brother until he grudgingly uncocked the gun and put the handcarved grip in her palm. She curled her hand around it, her thumb resting on the hammer and her forefinger on the trigger.

"That's a hair trigger, ma'am." J.B. was smiling, but his eyes were as dark and hard as river agates. "This is some thanks I'm getting for helping you."

The barrel of the gun shook in her hands. Helping? Did he think she was an idiot? Keeping a wary eye on him, she got to her feet.

"Luke Reynolds hired you, didn't he?"

"Nobody hired me." J.B. inched toward the sofa. "Who the hell is Luke Reynolds? That's the second time I've heard you speak that name. The first time you told me *your* name was Luke."

Brandy raised to her knees and wrapped her arms around Laura Lee's legs. "He says he's J. B. Wynthrop."

"Yeah, he's J. B. Wynthrop—" Laura Lee snorted in disbelief "—and I'm Robert E. Lee."

Tad moved to her side. "Do you really think Reynolds hired a gunslinger, sis?"

"I'm no gunslinger."

"You aren't a Wynthrop, either," Laura Lee said between clenched teeth. She held the gun with the barrel aimed at his belt buckle. What would she do if he refused to leave peacefully? Shoot him? The weight of the weapon and the thought of shooting a man in cold blood lowered the barrel of the gun several inches.

"At least raise it back to my belt buckle if you're going to shoot me," J.B. told her, in a voice as cold as the spring rain. When he observed the wild flush that swept up the armed woman's neck, his grin widened. "I can prove my identity. Send the boy to my horse and have him get what's in my saddlebags."

"And leave you here alone with the women?" Tad's eyes went from the tall stranger to his sister's face. "Gimme the gun, sis. I can shoot him."

"Go get the man's saddlebags, Tad. We aren't going to shoot him unless he makes a wrong move. Go ahead. Do what I said." She slowly moved the barrel up and down the length of the intruder. "Don't move a muscle. I don't want to shoot you, but I will if I have to."

Brandy pushed Tad toward the front door. "Hurry!"

While Tad slowly shuffled outside, Laura Lee stared bravely into the man's intimidating black eyes. He edged backward until his brawny shoulders were braced against the wall that divided the parlor from the entryway. Lazily, as though he hadn't a care in the world, he hooked his thumbs in his wide belt and crossed one leg over the other at the ankles.

His nonchalant pose didn't trick Laura Lee. He'd spring at her like a mountain lion if he sensed danger. His powerful hands could snap her neck as easily as they'd broken the twigs that got in his path when he'd chased her. She disliked the way he was scrutinizing her, as closely as she was him. And from his cocky grin she knew he didn't consider her a worthy opponent.

Uneasy with the conclusion she'd drawn, she snapped, "What's the name of the Wynthrop plantation?"

"Heavenly Acres."

"Anyone could have told him that," Brandy whispered. "Who sent you?"

"Who would want to harm two *ladies* and a boy?" he countered sarcastically.

"You, for one," Laura Lee said sharply. "Luke Reynolds, for another."

"I'd never heard the name until you mentioned it."

"I wouldn't expect you to admit it."

His patience slipped a notch each time she dared to call him a liar. "Lady—and I use the term loosely, considering you're aiming that gun at dangerous territory again—I don't murder women and children for anybody... including Luke Reynolds, whoever the hell he is."

Laura Lee nudged Brandy with her elbow. "Go see what's keeping Tad. Sending him out there may be some kind of sneaky trick."

"Suspicious, aren't you? I'm beginning to wonder what you did to warrant a man to hire a gunslinger to come after you?"

J.B.'s pride silently demanded action. He'd let a pint-size woman get the drop on him. She might wear the pants in this household, but she wasn't going to be allowed to buffalo him. Slowly, fluidly, like a cautious predator, he straightened.

"That's none of your business." She kept her eyes on him, listening as Brandy quietly closed the door behind her. "Just stay where you are, mister."

"You won't shoot."

"One more step and you'll be breathing through the hole in your chest." Unaware she was doing it, she took one step backward for each pace he moved forward. "Stay right where you are!"

"You don't have killer eyes, Miss Laura Lee." His voice was calm, and his hands hung loose at his sides. "You don't have what it takes to kill an unarmed man."

"You'll be the second man today who underestimated me."

"Luke Reynolds being the first?"

She nodded. "When I last saw him, he had his pants down around his ankles and his wife was banging a cake pan on his head. I set him up. Still think I can't pull the trigger?"

"You can't." He stretched out his hand, palm raised. "What'd he do to you?"

"Nothing." Suddenly she realized that he'd cornered her. "Back off."

"My name's J. B. Wynthrop, from the Rocking W Ranch, outside of Austin, Texas. Jacob Bradford Wynthrop was my father. Our parents made a deal. I'm here to keep my end of it. And I'm also here to collect on the Shannons' end of the bargain."

Laura Lee let the barrel of the gun drop to the floor. In one supple movement he disarmed her and holstered the weapon. When she saw the victorious glint in his devilish black eyes she instantly wished she hadn't relinquished it.

"I don't remember you," she said, in place of the apology that she could tell he was expecting. To her way of thinking, he should be down on his hands and knees, begging her forgiveness.

She folded her arms at her waist, and her belt buckle scratched the sensitive underside of her wrist. She glanced down and was appalled by what she saw. Pigs that wallow in mudholes are cleaner! she thought.

She crossed to the window nearest the door, and her reflection in the glass totally dismayed her. Bits of brown leaves dotted her straggly hair; a small clod of dirt clung to one eyebrow; black smears decorated her face like war paint. When she felt her shoulders start to sag, animosity strengthened her spine, and dignity held them erect.

She considered J. B. Wynthrop directly responsible for her disheveled appearance. If he'd arrived in time she wouldn't have had to 'borrow' Luke Reynolds's money. If he hadn't collided with her she wouldn't have eaten mud. If he hadn't stalked her she wouldn't be standing here feeling water squish between her toes!

The rancor she felt toward the copperhead banker paled in significance compared to the hatred she felt toward the man directly in back of her. Everything that had happened was his fault.

Her eyes narrowed. She couldn't right the wrongs done to her by the bigwigs in Washington, but she'd gotten her revenge on Luke Reynolds—and she'd do the same for J. B. Wynthrop. One way or another, she'd set him up, too.

J.B. relaxed. His gun was back where it belonged. And any remaining doubts concerning his identity would be dispelled shortly.

He regretted having manhandled Laura Lee, but how was he supposed to know that this urchin who'd fought him like a wildcat was a woman? He'd been in a dozen barroom brawls, and he'd never been punched where she'd hit him.

He studied her from behind. Cultured Southerners considered Texas wild, but in all his days he'd never laid eyes on a woman dressed in men's clothing. The trousers gathered beneath her leather belt thickened her waist, and yet he felt certain he could still span it with his hands. Only a slight curve hinted at the shape of her feminine buttocks, but it was enough to tease his imagination. Bustles should be banned, he decided, liking what he saw.

His eyes ran down the length of her legs to her mud-caked boots. For such a small thing, she had incredibly long legs, and her feet were absurdly big. The length and width of her feet made him wonder if her ankles were thick, too. Then her toes, wiggling a couple of inches back from the tips of her boots, made him grin appreciatively. Tiny feet and well-shaped ankles, he thought, revising his first impression.

His brother wouldn't be disappointed—if he could deliver her gagged, with her hands bound behind her back.

"Here they come," Laura Lee murmured. Anxious to settle the dispute and retire to her room to get cleaned up, she moved to the front entry.

J.B. remained stock still. His perusal of her when she'd been motionless hadn't prepared him for the effect her gently swaying hips had on the tender place where she'd injured him. Groaning silently, he forced his eyes to the portrait hanging over the fireplace.

"What took so long?" Laura Lee asked.

"The leather was wet! I couldn't get the buckle undone. When I did, I reached inside and pulled out a wad of money!" Tad hopped excitedly from one foot to the other. His apple-colored cheeks dimpled. "The wind blew some of it out of my hand. Brandy and me had to chase after it. He must be a Wynthrop, sis. Who else would be bringing us saddlebags full of money?"

Laura Lee looked at Brandy, one of her eyebrows raised skeptically. Before she could stop Tad, he burst into the parlor and threw his arms around J.B.'s muscular thighs.

The boy's head buried the buttons on his trousers in the exact spot his sister had lambasted, and J.B. groaned inwardly. Was the whole family determined to destroy him?

"Thank you! Thank you, Mr. Wynthrop!" Tad babbled with an odd mixture of excitement and relief. "Now my sister won't have to go to jail for robbing the bank!"

Louisiana mud had a better flavor than the acid taste caused by her brother's demonstrative defection to the enemy camp. Laura Lee considered what she'd done a privileged family secret, not general information to be blabbed to a virtual stranger.

"That's enough, Tad," she snapped. "The Wynthrop money arrived too late to be of help." She glowered at J.B., then turned to Brandy and murmured, "Even if I pay Reynolds back, he can still press charges."

Brandy's amber eyes widened. "Sheriff Winters wouldn't arrest you, would he?"

"Are you kidding? The Underground Railroad stopped at his house. He has an ax to grind with anyone who owned slaves before the war. He'd toss me in jail and throw away the key! Meanwhile, Reynolds would be out putting together a lynch mob."

Tad rushed to his sister's side. "We'll hide you. We'll tell everybody you left town."

"She is leaving," J.B. said. He removed an envelope from one of the saddlebags Tad had brought in. "I have three reasons for coming to Blythewood. One, to honor a family debt. Two, to check on Heavenly Acres. And three . . . to take Laura Lee back to Texas."

"Like hell you will," Laura Lee said. This man's manhandling of her, and his unmitigated arrogance, had already made her decide that following her plan to go to Texas would be impossible. They'd kill one another before they were a mile from Blythewood! "He's demented if he thinks I'm going with him. Did Foxfire make it back to the stable?"

"She won't be needing her horse," J.B. said. "She's staying right here until I get whatever mess she's made cleaned up."

Bristling, Laura Lee circled Tad's shoulders with one arm. This was obviously a man who thought everyone should obey his commands, but her plans hadn't changed, only her destination. She wasn't going to Texas, that much was certain.

"Go take care of Foxfire, Tad." She shot the intruder a dirty look. "He ran off when I was unseated. Unsaddle him and give him some feed. After he's eaten, put a dry saddle blanket on him. I'll be leaving within the hour."

"But, sis—"

"Don't argue." Brandy's tight-lipped expression communicated her opinion of Laura Lee's abandoning them with an irate stranger in their midst. "Don't get upset, Brandy. Mr. Wynthrop won't be staying, either."

Spreading his legs and folding his arms over his massive chest, J.B. chuckled. It would take an army of men her size to budge him an inch from where he stood.

"You're going to make me leave?" he asked skeptically. He tapped the envelope against his biceps to illustrate the folly of any such attempt. "I'm staying, and so are you. Do you honestly believe I've come here to stick my hands in my pockets and watch you blithely ride off to who knows where?"

"You haven't been consulted, Wynthrop," she replied. Then she added, "Whether you watch me leave or not is up to you."

He waved the envelope under her nose. "Read this, Miss Shannon. As you can plainly see, it's in your father's handwriting."

"Whatever our fathers agreed to before the war has been nullified—by you."

"The hell it has."

He lifted the flap of the envelope and extracted the folded sheets within. He'd promised his older brother that he would control his quick temper. Women aren't cattle, so don't ride roughshod over them, John had said. J.B. kept the smile on his face, but he couldn't control the sarcasm that dripped over his voice like honey on corn pone. "Read these. I assume you can read."

"Ignorance isn't my vice," she retorted pointedly, deigning to take the document but turning her back on him and motioning to Brandy to precede her up the steps. The mud on her face had dried, and her skin felt as taut as her nerves. Under her breath she muttered, "Don't fret. This big Goliath is leaving, immediately." Taking Brandy firmly by the elbow, she marched up the steps, without a backward glance at the tall Texan who claimed to have rescued her.

A few minutes later, Laura Lee was pouring water from a daintily painted pitcher into a matching water bowl. Her coat, trousers and boots had protected her from the worst of the filth, but she still longed for a long soak in the tub in the kitchen. It was ridiculous, she mused. She'd be muddy again within the hour. She splashed water on her face. Brandy was sitting on the edge of her canopied bed, silently reading the papers.

"It's the agreement between your father and Jacob B. Wynthrop. Do all the Wynthrop men have the same initials?"

"Family tradition." She glanced over her shoulder at Brandy. Her cousin was staring at her with a most peculiar expression on her face. "You're wondering if the Texan downstairs is John, aren't you?"

Brandy nodded and asked, "Is he the one you agreed to marry?"

"No."

"No, he isn't John Wynthrop, or no, you aren't going to marry him?"

"No, to both questions. John has dark hair and dark eyes. But if he were John, I still wouldn't marry him." She turned to the washbowl again, wondering why John had sent his brother to fetch her back to Texas, though she knew it was a moot point. "I stipulated in the letters John and I exchanged that Blythewood has to be on a profit-making basis. Unless we expand the size of the garden beyond our own needs and hawk vegetables in town, Blythewood won't make one red cent this year."

Brandy glanced at the papers and shrugged. "I don't see anything in your handwriting, but these papers do look authentic. You ought to at least read them."

"Nonsense. It would be a waste of time. I'm telling you, there weren't any documents drawn up. A gentleman's agreement is completed with a handshake."

"This does look like your father's writing, Laura Lee. I think you ought to read it."

"Why? What difference does it make? As far as I'm concerned, there is no agreement."

Water dripped off her nose onto the towel as she turned toward her bed. She longed to throw herself on the bed, cover her head and sleep for a week. She ached clear to the bone, which wasn't surprising, since she'd fallen off a horse twice. Her pale skin didn't show signs of bruising yet, but by tomorrow she'd be various shades of black and blue.

One more black mark against Mr. Wynthrop, she thought, drawing up a mental tally sheet listing his transgressions.

Go to Texas with him? She'd strangle him with her bare hands first—if she could get her fingers around his muscular neck, that is. She should have shot him when she'd had the chance. His hide was so thick, the bullets would probably have bounced off him.

"You're honor-bound to carry out your father's wishes," Brandy reminded her softly.

"Mister Wynthrop didn't!"

Brandy stopped reading before she got to the last page. "I imagine he arrived late because of the weather—because of circumstances beyond his control."

"Horse puckey!" Laura Lee spit the vulgar expression into the towel to keep her cousin from hearing it. Brandy didn't approve of slang; she wouldn't openly reprimand Laura Lee, but she was known for her withering looks.

"What did you say?"

"Bad luck-y," Laura Lee improvised agilely. "He reneged on whatever it is those phony papers say. I wouldn't be in this fix except for that slowpoke cowboy."

"Does that mean you aren't going to take the money?"

Laura Lee stared at the faint red marks on her arm. A get-even smile curved her lips. "No, my dear. That means I'm planning on staying out of Luke Reynolds's clutches, as planned, but tomorrow morning you're going to instruct Mr. Wynthrop that I'm spending the day in bed—recovering from our unfortunate meeting—and he's to take the money into town to pay off the loan at the bank."

"But that's dishonest!" Brandy protested.

Laura Lee grinned. "You're talking to a bank robber, remember?"

"You didn't actually rob the bank—not really. Mr. Reynolds did give you the money. It's not like you held him at gunpoint."

Laura Lee lay back on the bed and stared up at the eyelet-lace canopy. "Make no mistake about it—I was within seconds of pulling the derringer out of my purse."

"Your intentions were noble...honorable. You only did what you had to do."

Laura Lee braced herself on her elbows and stared at Brandy. "Brandy, much as I'd like to accept your innocent verdict, that's not how others will view it." She reached over and flicked the corner of the papers. "Reynolds has everyone in his pocket. He even knew about the Shannon-Wynthrop agreement."

Laying her hand over her cousin's, Brandy said, "You already planned on going to Texas. You'd be safe if you went with Mr. Wynthrop."

"Safe? He's a barbarian! Aside from my personal dislike for him, you and I both know that the reputation of a woman traveling alone with a man is almost worse than of one who's robbed a bank." The muscles in her arms and legs protested silenlty as she heaved herself off the goose-down mattress. She paced from one end of the room to the other, muttering, "First Reynolds, now Wynthrop. Why do men keep interfering with my plans?"

"Because they're uninformed regarding your intentions?" Brandy suggested lamely.

Laura Lee gave her a dirty look. "Whose side are you on?"

"Yours, but—"

"Then help me decide where I can hide out for a month or two. Luke will get his money back. Maybe he'll calm down."

"I can't persuade you to stay here and work something out with Mr. Wynthrop?"

"I don't bargain with people I detest or make deals with blond-headed devils."

"You're stubborn as a Missouri mule, Laura Lee Shannon!"

"St. Louis?" Laura lee snapped her fingers. "That's a great idea. Once the floodwaters have receded I can catch a boat going upriver."

Unbeknownst to the women, J.B. had stealthily tracked them upstairs. He leaned against the wall, eavesdropping on everything being discussed. Had John been there and been able, he'd have stripped an inch off his backside for his unchivalrous behavior. But John wasn't there, and he wasn't able to climb steps, anyway.

Listening to Laura Lee vilify the entire Wynthrop family justified his conduct, he silently told himself. Each word she spoke had him grinding his teeth. The impudent little cuss hadn't bothered to read what her own father had written. Didn't she realize that in time of war gentlemen's agreements were put on paper? Bullets didn't discriminate between gentlemen and . . . barbarians!

He leaned closer, catching only snatches of their conversation. Stipulation? What stipulation? John hadn't mentioned anything to him about putting Blythewood back on a paying basis. That could take years...decades. He'd have to see that in writing before he believed her.

Right, Brandy—talk some sense into her head. She would be safer going to Texas. Poor little darling, he thought unsympathetically. The banker and the barbarian spoiled her plans. If those plans were anything like what she was talking about doing—absconding while he pacified the banker—they ought to be ruined.

Nobody made a fool of Jack Wynthrop.

It was a lesson he'd teach her the hard way if necessary. Women! Too illogical. Too emotional. This one in particular needed the firm hand of a husband to keep her on the straight and narrow. He hadn't met the woman who fit the mental picture of the woman he'd wed, but he knew she'd be sweet and biddable, tall and busty, with a pioneer spirit to match his own. A Southern magnolia might be John's ideal woman, but he wanted a wildflower—a Texas bluebonnet.

He heard fingers snapping and heard John's intended announce that she was going to St. Louis. Turning silently on the balls of his feet, he Indian-walked back down the hall to the steps.

Miss Shannon wasn't going anywhere—except straight into his brother's loving arms.

Chapter Four

From the bottom of the steps, Tad demanded, "What were you doin' up there?"

"I thought I heard somebody faint and hit the floor." Telling even a white lie to a kid bothered J.B.; he prided himself on being a straight shooter. "Must have been her boots hittin' the floor."

"She isn't leaving tonight?"

J.B. shook his head. "She's staying." Like it or not! he added silently.

"I fed Foxfire and changed his blanket, but he's being cantankerous. He'll be glad she's changed her mind. Guess I'd better go take care of him."

"I'll do it." J.B. frowned at the thought of telling another fib. Laura Lee would throw a conniption fit should her brother tell her he'd countermanded her order. "Your sister said for you to run on up to bed. She'll see you at breakfast."

Yawning, Tad put his foot on the first step and watched as the tall Texan pulled his rain poncho over his head. "Where are you sleeping?"

"I'll bed down in the barn. Where's the lantern?"

"I left it on the front porch."

Tad had climbed three steps before he began to wonder what Brandy would say if she knew that the master of Blythewood had let company sleep in the barn. She'd scold him for certain. He took a swift look back and sized J. B. Wynthrop up. There wasn't a bed in the house long enough for him.

"I'll see you in the morning," J.B. said, aware that the boy was struggling with some inner conflict. He squared his hat on his head and opened the front door. "G'night."

The rain had stopped, J.B. noted, stooping and striking a match to light the lantern. A smile tugged at his mouth as he rose and lifted the lit lantern high.

The livery stable where he'd rented Hoss had rein-trained him: reins dragging on the ground was a command to stay put. He'd patiently grazed on the grass near his hooves, waiting to be taken to the barn.

J.B. strode down the steps and picked up the horse's reins. He patted the white star beneath his forelock. "Good fella. Your owner trained you well. You'd think he could've given you a better name, huh?"

He stroked Hoss's long neck and watched him chew. J.B.'s stallion, Hellion, would have replied horse-style by flicking his ears or snorting or nudging his arm. Hoss was as bland as his name.

"Okay, Hoss, let's get over to the barn and get you unsaddled. Looks like the two of us will be sharing the same accommodations, huh?"

A vague sense of familiarity coursed through him when he raised the lantern and studied the front of the house.

Blythewood's French Colonial architecture had been duplicated by other Southerners who'd moved to Texas—though Texans called the gallery, the overhang surrounding all four sides of the house, a balcony. And Texans had adapted the style to fit their individual needs.

He started walking Hoss toward the barn. The Texas versions of Blythewood lacked these steps leading from the ground to the first floor. Must be the difference in terrain, he mused, recalling his father telling him how Blythewood had been moved, brick by brick, from the banks of the mighty Mississippi to its present location. Farther down-river levees had eliminated the need to raise the main floor off the ground, but not here. This area still flooded regularly.

As he strode toward the barn, he compared Blythewood to the Wynthrop home, a few miles farther north on the river road. His memories were a bit vague, because he'd been shipped off to military school at an early age, but there was a painting of Heavenly Acres in John's office.

The Wynthrop plantation house was a classic Greek Revival, with tall pillars in front that climbed the height of the two-and-a-half-story brick-and-frame structure. Imported marble floors, floor-to-ceiling windows and colorful Persian carpets made Heavenly Acres lavish in comparison to Blythewood.

Neither house resembled the ranch house at the Rocking W Ranch. The first cabin which they'd constructed of pine logs, had been as austere as Heavenly Acres was lavish. Like the Shannons, the Wynthrops had donated the bulk of their wealth to the Confederacy. It was only in the past two years, since his father's death and J.B.'s decision to remain in Texas, that the present big house had been built. Long, low and sprawling, with foot-thick sand-colored stucco walls and a clay tile roof, it suited the land and the climate, just as Blythewood suited the surroundings.

Hoss nudged him in the center of his back. "Not moving along fast enough? That's a common complaint around here," J.B. said dryly. "The boss lady would agree with you. She can't see the backside of us any too soon. But we're stickin' to our guns and staying here—and so is she!"

Carefully avoiding the third step from the bottom of the seldom-used steps at the back of the house, Laura Lee moved as quietly as was possible in her oversize boots. Like the rapidly deteriorating town house in Blytheville, the steps were low on her repair list.

She used them now to avoid passing by Tad's room. Tomorrow, when he woke, Brandy would tell him that she had stuck to her original decision to leave Blythewood. J. B. Wynthrop's arrival hadn't made it any less likely that the sheriff would be pounding on her door come morning. She'd decided that another sorrowful departure would only serve to distress Tad.

She paused, her eyes searching the darkness for Foxfire. Tad must have left him in the stable, she thought with a grimace.

Surefooted from years of going to the stable without a lantern to guide her, she lengthened her stride.

The clouds separated briefly. Moonlight pierced the darkness. Anxious to be as far upriver as possibly by daybreak, she sent a silent prayer heavenward asking God to hold off before he delivered another deluge.

Upon entering the barn, she automatically reached for the lantern on the hook beside the door and felt the heat of the lantern's glass globe. It should have cooled by now, she thought. Her eyes searched the darkness; her ears listened for unfamiliar sounds.

Foxfire should be saddled, ready and waiting for her, but he'd been put in his stall. By whom? she wondered, cautiously walking the length of the barn. Tad? Sometimes his softheartedness about animals conflicted with following her orders. Maybe holding J.B.'s money in his hands had convinced him that there was no reason Foxfire shouldn't be put away for the night.

Laura Lee gritted her teeth when she saw J.B.'s horse two stalls down from Foxfire's. Tad must have taken it upon himself to offer J.B. a night's lodging in the spare bedroom and bedded his horse down for him, too.

She slid back the wooden bar that held the gate to Foxfire's stall closed and removed his headgear from a nail on a nearby post. Foxfire made a snorting sound and continued to chew lazily on the hay Tod had provided.

The thought of J.B. snuggled in a feather bed both annoyed and relieved her. She wanted him off Shannon property, and yet she didn't want another chance meeting with him on the river road. She should have known he'd worm his way into Tad's good graces when he told her that he wasn't going anywhere.

"Bullheaded . . . arrogant . . ." she muttered, holding the bit in her hand, " . . . laggard!" He'll be dead and burning in hell's fire before I travel west with him, she decided.

Brandy had attributed his tardiness to the weather; Laura Lee suspected he'd gotten lost. He'd had to ask her for directions to Blythewood, hadn't he? Too dense to remember his way home. Even Foxfire was smarter than that cowpoke.

Pawing noises coming from the other stall brought her head around. J.B.'s horse is restless, she mused. Earlier she'd wrestled with the problem of leaving Brandy and Tad without any means of transportation. Now an alternate solution came to mind.

She'd "borrowed" money from Reynolds; why not "borrow" J.B.'s horse?

Her impetuous idea became increasingly appealing as she silently weighed the advantages of it. From what she'd seen of the animal, he was in better condition than Foxfire. With the Mississippi flooding its banks, few boats and perhaps none, would be moving upriver. She'd probably have to travel farther on horseback than she'd originally intended. Besides, she told herself—blaming J.B.'s tardiness for her scandalous departure—he could afford to buy another horse.

She ran her hand down Foxfire's flank, gave him an affectionate pat and moved outside his stall. On her way to the other stall she hung Foxfire's headgear on the nail again. Anyone raised around horses knew better than to enter the unfamiliar horse's stall without letting the animal at least become accustomed to her voice, so she started murmuring to J.B.'s horse as she approached it.

J.B. had wrapped a dark woolen blanket around his shoulders and hunkered into the corner of the deep stall while he'd waited for Laura Lee to carry out her plan to leave Blythewood. He heard her approaching footsteps and wondered what she was doing. He had the advantage of being able to see every move she made while remaining out of sight himself. He watched her reach over the railing and scoop a handful of grain from the food trough. She held it beneath his horse's mouth, gently murmuring nonsense words.

A kindhearted gesture, he mused, his esteem for her rising fractionally. She evidently liked his horse a whole hell of a lot more than she liked him. He had the teeth marks and the bruises to prove it.

The clatter of the horse's headgear being removed from the hook where he'd placed it made him doubt his assumptions. What in blazes? He hunched deeper into the shadows of his hiding place when he heard the gate being opened.

Her intentions became as clear as the crystal decanter he'd seen on the sideboard in the dining room. He'd expected her to attempt to run off, but not on his horse! In Texas, stealing a man's horse was a hanging offense.

"Take it easy, big fella," Laura Lee said soothingly.

Suddenly what had at first struck her as an ingenious plan no longer seemed such a good idea. The vast difference between "borrowing" money to save Blythewood and stealing a horse so that her family would have transportation made her stop and think twice.

She wasn't a cold-blooded thief.

She might be destitute, but until today she'd always been scrupulously honest.

Her hand slithered down the horse's flank. She couldn't steal this man's horse any more than she could shake the coins from Tad's piggy bank to buy ribbons for her hair.

"Take it easy, big fella," she crooned when he shifted backward.

J.B. raised himself up on his haunches. "You put that bit in his mouth and you'll be singing angel hymns."

Caught red-handed, she dropped the incriminating evidence as though the leather reins had burst into flames. She'd changed her mind, but J.B. had no way of knowing that his horse was safe.

"What are you doing here?" she blustered.

"Protecting my horse from a horse thief? Bedding down in the barn because the mistress of Blythewood shut me out of the house?" Slowly he straightened to his full six feet two inches. With measured steps meant to intimidate her, he closed the gap between them. "Or maybe I'm waiting for my horse to finish eating so I can hit the trail back to Texas. Take your pick, Miss Shannon."

His voice was colder than sleet in wintertime. It was all she could do to keep from scurrying out of the stall like a frightened mouse. Wouldn't that amuse him, she thought, bracing her shoulders against the gate of the stall.

"The latter, I hope," she replied wryly. Her throat felt as dry as her reply, but she stood her ground, refusing to let him back her into a corner the way he had in her parlor. "Maybe I'm saddling up your horse to escort you off my property."

"Your property?"

"My brother's property." She strained her eyes to see in the darkness. Was that ham-hock-size hand of his empty? His type probably slept with his holster and gun as a pillow. "I'm his guardian. I have some say in who stays at Blythewood. I ordered you to leave."

Once again he couldn't help but admire her gumption. He'd caught her in the act of stealing his horse and she'd neatly switched from defending her actions to being in command of the situation.

His voice dropped to a low growl. "I'm not going anywhere tonight. You aren't, either." He reached over her shoulders, braced his hands on the railing and pinned her against the slats. "Understand?"

"You're the one who's having difficulty understanding, Wynthrop. You may be used to giving orders to empty-headed muscle-bound cowboys, but your orders don't amount to a hill of beans here."

The nearness of him was making her knees weak. The short breaths she was taking filled her senses with the smell of danger, mingled with leather, rainwater and horseflesh. She turned her head aside to keep from staring at the shadowed tuft of masculine hair peeking from beneath his open-necked shirt.

"Just back off, mister."

"Dammit, Laura Lee! I came to Louisiana to help you."

"You're too late to help."

She flinched when he cupped the side of her face with his callused hand; her neck stiffened as she tried to keep from looking him in the eye.

"Would you excuse my tardiness if I told you that when I realized I wouldn't reach Blytheville in time I tried to telegraph you but the wires were down?"

"Miserable excuse." She wasn't going to be swayed by the warmth of his hand or the warmth in his voice. It was his fault she had to leave Blythewood. She tossed her head. "You could have informed us of your intentions. The lines weren't down two weeks ago."

The sharp motion dislodged one of Brandy's precious hairpins from her hair. A long, curly lock of fine blond hair tumbled from beneath her hat, coiling between his fingers. The silky strands caught on the rough texture of his skin. Her scalp tingled, not with pain but with awareness. A woman of less mettle would have become flustered, would have swept the traitorous lock of hair up with her hand and pinned it back in place.

Laura Lee remained motionless. The blood pounding in her ears proved that she was flesh and blood, but she could have been carved from a solid block of ice. Her heart might burst and her hair might fall out, but he would never have the satisfaction of knowing he'd shaken her!

She had every reason in the world to dislike J. B. Wynthrop. He'd broken the terms of the very document he'd insisted she read. Dammit, she wouldn't allow herself to think of him as a man. She bit the inside of her cheek in an attempt to obliterate the pleasurable sensations percolating through her insides.

"Nothing I say will convince you to forgive me for my late arrival?"

"Nothing."

"Nothing I say can convince you to keep your father's end of the bargain and go to Texas with me?"

"Absolutely nothing."

He's weakening, she thought. He's resigning himself to the fact that I can't be bullied or coerced. Her determination had beaten him. She'd won!

"I'm leaving by myself. You can take the Wynthrop money and . . . and . . ." She saw that his eyes had taken on a strange glitter. "And pay your debt by giving it to Luke Reynolds . . . if you're concerned about the Wynthrop honor."

In one swift motion he pulled her to him. Her boots left the straw-covered dirt floor, her stomach hit his shoulder, and her nose crushed against the muscles of his back. The wind had been knocked out out of her, or she'd have screamed bloody murder. Dangling upside down, dizzy, she gasped for air. Her lungs nearly exploded when she felt him place his hand firmly on her derriere.

"Put me down!"

"Why? There's absolutely nothing I can say that will change your mind. Maybe your ears work better upside down. In any case, I'll risk repeating myself. Neither of us is going anywhere tonight."

Her fists began beating a steady tattoo of rage on his back as she squirmed and tried to kick him. But as soon as she spoke again she could tell that the bite of a horsefly would have done greater damage.

"You dress and act like a boy," he warned her. "Keep fighting and you can expect to be treated like one."

Her eyes widened and her arms stiffened against his back when she felt a solid wallop on the backside. Her brother's bulky cloak prevented her from being hurt in the slightest, but her temper flared. "I should have shot you when I had the chance! You can't treat me like this!"

J.B.'s chuckle was far more damaging to her pride than corporal punishment could ever have been. There was laughter in his voice when he said, "Stop bellowing like a wounded heifer. Do you want Tad and Brandy to see you hanging by your heels over my shoulder?"

"The minute you put me down I'm going to...to..." She was sputtering in her outrage. She couldn't even think of a punishment vile enough to suit his perfidy.

He pivoted to close the stall gate, and she tried to scratch and bite him. She was rewarded for her futile efforts with a mouthful of fabric and a broken fingernail. His coat protected him as well as a medieval suit of armor would have.

"You're going to remove those oversize clothes you're wearing," J.B. said, "and climb into bed like the sweet young woman I expected to find when I arrived at Blythewood."

He strode from the barn toward the back steps.

"I'll do nothing of the kind," she snapped. "Nobody, especially you, tells me what to do and what not to do. I'll do as I damn well please . . . and you can't stop me!"

He'd climbed two steps, and he had his foot on the third. She heard the board crack and clutched at his coat, preparing to be pitched headfirst onto the next step. That board had been rotten for two years now.

J.B. avoided a nasty fall by removing his left foot from the step and springing lightly on the ball of his right foot, skipping the rotten tread. He made less noise climbing the rest of the steps than she'd made coming down them. "I'll fix that tomorrow."

"You aren't going to be around long enough to fix anything."

"Is Heavenly Acres in the same state of disrepair?"

His question took the fight right out of her. Heavenly Acres was charred rubble. In her present position she wasn't about to break that piece of news to him. Brute that he was, he'd probably whale the daylights out of her for not protecting the Wynthrop property.

"I said, is Heavenly Acres as run-down as Blythewood?" he repeated.

She considered the matter. Run-down? No. Burned down? Yes!

"Heavenly Acres isn't the way your family left it," she admitted, expecting his hand to rise and fall on an unmentionable part of her anatomy. Her blood rushed to her face, and her brain felt as though it had been jarred loose from her skull, but her survival instincts rescued her. She knew it was always best to attack in times of danger.

"Are you blind? You came upriver on horseback. Didn't you notice that most of the homes are decaying or gutted by fire? Farther north, whole cities are nothing but piles of brick rubble! Did you expect Heavenly Acres to be unscathed?"

"No." He turned right at the top of the steps and paused beside the French door. "Is this your room?"

She clamped her lips shut.

He waited for her response. When it became clear that none was forthcoming, he advised her, "Don't make me wake up the household, unless you're willing to face the consequences."

Fear of the unknown prompted a curt "Yes."

J.B. pushed the door open with his foot. Inside, her bed's white canopy and pristine bed clothing made an easy target for his burdensome load.

"I'm going to put you down, but I want your word of honor that you won't poke me or kick me once your feet touch the floor."

"The Wynthrop honor, Confederate money and swamp mosquitoes have one thing in common—they are all worthless. Why should I give my word to a man like—Wha—!"

She was flat on her back before she could finish, lying in an unladylike sprawl with her knees spread apart and J. B. Wynthrop standing between them.

"I'm not a patient man, Miss Shannon. Conservatively speaking, I'd estimate that you've used up about ten-years' supply of patience."

He would have shaken some sense into her, but the sight of her unbound hair fanning around her face and spilling over the side of the bed made her appear suddenly vulnerable, and he was stirred by a feeling of pity for this feisty child-woman.

"Buy some. You've got plenty of my money." She expected him to give ground when she started to roll forward. He didn't. Realizing within seconds that she'd be pressed up against him, closer than spoons in a silverware chest, she settled for pulling her legs onto the bed. "You're short on patience, but you've stockpiled hair triggers for your temper, haven't you?"

His black eyes raked over her. "We won't discuss what short-comings *you* have and don't have, Miss Shannon. It'd take weeks."

He'd retaliated before he'd been able to stop himself. What was there about her that reminded him of a tiny burr caught under his saddle blanket? At first he'd been able to ignore the needlelike pricks, but after a while she'd begun to rub him raw. No man—and certainly no woman—had ever dared to question his honor without facing dire consequences.

"Your low opinion of me doesn't bother me in the least." She sniffed indignantly. It did. She had always been held in high regard by those who knew her. He'd wounded her pride—and her backside. She wouldn't listen to any more of his vile insults. "You're in my bedroom. Leave."

"Get undressed and go to sleep."

He backed across the room to the wardrobe, keeping a close eye on her. As though he had eyes in his fingertips, he had her nightgown and the extra blankets she'd stored there in his hands within seconds. He flung the cotton gown on the bed. "You may not be exhausted after your day of bank robbing and horse thieving, but I am."

She gasped, astonished, when he kicked off his boots and spread the blankets on the floor. "Just what do you think you're doing? You can't sleep in here!"

He shed his coat and began unbuttoning his shirt. "I've slept in worse places."

"Indubitably! That is not what I meant." Laura Lee turned her face toward the flowered wallpaper. He'd admitted he was short on patience. Didn't he have an ounce of modesty, either? Was he going to shuck his clothes right there in front of her? She grabbed a pillow and tossed it at him. "Have you no sense of propriety?"

He snagged the pillow with one hand and dropped it to the floor. Exasperated by the way she had suddenly turned from hellcat to prude, he said, "Look, Laura Lee . . ."

"No, thank you!"

Amused by her quick response, J.B. had to grin. "Then don't look. Just listen. I'm not going to spend the entire night chasing you between the bedroom and the stable." He spread out both blankets, one on top of the other, kicked the pillow she'd thrown to the top end and lowered himself between them. "You brought this on yourself. You're good at pretending you're a boy. Keep pretending. Night."

Her plans for returning to the barn and escaping were evaporating faster than morning fog struck by the sun's rays. "I dare not close my eyes with you in here!"

Silence came from his side of the room.

"Your name isn't Jackson," she said sharply. "Don't you stonewall me!"

Her ragged breathing and the muffled sound of her fist pounding the pillow into shape were all that could be heard. Several explicitly rude names rattled through her head. Her nose tilted upward, as though he'd fouled the air she breathed. She wouldn't waste her breath on a man who'd gone deaf and dumb the second his head had hit the pillow.

Frustrated, she tossed under the coverlet. Didn't that uncouth cowboy stretched out in the middle of her floor realize that Luke Reynolds and the sheriff would be at Blythewood at dawn? Did he want her thrown into jail? Granted, she hadn't exactly been a gracious hostess from the moment he'd introduced himself, but she didn't think even a loathsome cowpoke would want to see a woman put in prison for robbing a bank, would he?

Yes, yes and yes, she silently groaned, flopping back on the remaining pillow. She refused to follow his orders, so he didn't care what happened to her. He'd probably smile when they put the handcuffs on her!

Calm down and think, she told herself. There had to be a way to escape. He'd proven she was no match for him physically. She'd have to outsmart him. Until now she'd underestimated, thinking he was all muscle and no brain. She wouldn't make that mistake again.

Her troubled eyes moved to where J.B. slept. Mentally she measured his height and breadth. Anybody that tall belonged on the floor. In a regular bed his feet would have dangled over the footboard. It's a good thing he didn't ask to share my bed, she mused. I'd be clinging to the edge of the mattress with my fingernails.

Not true, she said to herself. He outweighs you by a hundred pounds. The mattress would have caved in at the center, and you'd have rolled on top of him!

Her eyelids drooped from fatigue; a mental image of J.B. in the bed with her, curled up on top of him, came vividly to life. Her imagination altered reality. He wasn't stretched out on his back; his muscular body curved toward her. And his arms weren't folded under his head, either. His arm was draped over her waist, and his hand moved up and down her spine.

A pleasant tingling sensation crawled up her back. She shifted closer to the edge of the bed, closer to the sound of J.B.'s rhythmic breathing. Wouldn't it be wonderful to have a man's strong arms around her? She'd be safe, protected, cherished.

She opened her eyes, suddenly aware that her wayward thoughts were leading her down a forbidden path.

Safe and protected? Only if she had the barrel of her gun centered on his belly button!

She sent a deadly glance in his direction, as though he were directly responsible for her naughty image of the two of them sharing her feather bed. She'd make him damn sorry if he tried anything with her!

She rolled onto her side, hoping she could see his face, certain she'd find a lascivious grin quirking the corners of his mustache. What she could discern in the shadowy darkness had her fingers clutching the remaining pillow to throw it at him.

Damn his rotten hide! He was smiling . . . with one eye open, watching her every move!

He wasn't the only one who could feign sleep. She crawled under the bed covers, savagely yanking them up around her neck. Concentrating, she slowed her breathing to an even pace that matched his. After what seemed like hours, she managed a few feminine snores for good measure.

Her normal cheeky grin curved her lips when she heard echoing snores, louder, with a few masculine snores as he inhaled.

Nobody could fake anything that awful, she decided, swallowing a snicker. But she wasn't taking chances. She'd wait. The minute she felt certain he'd fallen into a deep sleep she'd be out of there quicker than a rabbit with his tail caught between a gator's teeth.

She allowed herself the luxury of relaxing for the first time in a dozen hours. Her reservoir of strength had been depleted. She stretched out one leg, then the other. Her arms snaked beneath her pillow; she drew her knees up to her chest.

It won't be long now, she thought, breathing easily. Not long at all. He'll be sleeping like the dead, and I'll leave. She yawned. Not much longer.

Long years of sleeping under the stars in hostile terrain meant that J.B. slept with one eye open and was fully awake at the slightest unusual sound. The whisper of cautious barefoot steps in the hallway had him sitting bolt upright.

Instantly taking in his surroundings, he glanced from the bed to the door. Laura Lee was sleeping undisturbed. Judging from the sound, he guessed Tad would be bursting through the door momentarily.

He'd presumed to sleep in the middle of her floor. Unless he wanted Tad pointing a shotgun at his midsection he'd better vanish immediately. Quiet as a marauding Indian, he gathered the blankets and shoved them into the wardrobe. He picked up his discarded clothing and his holster and made it through the galley door just as the bedroom door slowly opened.

J.B. wasted no time waiting to see who would poke his head through the opening; he scampered down the back steps. There was little reason to risk being seen running toward the barn. He sat on the back step long enough to get his feet into his boots.

Daybreak at Blythewood, he decided, was a sight to behold. The sun was a brilliant yellow-orange ball of fire that silhouetted the trunks and branches of twisted oaks. He wished John could see it. Since the accident his brother had spent many hours drawing with pieces of charcoal or painting. He'd have captured the glorious moment, the gnarled trees and the rays of sunlight, on canvas.

J.B. raked his hand through his ash-blond hair, as was his habit whenever thoughts of John entered his head. He was resigned to the fact that he would never get over the gut-wrenching guilt he felt every time he thought of him. Even this trip from Texas to Louisiana testified to his desire to make amends.

John had saved his life, and in doing so he had lost the use of his legs. J.B. would have cut his own off to replace them if he could have. That wasn't possible, but there was something he could do for his brother. He could bring John the bride he'd been promised. It was what John wanted, and, by damn, whatever John wanted, J.B. got for him.

He stood, stretching his arms upward and yawning. He heard Laura Lee's gallery door open overhead. Smiling smugly at having accomplished the task of keeping her at Blythewood, he stepped into the backyard and lifted his face upward. His eyes widened, his smile collapsed, and his arms raised to cover his face.

A rush of water drenched him.

Chapter Five

Sniffing his drenched sleeve, J.B. raised his eyes to the gallery. "Good shot, Miss Shannon."

"Thank you, Mr. Wynthrop," Laura Lee replied civilly. Considering the fact that he'd blocked her escape route last night, he was lucky she hadn't dumped the chamber pot on him. "Next time I'll choose a more appropriate weapon."

A good night's sleep hadn't blunted her sharp tongue or cooled his temper, he decided, preparing for another battle of wits. "After I've changed, would it be possible for us to discuss the papers I gave you last night?"

His smart remark about her reading ability still stuck in her craw. Blessed with a natural aptitude for reading and figures, she'd escaped the drudgeries of being groomed to be a lady by sharing the attic classroom with Beau. She'd wager she could read circles around some slowpoke cowboy.

Still, she was aware of the prevailing attitude among men that women with learning were unattractive, and she decided to use it to her benefit. J.B. expected her to be a scatterbrained nitwit. She'd watched the Betsy Maes of the South often enough to be able to imitate their empty-headed poses.

Fluttering her long lashes, she smiled sweetly and said, "You'll have to pardon me for being such a slooow reader."

"Tonight, after we've retired for the evening, I'll read it to you instead of telling you a bedtime story," J.B. promised, wiping a dribble of water from his face with the back of his hand.

Her eyelids ceased their fluttering. Beneath his thick mustache he was grinning like a man who had shared a lot of women's beds and thoroughly enjoyed pillow talk. She gawked at him, furious at his silent insinuation. She propped the rim of the bowl on one hip and her hand on the other.

"I'll read the papers and meet you in the dining room, Mr. Wynthrop," she told him, coolly.

She spun on her heel, having had the last word, but his chuckle rasped up her backbone. Why did he make her feel like a pesky kitten who enjoyed having her fur stroked from tail to head? she fumed, slamming the door to her room.

There wasn't a doubt in his mind when he heard the sound of her heels striking the boards overhead and the rattling of the windowpanes that she'd gone inside to get the chamber pot. J.B. moseyed out of range just as Tad burst through the back door.

"Hey, Mr. Wynthrop, are you gonna go into town right away to pay the banker? I'll saddle your horse for you."

J.B.'s cocky grin changed to a genuine smile that reached his dark eyes; laugh lines crinkled at the corners of them. This boy didn't waste time—either by walking or by being subtle.

"Hold on, Tad." He hooked Tad by the shirt collar to keep him from rushing by him in too much of a hurry to wait for a reply. "The bank won't open until ten. Don't we have time for breakfast?"

"You hungry?"

"I haven't eaten a decent meal in days."

"Brandy is gonna fix eggs, soon as I collect them." Tad's china-blue eyes raised toward his sister's room. He shook his head and shrugged, as though he couldn't figure out what was going on between his disgruntled sister and this man who'd brought them saddlebags filled with money. "I guess it wouldn't cause too big a fuss if you ate breakfast with us."

Nodding his acceptance of the boy's reluctant invitation, J.B. released his hold on Tad's shirt. "Where's the chicken coop?"

"In back of the barn."

"I've got to change clothes. Mind if I walk with you?"

"I'm kinda in a hurry." Tad's eyes measured the stranger's long legs. They'd have made four or five of his. In broad daylight the newcomer seemed much taller.

J.B. grinned. When isn't this kid in a hurry? he thought. He dropped to his haunches and sat back on his heels. "Want a ride?"

"On your shoulders? Yeah!"

"Put your foot here—" he pointed to his thigh "—and swing aboard."

With a little help, Tad mounted his shoulders. Twisting at the waist, he saw his sister in the upstairs doorway. "Hey, sis! Look at me! I'm bigger than a giant!"

Laura Lee retreated farther into the room. Blast! She didn't want that insufferable man to know she'd been watching and listening. If J. B. Wynthrop thought he could get in her good graces by establishing a friendship with her brother, he had better think again. She wasn't as soft-hearted or as gullible as Tad.

"Guess she's gone downstairs," Tad said, making a clicking noise between each word as he looped his arms around J.B.'s forehead. "I bet if there were clouds today my head wouldn't get wet! It would be above them."

"That's how I used to feel when my big brother put me on his shoulders."

A circle of pain tightened around J.B.'s heart. He had looked up to his brother back then; now he had to look down to see him in his cumbersome wheelchair.

"Wow! You've got a brother bigger than you?"

"One way or another, yeah, he's bigger than me."

"I had a brother, but I don't hardly remember him. He's missing."

"Missing?"

He'd heard Beau had been killed at Shiloh. Although they'd been the same age and their families had been staunch friends, they'd never formed a close friendship themselves. As the oldest son and heir, Beau had been educated at home; as the second son, J.B. had been sent to the Citadel, a military academy in Charleston, South Carolina.

It was ironic, J.B. mused. Beau had been killed in action, while he'd spent the war looking after the crops in Texas.

"Yeah. I thought he got lost up north, but Laura Lee said it meant he was missing in action. She was crying like she did when Father was killed, so I guess that means Beau and Father are in heaven together." Tad sighed. "I wish things could be the way they used to be."

J.B. tightened his grip on the boy's legs when his voice dwindled away into sad nothingness. He'd made similar wishes himself. "Yeah, I know."

"Laura Lee says someday things will be better, but I don't think so. Look around." Tad flung one thin arm wide in a sweeping gesture that took in the weed-choked fields and the deserted brick cabins down the narrow lane. "The place is empty. Who's gonna plant the cane? Harvest it?"

"What does your sister say about that?"

"She says everybody'll be back. What do you think? Will they?"

"Maybe." J.B. didn't like holding out false hopes. "Maybe not," he said honestly.

Tad sighed. "We don't have the money to pay workers if they do come back."

War had made Tad old beyond his years, J.B. thought regretfully.

"Still in an all-fired hurry to get the eggs?" J.B. asked, suddenly wanting to put some fun into the boy's life.

"Uh-huh."

"Then hang on, broncobuster, we're gonna gallop."

As he rounded the corner of the barn he began to trot. Tad giggled childishly, bouncing on his broad shoulders.

An hour later the four of them were sitting at the kitchen table. Scrambled eggs, biscuits and red-eye gravy were passed around the table in silence after the blessing was given.

The makeshift table they'd carried down from the attic months ago had been adequate for the three of them, Laura Lee mused, but now, with J.B. seated there, it seemed to have shrunk in size. She had drawn her legs back until her heels touched the rear rung of the chair, and yet her knees were perilously close to bumping those of the long-legged man seated across from her.

Laura Lee glanced furtively across the table.

Eyes that were as black as sin and twice as devilish studied her.

She chased a forkful of her eggs around her plate, suddenly self-conscious about her table manners.

"Do you want to ride into town with me?" J.B. asked her suddenly.

Her fork clanked against the rim of the plate. To cover her awkwardness, she took her napkin from her lap and dabbed at her lips. "I have no intention of voluntarily turning myself in to the sheriff."

"No charges will be pressed," J.B. replied.

The raising of her eyebrows plainly expressed her doubts.

From what he'd pieced together from the conversation he'd overheard last night, he could understand her reluctance to return to the scene of the crime. To reassure her, he added, "Bankers are in business to make money. Luke Reynolds will be repaid, with interest. He won't be bothering anyone."

Brandy nudged her cousin's foot to get her attention. Without saying anything, she communicated to Laura Lee that she thought she should tell J.B. about the prank she'd pulled. The damage Laura Lee had inflicted involved more than depleting Luke Reynolds' bank vault. Laura Lee had done the unforgivable; she had robbed him of his masculine pride—and in front of his wife.

"I'll go with you," Tad said, anxious to protect his sister.

"Don't talk with your mouth full," Laura Lee told him.

The thought of J. B. Wynthrop encountering Luke Reynolds knowing only half of the circumstances held a vast appeal for Laura Lee. Reynolds would get his money, and at the same time she'd be paying J.B. back for the purple thumbprint he'd left on her upper arm.

And J.B.'s visit to town would also tell Luke Reynolds that the Shannons had male protection. He could bully two women and a child, but J. B. Wynthrop was another matter. Another matter indeed, Laura Lee thought, her disposition improving greatly at the prospect of J.B. permanently altering Luke's nose.

Brandy nudged her foot, harder, and shot her a withering glance.

"I guess I should warn you," Laura Lee said, choosing her words carefully for Tad's sake. He was too young to hear what sort of collateral Luke Reynolds had had in mind when he'd given her the money. "I deflated Mr. Reynolds's ego... in front of his wife."

"Betsy Mae caught him with his pants down at her house in town is what she means." Tad grinned at his sister and explained, "It embarrassed him like it used to embarrass me when she'd want to wash behind my ears while I took a bath."

Blessed innocence, Laura Lee mused, returning Tad's smile.

J.B. wasn't amused. A man who coerced a woman into bed wasn't much of a man. "I'll take care of that problem, too."

"While you're gone, I could start reading those papers," she said.

"You do that." J.B. mirrored her grin, wiped his mustache on his napkin and got to his feet. "We'll start making preparations as soon as I return. Excuse me, ladies."

He'd barely made it through the back door when Tad jumped up. "I'm not gonna miss this!" he declared, trotting his empty plate to the sink.

"Tad!"

"He can go," Laura Lee said to Brandy as she began scraping the remainder of her uneaten breakfast into the slop bowl. "I'll do the dishes for a change. Why don't you go get those papers off my nightstand?"

She disapproved of the bond growing between her brother and J.B., but the mulish expression on Tad's face when he'd announced his intention to ride into town had reminded her of their father. Their mother had known better than to argue at times like this, and a puny excuse given to keep Tad at home would have resulted in her brother sulking until J.B. returned.

She'd done the right thing. No harm would befall her brother while he was with J.B., and Tad would give her a firsthand account of what happened between Luke Reynolds and J. B. Wynthrop.

"I'm here to pay off the note on Blythewood."

J.B. had let the banker have the satisfaction of seating himself behind his desk, in the seat of authority—a ploy meant to intimidate lesser men who came begging for money, hat in hand. Now he emptied the money from one saddlebag, then laid his palm flat on the man's desk, letting the other rest loosely on his six-shooter. Leaning forward, he created the opposite effect that Reynolds desired.

"Count it," J.B. told him in a voice that was deadly soft. "Whatever is left over is to be credited to the Shannon account. There won't be any problems, will there?"

Luke rubbed his forefinger thoughtfully over the plaster tape on the bridge of his nose. The Shannon brat had smugly introduced him to the Texan out in the lobby. He'd already been on the receiving end of J. B. Wynthrop's knuckle-busting handshake. Only a fool would risk looking down the barrel of the six-shooter that was riding on the man's hip as though it were part of his body. His feud wasn't with the man looming over him; it was with Laura Lee Shannon.

"Won't you be seated, Mr. Wynthrop?"

"This isn't a social visit." J.B.'s eyes dared the banker to go ahead and reach for the gun that he felt certain was hidden in the desk drawer. Before he could fill his hand, J.B.

would have the pleasure of winging him. Women, children and desperate men were obviously the banker's preferred customers. "I won't be here long . . . will I?"

Luke wisely laced his hands together on the desktop. "There isn't an IOU to sign over to you."

"A receipt will do nicely."

"Made out to you or Laura Lee?"

Luke realized from the murderous glint in the other man's eyes that he'd almost made a fatal error. By admitting that there wasn't an IOU he had nearly confessed to having attempted to exchange money for Laura Lee's favors. He plucked his pen from the inkwell in such haste that black blobs dripped off the point and onto his desk. Automatically he reached for his handkerchief, but he had second thoughts when he saw the stranger's hand tighten on the butt of his gun. He blotted the spots with a blank sheet of paper.

"That will be *Miss Shannon* to you," J.B. said grimly.

Hastily, Luke scribbled Paid, the amount and his signature on another piece of paper. "Anything else I can do for you? I understand the Wynthrop property, Heavenly Acres, burned to the ground. We're a small bank, but I'm confident we could arrange something."

"Nothing."

The granite hardness of J.B.'s square jaw didn't so much as twitch, but the knowledge that his family home lay in charred ruins tempted J.B. to reward this bearer of bad tidings in the same manner as the ancient king who had beheaded a messenger who had dared to deliver bad news. His trigger finger itched.

"Well, in that case, I won't detain you," Luke said, only too glad to be rid of the man. It was obvious that one wrong word was all Wynthrop would need to clear his holster and empty his gun. Slowly, not making any sudden moves, Luke handed the Texan the slip of paper and stood. "It's been a pleasure doing business with you."

Silent messages passed back and forth between the two men.

We do understand each other, don't we? J.B.'s eyes said.

Luke nodded and managed a polite smile.

And you won't bother me or my friends, will you?

Luke shook his head. His smile faded, but he raised his hand as if to seal the bargain with a handshake.

J.B. scowled, then turned on his heel and strode toward the office door. When he spun around unexpectedly, he knew from the malice glimmering in Reynolds's eyes that he was a true copperhead—he'd strike without warning.

"As Miss Shannon's former employer, you'll be receiving an invitation for a farewell party. Soon."

J.B. saw Reynolds's eyes blink, then widen in surprise.

"She's leaving Blythewood?" From Laura Lee's reaction yesterday, when he'd mentioned her intended and she'd seemed surprised, Luke had jumped to the conclusion that his source of information had been misinformed about that part of the Shannon-Wynthrop agreement.

"She'll be marrying my brother. As her future brother-in-law, I've come to escort her back to Texas." He thumped his chest meaningfully. "She's family now, as far as I'm concerned. I wouldn't take kindly to anyone who stepped over the boundaries of propriety—in the past or in the future."

Only a man who'd been taught to keenly observe the lay of the land would have seen the banker's imperceptible shudder. J.B. saw it. His lashes lowered, hooding his eyes.

Luke nervously ran his hand over his scalp, wincing at the tender lumps there. "My wife and I will be honored to attend the party."

Without another word, J.B. reached behind his back and opened the door as though he had eyes in the back of his head. He opened it, stepped backward and closed it. His teeth clenched as he digested the unexpected news the banker had revealed.

Giving the one-armed man behind the counter a curt nod, he glanced at the clock over the outside door and called to Tad, "Come on, son. We've business to tend to before we return to Blythewood."

"Where we going?"

"To Heavenly Acres."

Like two sentries guarding a palace, Laura Lee and Brandy paced from one end of the wraparound porch to the other. Family honor rested heavily on Laura Lee's shoulders.

"Your father gave his word of honor," Brandy said softly. "It isn't as though you didn't agree to marry John."

"You know I'd never laid eyes on that written agreement until J.B. arrived with it. How was I to know if John would honor *his* father's word? I barely remember John!" From the skeptical look Brandy gave her, Laura Lee knew she wasn't swaying her. "The Wynthrops are the ones who interpreted 'keeping my wife and daughter safe' as being synonymous with John marrying me."

"You will be safe married to John."

"But . . . if I'd known Father hadn't put marriage in the written agreement, I wouldn't have agreed to marry John."

"But you did agree to marry him?"

Laura Lee grimaced. Her logic was wasted on Brandy.

"Promising and doing are two different things entirely." Laura Lee examined the scuffed toe of the petite button shoe on her foot to keep from looking Brandy in the eye. "It's like the summer visit you made when I was five.

You promised to teach me how to use the buttonhook so I could get a grown-up pair of kid boots. We both know you intended to do what you promised, but I was too little. My fingers just couldn't handle that pesky buttonhook. You'd promised to teach me, but I still couldn't use a buttonhook. On a grander scale, that's what's happened here."

"You're comparing buttoning a shoe to getting married?"

The thin leather of Laura Lee's sole scuffed at a knothole in the worn planking. Analogies were often beyond Brandy's comprehension. Patiently Laura Lee explained, "No, Brandy, I'm showing how some promises are harder to keep than others. In both cases, we meant well. Regardless of what my father promised or what I agreed to, this isn't the right time for me to leave Blythewood. I can't understand why the big rush is necessary."

"John wants a wife. You agreed to marry him."

"After Blythewood was back on its feet. Doesn't it strike you as peculiar that John didn't come for his bride?"

"No, not really. He's running the ranch."

"What about his letters? I can read them aloud to you without the least bit of embarrassment on my part. Do they sound like the letters of a man eager to be wed?"

"Maybe he's shy?"

"Hmph!"

"I imagine ranchers can't be expected to spout poetry. They're busy outdoors."

"Listen to yourself, Brandy. Neither of us knows what John Wynthrop is like. Would you marry a man you didn't know?"

"I considered becoming a mail-order bride before I came to Blythewood." The gleam in Laura Lee's eyes told Brandy that she'd have been better off not telling that secret. "I came here."

"Point proven." Laura Lee looked Brandy straight in the eye. "You thought about marrying a stranger, but you opted to come to Blythewood."

"But my father didn't sign papers promising I'd go west. I didn't, either."

They were right back where they'd started. Giving up hope of convincing Brandy that an injustice had been done or enlisting her support in finding a loophole, Laura Lee raised her hands waist-high, then dropped them into the folds of her dress.

Sure she was right, Brandy said, "Marrying John Wynthrop will solve all your problems."

"I can solve my own problems, thank you very kindly."

Brandy gawked at her cousin as though she'd just blasphemed. What woman in her right mind would want to worry about money and land and the unwanted attentions of someone like Luke Reynolds when she could marry the man her father had chosen for her? "Marriage is a woman's sanctuary."

"Prison. Captain Bligh lives in a gilded cage. His wings have been clipped. Is that what you think I want?"

"Hmph! He's taken care of. I'd love to have someone take care of me. You would, too. You're being contrary because—"

"Because I thought I'd be in love with the man I married?" Laura Lee injected with ill-concealed bitterness in her voice. "The slaves were freed by the Emancipation Proclamation, but women remain men's chattel. I won't be subservient to any man—especially to a man I barely remember."

"How can you say that? You've known John most of your life. You yourself agreed to marry him!"

"With a long-term stipulation. I thought that John would come to his senses after a few years and realize that he didn't want to marry a stranger any more than I do. John must have known I'd be reluctant—that's why he sent his brother to do his dirty work."

"The only dirty work J.B. is doing is cleaning up the mess you made. He's saving your reputation from your own scandalous behavior."

"The Wynthrops *caused* my scandalous behavior!"

Laura Lee lengthened her stride until she was several paces ahead of Brandy's mincing steps. Her cousin's yammering was getting on her nerves. She needed to be clear-headed, needed to think rationally. She stroked her temples as a twinge of pain darted behind her eyes.

"Be reasonable, Laura Lee. It'll take years to restore Blythewood to its former glory. Think of Tad! Think of Blythewood! You were willing to borrow money... to exile yourself from your home... to do anything you had to do for both of them. Why are you being so pigheaded about marrying a man who could take care of you, your brother and your home?"

Guilt slowed Laura Lee's steps, and Brandy caught up with her. Her conscience was silently scolding her for being selfish. She felt as if she were swimming against the current of the flooded Mississippi. She hated being sensible. It was sensible for a genteel woman to learn to manage a house: supervise servants, count silverware and linens, sew a fine stitch. She despised such feminine chores. As surely as the Confederacy had fought for independence, she had waged a lifelong war against being dominated.

Independence. Yes, she thought, savoring the feel of the word on her tongue. There were few good things she could attribute to the war, but the absence of the Shannon men at Blythewood had allowed her to take the reins of power. Laura Lee Shannon had become a woman in her own right, she mused. She couldn't go back to letting a man dominate her any more than the liberated slaves would welcome a return to chains and manacles. She'd had a taste of freedom; she wanted to continue savoring the flavor.

"I can manage without a Wynthrop telling me what to do and when to do it," she countered staunchly, her spine growing rigid. "Don't worry, Brandy. I'll take care of you and Tad somehow."

"Oh, Laura Lee, I'm not complaining. I just don't want you to get another wild idea into your head about trying to stop the inevitable. Why do you think your father promised you to John? He knew what was best for you. That's why he put it in his own handwriting."

"You think he made a wise decision—arranging for a marriage between his darling daughter and a man she can barely remember?" Laura Lee pushed up one of her sleeves. "See what his brother did?"

"J.B. did *that*?"

"And there's another set of his fingerprints on my other arm!"

Shocked by the faint bruises she saw, Brandy faltered, "Oh, honey, what did you do to earn those ugly marks?"

It's hopeless! Laura Lee thought despairingly, yanking her sleeve down. Utterly hopeless! I prove what kind of brutes the Wynthrop men are and she wants to know what I did to deserve the bruises!

"What would you do if J.B. yanked you off Foxfire and manhandled you?"

"Faint or cry. A man can't cope with the oldest weapons known to women. What did you do?"

"I defended myself!"

Brandy clucked her tongue. "J.B. must have dozens of bruises."

"Why do you keep taking his side?"

"I'm on your side, Laura Lee. Like your father, I love you. I only want what is best for you. Once you get over your obstinacy, you'll thank me for caring about your welfare."

Like Tad, Brandy thought J. B. Wynthrop was a knight in shining armor who'd arrived on a white charger to rescue distressed women and children! She could talk to Brandy until she was blue in the face and still be unable to convince her that J.B. was a cowpoke wearing ordinary clothes astride a rented horse.

"You haven't heard a word I've said," Laura Lee muttered. Resigned to having to find a way out of this mess by herself, she added, "I'm going to the barn."

"I'll start packing your clothes."

"Don't bother" was on the tip of Laura Lee's tongue, but she kept silent. She'd think of something. She always did.

Dismounting in front of Blythewood's barn, J.B. let Tad run into the house to tell the womenfolk that they'd returned while he unsaddled Hoss and Foxfire and led them into their stalls. His hands shook with pent-up rage as he used the pitchfork to toss hay to the horses.

The last few days, as he'd traveled along the river road and seen the ghostly shadows of other homes that had been gutted by fire, he'd convinced himself that Heavenly Acres sat far enough back from the river to be safe. He'd intentionally delayed riding over to his home until his hopes were confirmed.

Before he'd gone to the bank he'd looked forward to returning to Heavenly Acres. The memories he cherished were those of a homesick eight-year-old boy, memories that had been embellished by one of John's paintings.

He'd looked forward to stepping out from under the canopy of oak branches lining the lane leading to Heavenly Acres and walking across the wide expanse of lawn. His imagination had provided him with the scent of gardenias and jasmine, although he'd known it was too early for them to be in bloom.

Luke Reynolds had shattered his mental picture as thoroughly as a cannon aimed straight at his heart. He'd hidden his vulnerability behind a poker face but animosity had burned in his stomach. The banker had no idea how close he'd come to meeting the grim reaper. But as much as he wanted to find a release for his pent-up anger, he couldn't plug Reynolds any more than he could blame Laura Lee for the disaster.

Frustration shook him, but what could a tiny woman and a boy have done to stop a marauding army of men hell-bent on destruction? J.B. knew he couldn't have stopped them if he'd been there himself.

Laura Lee might have warned him a little more thoroughly, but nothing she could have said would have prepared him for actually sifting through the black ashes, kicking burned timbers aside, searching for some small memento to assuage his grief and anger. Looters must have pilfered the ashes long before he'd arrived. Nothing of value remained. Perhaps it was better that she had kept silent. With his short temper, he knew, he'd have taken out his rage on her.

He closed his eyes, and a picture of Heavenly Acres loomed up in his mind. Like a tombstone, the smoke-stained remains of the brick fireplace rose from the sodden rubble. Strange, but it was Tad's small hand curling around his that had given him the strength to turn and walk away from Heavenly Acres. He'd looked down into the boy's eyes—eyes that were bluer than the sky overhead, and twice as old—and found solace.

"She couldn't stop them. She tried," was all Tad had said.

J.B. knew he had to accept the desecration of his home with the same brand of heroic stoicism his brother had summoned up when he'd had to accept the loss of the use of his legs.

He opened his eyes and leaned the pitchfork against the wall. He knew a grown man shouldn't cry, but he could taste the salt of his tears. Slowly he curled his hand into a tight fist and slammed it into the wall, welcoming the pain that reverberated from his knuckles to his shoulder.

"Oh, John, how am I going to destroy your dreams by telling you what has happened? You'd be better off not knowing!"

It was against his nature to avoid facing hard truths, but now he could understand why John had insisted on keeping his handicap a secret from Laura Lee.

Back in Texas, when he and John had discussed bringing the Shannon girl to the ranch, John had insisted on not telling Laura Lee the bald truth about his being crippled. Hiding the whole truth had bothered J.B. But now he was glad he'd given his word not to tell her.

Fear might have kept her from telling him that Heavenly Acres had been destroyed, but she'd been wise not to do so. She'd done the right thing.

He would do the same for her.

She'd adjust. Not for a second did he doubt her inner strength. She'd make the best of a bad situation.

J.B. swiped his sleeve across his damp cheek. Undoubtedly Laura Lee was as guilt-ridden about Heavenly Acres as he was about his brother's injury. He'd do his damnedest to control his temper and be patient with her.

A wry smile crossed his face. "Don't make promises to yourself that may be impossible to keep. Laura Lee Shannon is one lady who can make being a gentleman damn difficult."

Chapter Six

"What happened at the bank?" Laura Lee demanded the moment J.B. stepped through the back door. She'd been busy setting the table for dinner when Tad had dashed through the kitchen and run straight up the stairs to his room.

"Everything's gonna be okay. I forgot to feed Captain Bligh," was the extent of what he had shouted over his shoulder.

"You can stop worrying. Mr. Reynolds has lost interest in arriving with a hanging rope in his hand."

Her ice-blue eyes melted under the sizzling heat of his charcoal-black eyes.

Unrestrained by hairpins, her blond curls swirled with enticing vitality as she whipped a sharp glance up at him. Why wasn't her hair parted down the middle and skinned back into a knot at her nape? Why were all ten of his fingers tingling from wanting to tunnel into the beckoning softness of her hair? Why wasn't she wearing those infernal britches he hated? She'd transformed herself from a runaway hoyden into a fragile woman. The blue hue of her dress reminded him of hills and valleys covered with Texas bluebonnets. The white lace edging the demure neckline and her trim waist accentuated the fullness of her breasts and a waist he could easily have spanned with his hands. His throat constricted.

Gruffness exposed his inner turmoil as he asked, "Do you want to join me in the library to discuss what I've planned?"

Although she'd broken eye contact with him, Laura Lee felt drawn to him. It's natural, she told herself silently, to feel gratitude toward someone who's rescued you from financial ruin...saved your reputation. Of course...that explains the attraction. She stepped back, as though some inner warning system had automatically rejected her simple explanation.

"Are we back to me throwing you over my shoulder?" J.B. asked, unaccountably stung by her withdrawal.

She bristled like an angry porcupine. Determined to goad him, she muttered an explicit phrase she'd heard Beau use when he'd been kicked between the legs by a horse.

"Lye soap, Miss Shannon," he said, and she could see that she had shocked him. "Get in there. Now."

Laura Lee gave him a sugary smile. Whatever Beau's words meant, they'd certainly riled J.B. Lovely! She'd have to search her memory for a few more choice phrases that weren't meant for her tender ears. Better to feel animosity than that peculiar sensation in the pit of her stomach she'd felt moments ago.

The solid oak door clicked ominously as J.B. shut it behind them. He pointed one imperious finger toward a leather wing chair. "Sit."

Speak. Roll over. Play dead. Does he think he'll have me licking his boots and wagging my rear end? Laura Lee raged silently. I'm not some dumb animal to be ordered around by the master of Heavenly Acres!

Her father's sanctuary remained much as he'd left it. Heavy emerald-green velvet drapes with tasseled gold tie-backs partially blocked the sun's bright rays. She paced the perimeter of the room, running her fingers over the leather-bound volumes in the bookcase, trailing them over the polished mahogany desk, brushing them against the arm of his desk chair to remind herself of what she'd be leaving behind.

In the past few months, when worrying over the ledgers had drained her emotionally, she would raise the lid on the humidor. The faint odor of the Havana cigars he'd smoked lingered inside it. Somehow, one whiff always bolstered her stamina, making it possible for her to keep food on the table and shelter over their heads.

Here she could almost feel her father's presence.

J.B. felt it, too. He sat on the corner of the desk with his legs stretched out and crossed at the ankles, his arms folded on his chest. He tried not to let those little hands of hers tug at his heartstrings, but his eyes lost their glittering hardness as he said, "He arranged for you and Tad to be provided for."

"I've read the papers. They're self-explanatory. Nothing I wasn't aware of before you arrived."

"And you're agreeable to the marriage?"

She raised her chin and circled the desk until she stood directly in front of him. Out of nowhere, like a streak of lightning from a clear summer sky, came a wild thought: Why didn't my father specify you instead of your brother to be my husband?

She was only inches away from him. J.B. had to remind himself of how close he was to making restitution to his brother to keep from pulling her into his arms.

He was taking her back to Texas for John to marry.

"Yes."

Her simple reply astounded him. He'd thought there would at least be recriminations and dire threats attached to her answer. His brows drew together in consternation.

"What about . . . l-love?" His tongue stumbled over the unfamiliar word as he looked into sky-blue eyes that beseeched him to find an alternative solution.

"Love?" Their eyes met and clashed. "What's love got to do with an arrangement of this nature?"

J.B. reckoned that his brother's fantasies about Laura Lee were love in its purest form. "You'll be admired and respected. Out west, refined ladies are scarce as pure water."

Take off your blinders and take another look, Laura Lee thought, unable to believe he was serious. She'd be the first to admit she'd acted like an obnoxious brat from the moment they'd met, and she knew how little she resembled most men's picture of the ideal submissive Southern woman. How could he compliment her with a straight face? Why weren't his black eyes dancing with ill-concealed humor? Why wasn't his mustache quirked up on one side? His carved, aristocratic features were set in a deadpan expression.

"I can't imagine John and me sharing the same house, much less the same bed." Mention of the intimate side of marriage triggered a blush that she couldn't conceal. Flustered, she let her gaze drop to her toes, but, determined to prove her point, she stammered, "I mean . . . well . . . he'll expect children, won't he?"

"Do you?"

This marriage would be childless. J.B. would have to provide the heirs to the Rocking W Ranch. In fact, one of John's reasons for sending him to fetch Laura Lee centered around his belief that marriage would be contagious.

J.B. remembered chuckling at that unlikeliness of that and telling John he'd rather have the pox.

Laura Lee flinched inwardly when she saw his black eyes flicker with amusement. Mother warned me, she thought. Men derived pleasure from their conjugal rights; women resigned themselves to performing their wifely duties.

She peered through her dark lashes at the virile man in front of her. No doubt about it; he'd want children—a score of them. Her heart pounded as forbidden thoughts of his callused hands stroking her intimately spread goose bumps beneath the bodice of her scoop-necked dress.

Trying to keep her voice as frosty as a January morning, she croaked, "No. He'll want children though, won't he?"

J.B. only shrugged, unwilling to prevaricate when it wasn't necessary. She's an outspoken little chit, he thought. Other women would have swooned to avoid discussing what would or would not be taking place in the bedroom.

"Was that a yes or a no?" Laura Lee demanded.

"I imagine he'd concede to a stipulation that there be no children from this marriage. John isn't a callous brute like me. He's refined...sensitive...." He was crippled! The vow he'd made to conceal that fact from her weighed heavily on his conscience. If she didn't want children, why shouldn't he tell her she had nothing to worry about on that score?

It was too easy, Laura Lee thought, but she couldn't figure out how he was tricking her. "I might change my mind, but in case I don't, I'd like that in writing."

"You have my word of honor."

"Wynthrop honor?" She snorted and stepped to the desk where she'd placed the agreement her father had signed. "There must have been some reason my father felt it necessary to put this in writing. Since there are no witnesses to our discussion—"

Her words died in her throat when his fingers bit into her wrist. Anger, an emotion she trusted, cleansed the befuddlement from her eyes.

"Let go of me!"

"You dare to question Wynthrop honor? By God, woman, you're treading on dangerous ground." He lost the perilous hold he had kept on his temper and searched for a way to hurt her. "I've been to Heavenly Acres," he snarled.

"Oh." Her face turned bright pink, then paled.

"Oh? That's all you have to say about allowing the Wynthrop home to be reduced to ashes and cinders?"

Genuinely distressed, she let her balled fist go limp. He has every right to blame me, she thought. She chewed on the soft inner lining of her lip to keep the memory of that hideous night from engulfing her.

"I didn't lie. I could have." Laura Lee tugged her wrist free. "You asked me if Heavenly Acres was run-down, like Blythewood. Would you have told me the whole truth if *you'd* been slung over *my* shoulder?"

"Clever, but not clever enough." He reached behind himself and picked up the papers her father had signed and read aloud, "In exchange for one-third interest on all property purchased in Texas, the Shannon family will be caretakers of Heavenly Acres."

"I couldn't stop them! They were like maggots on rotten flesh—everywhere!" She waved her hands wildly, knocking the papers out of J.B.'s hand; they fluttered to the floor unnoticed. "I tried to stop them. God knows I tried!"

Her eyes had rounded in unspoken horror. Sorry that her slur on Wynthrop honor had goaded him into losing his temper, he said, "I don't expect a woman to hold off the Yankee army more than I'd expect you to risk bodily harm by telling me Heavenly Acres was destroyed. I wouldn't have tossed you over my shoulder if you hadn't riled me by trying to steal my horse. I apologize."

"Keep your damn apology!" She stood on tiptoe to diminish the difference in their heights. Even perched on the desk, he towered over her. "You misjudged me when you thought I was going to steal your darn horse, too!"

J.B. grinned and stood up, tucking his thumbs under his belt buckle. He seldom apologized for his behavior, and she'd flung his apology back in his face. The sting could not have been greater if she'd slapped him. Despite his smile, his temper was at its flash point.

"I gave my word to John that I'd bring you back to Texas. Well, my dear, against my better judgment, I'm sticking close to you until you've changed your name from Shannon to Wynthrop, though I'd rather tame wild mustangs blindfold than have you as a sister-in-law."

Laura Lee turned as pale as a ghost. She'd been unable to comprehend why he'd insisted on her marrying his brother, but now she thought she knew the reason. Blythewood would be lost to her, just as Heavenly Acres was lost to him. A loveless marriage would be the cruelest form of revenge.

She lifted her skirt with one hand and kicked at the hateful papers strewn on the floor. "I'll make each and every day of your brother's life total hell if you force me to abide by this agreement!"

"You can try, but you'll fail there, too," J.B. countered, his voice as steely as the bowie knife strapped to his leg. "He might put up with your impudence, but I'll be there to make certain you're a good wife."

Those sinfully black eyes of his traveled over her as though he were anticipating the pleasure of handing her over to his brother. He'd called her impudent? She could have sworn that his eyes had unbuttoned the tiny buttons beneath the lacy edging of her dress in less than two seconds. Laura Lee resisted the urge to cross her hands over her chest.

The air seemed too hot, too thick, for her to breathe. And then something totally flabbergasting happened. She could feel the tips of her breasts pucker in response to his shameless scrutiny. They pressed against her chemise, growing hard and heavy. She squeezed her eyes shut, willing her body to return to normal. She clenched her knees together to stop the achy feeling that was invading her lower limbs.

"I wish I'd never heard the Wynthrop name."

Her voice betrayed her, too. Hollow and breathy, it sounded more like a caress than a threat. Maybe there was something physically wrong with her. Her stomach felt as though it had completed a somersault.

J.B. was fighting his own inner battle as ferociously as Laura Lee was waging war against her reactions. Her lips were parted, inviting him to bend down to taste them. Fascinated, he watched her nipples harden and strain against the soft fabric of her demure dress.

Saliva pooled in his mouth as he wondered how they'd look after he'd laved them with his tongue. Pink and pearly, like her lips? A toasty brown, with dark centers? He swallowed hard, nearly choking.

His eyes lingered, then dropped to her willow wisp waist and lower. He had seen her in boy's pants, so he knew her legs were long and shapely. He groaned silently as his active imagination provided him with a detailed picture of the two of them in her canopied bed: he with his lips suckling her breasts; she with her legs twined around his middle, writhing, begging him to sink deep into the heat of her womanly softness.

Laura Lee licked her lips, unable to trust her voice. Say something, anything, her puritan mind silently screamed in protest. Women of good breeding didn't allow a man to stare at them! She searched for one icy remark to cool the flames in his eyes. From the neck up she was numb. From the neck down she felt as though she'd been seared by his flaming eyes.

"Supper!"

Brandy's voice echoed without meaning in her mind for several seconds, but then offered a welcome escape. Murmuring an incoherent excuse, she hastily turned away.

J.B. watched her gather her skirts and flee. He wanted to deny the mesmerizing effect she'd had on him, but only fools lied to themselves. He ached for her, plain and simple. He wanted her. And damned if he didn't think she wanted him, too.

She belongs to John, he reminded himself. You've done some low-down things in your life, but this time you're going to keep your hands in your pockets and your eyes on your boots.

"There you are," Brandy said when her cousin rounded the corner and came into the dining room. "I was just going to call you again."

Laura Lee covered her face with both hands. "Oh, Brandy, I can't go anywhere with him!"

"Now, now, Laura Lee. You're just being stubborn." Brandy set down the bowl she'd carried to the table and went to Laura Lee's side. "You'll get used to the idea of marrying John."

"Never!"

Brandy patted her shoulder. "You'll adjust. In a day or two you'll be looking forward to leaving with J.B."

"I can't go anywhere with him. I can't stand the sight of him!"

Liar! her conscience nagged. He stared at you and you melted like butter on a hot summer's day!

Tad skittered into the room with a bowl of black-eyed peas clutched in his hands. "Brandy said you were upstairs getting ready for dinner. How come your hair looks like you combed it with the eggbeater? Brandy made me put water on mine."

"She's been in the library talking to J.B." Brandy said, giggling behind her hand and winking at Laura Lee.

She gave Tad a weak smile. His hair was damp, and yet the stubborn cowlick on the crown of his head stuck up like a rooster's tail. "We both have unruly hair. I'd loan you some hairpins, but they'd fall out of your hair like they fall out of mine."

"Men don't wear hairpins, sis." Tad grinned and plopped the bowl in the center of the table. "I'm starving. Want me to call J.B.?"

"Mr. Wynthrop." Laura Lee corrected.

"Uh-uh. He said since we're gonna be brothers-in-law I should call him J.B." He held his sister's chair out for her. "Isn't that what you two were holed up in the library talking about?"

"Yes, it is," J.B. said coolly from the hallway. "We'll be leaving for Texas in a couple of days."

"Nothing is settled." Laura Lee seated herself, calmly spreading her skirts, seething inwardly at his high-handed announcement. He might be able to prod a mindless heifer into the slaughterhouse, but he'd find that getting her to follow in his tracks was more of a challenge. "Aside from the stipulation John agreed to, what you read to me mentioned the property holdings of the two families."

"John and I are willing to sell Heavenly Acres to keep Blythewood financially stable in exchange for the Shannon's share in the Rocking W Ranch." J.B. courteously held Brandy's chair out for her, directing his remarks to Tad. "You'll be able to afford hired help and make the needed repairs—which should get Blythewood back on its feet."

His generosity had Tad beaming, Brandy gasping and Laura Lee scowling.

He'd spiked her cannon again, he thought as he seated himself to the right of Laura Lee, across from Tad.

Instantly rebounding, Laura Lee inverted his lopsided grin by saying, "We could achieve the same goal by selling our share of the Rocking W Ranch. It's probably more valuable than Heavenly Acres."

"Without a house on the property, you're probably right," J.B. agreed. "There is no contingency clause in the agreement for destruction of the Wynthrop property. In all fairness, though, I don't think the Wynthrops should be penalized for Heavenly Acres being ransacked and burned."

Tad jumped to his sister's defense. "I told you she couldn't stop them. A bluebelly had her trapped in the barn, and he—"

"Hush, Tad!" Horrified at the thought of anyone else knowing what had taken place in the barn, she blushed bright red. She'd made Tad swear he'd never tell anyone what had happened. "Mr. Wynthrop isn't interested in the details."

"The food is getting cold," Brandy said anxiously. "Tad, will you say the blessing?"

Heads bowed in unison.

While Tad recited a prayer by heart, Laura Lee twisted the linen napkin she'd put in her lap. Why, oh, why, Lord, does he insist on me marrying his brother? Please, please, send him back to Texas! Alone!

"Amen."

"Can I have the slice of ham with the sticky stuff on it, please?" Tad was eager to commence eating as he was to start everything else.

"Brandy makes a delicious honey and mustard sauce," Laura Lee explained, spearing the choice end slice and putting it on a plate to be passed to her brother. "She's an excellent cook."

Tad crammed a wedge of ham in his mouth and said, "Laura Lee isn't much in the kitchen, but she can add numbers in her head. Show him, sis. J.B., give her five numbers."

"Never mind, Tad. I'm certain Mr. Wynthrop—"

"Twelve. Eighty-three. Forty-one. Twenty-five. Seventy-six." J.B. passed the black-eyed peas to his right. His eyes danced wickedly, daring her to come up with the correct answer.

Laura Lee saw no danger in showing off her mathematic skills. A man was more interested in his stomach than in totaling up numbers. "Easy. Two hundred thirty-seven. Candied yams? Another of Brandy's specialties."

"Is she right?" Tad asked J.B., unable to calculate the double-digit numbers on the fingers he had raised in front of his face.

Somewhat amazed, J.B. shrugged. "I'd need pencil and paper to add them up."

Laura Lee grinned. Men hated women who could outdo them. Bluestockings were unfashionable. "Wait until you taste the corn bread Brandy made."

"My sister collected the honey from the beehive."

Laura Lee knocked her foot against her brother's shin. She wanted J.B. to see her in an unfavorable light. It was her last slender hope of dissuading him from taking her west.

"Ouch! Why'd you kick me?"

"Don't talk with your mouth full."

Tad opened his mouth wide. "It's empty!"

Don't talk with your mouth empty, she thought, giving him a dirty look. Tad dropped his fork on his plate, and his eyes clouded with tears.

Instantly contrite, she decided to give him credit for his part of the meal. "Tad milked the cow and churned the butter. He's a big help around here."

"They make me do chores," Tad muttered.

"On a ranch one of the most important jobs is taking care of the livestock." J.B. buttered his corn bread and glanced around the table. The thought of asking Tad to join them on their trip entered his mind. There wasn't much a boy could do to save Blythewood, and it would put someone between himself and Laura Lee. From what he'd seen and heard since he'd left Texas, he was beginning to believe Tad would be an old man before the South recovered, so it might be best for the child. "How'd you like to be a cowboy, Tad?"

Tad's face brightened considerably.

Laura Lee glowered at J.B. "Wait just a minute. Who would take care of Blythewood?"

"I plan on hiring an overseer before we leave."

"What about Brandy?" Laura Lee asked. "She's part of the family, too. Are you going to make her a cowgirl?"

J.B. smiled at the horrified expression on Brandy's face. "Brandy would be welcome in your new home."

"Could I wear spurs and a six-shooter?" Tad scooped up black-eyed peas with his fork and shoveled them into his mouth. "And fight Indians?"

"Indians?" Brandy gulped, skipping her hand over her bright-colored hair as if she were in immediate danger of being scalped. "I've heard horrible stories about what has happened to some wagon trains attacked by Indians."

"You'd be safer at the ranch than you were in Atlanta during the siege."

"But I'm *safest* here," Brandy retorted, unconvinced.

"Last week you were lamenting the lack of suitable men around here," Laura Lee grumbled. "Didn't you say every man we meet is either physically or mentally lame? Or destitute? Or married?"

Brandy had the good grace to flush with embarrassment. "Well, yes, but I was reflecting on the lovely picnics and parties we used to have here when I visited. It's such a pity to see the same handsome men who escorted us from one fete to another penniless or crippled or both. When I think of that poor one-armed man who worked with you at the bank I could just cry my eyes out. Every girl in the parish wanted to do the Virginia reel with him. He used to be dashing . . . exciting. Now look at him. He's keeping books for Luke Reynolds, a man who made his fortune from our pain." She dabbed at the corner of her eye with her napkin. "It just breaks my heart to see those strong, fine, proud men reduced to poverty . . . missing an arm or a leg or an eye . . . begging for a job."

"We aren't beggars. Tad and young men like him will make the South thrive again," Laura Lee stated unequivocally. "The men who are worth their salt will fight to save what's rightfully theirs."

"How?" Brandy asked. "Tad is wonderful, but he's a child. It'll be years and years before he's able to get the crops planted, harvest them and get them to the wharves. What'll we do in the meantime? Who's going to teach them what they need to know?"

"Those men who returned, with the help of their wives and children. We'll survive." Laura Lee knew she sounded as though she'd stepped up on a soapbox, but she couldn't stop. She had to voice her convictions over and over again to keep believing in them herself. "You act like losing the war is a terminal illness. It isn't. We may be pockmarked, and it may take time for us to heal, but we will recover."

Brandy shook her head. "It'll never be the same. The men who are worth their salt won't sign the allegiance pledge. You know what that means. They can't vote or hold office. Carpetbaggers and copperheads make the laws. They've reduced us to being strangers on our own land. It'll never be the same," she said bitterly. Unable to check the tears streaming down her face, she excused herself from the table and raced up the stairs.

For several uncomfortable seconds, only the sound of forks scraping on china could be heard. Laura Lee considered excusing herself from the table to go and comfort Brandy, but she knew what would happen if she did. Brandy would make her feel rotten for not marrying John to permanently solve their financial problems. Guilt was already nagging at her.

J.B. thought over what had taken place between the two women. Laura Lee praised Brandy, and belittled herself. Didn't she realize that the courage she'd shown in fighting for what she believed in and the deep love she had for her family were of more value than Brandy's culinary expertise? A man could live on beef jerky and beans with a woman like Laura Lee at his side.

She had absolute faith in Tad, the South, and Southern men—a boy, a destitute land, and its penniless landholders.

He'd kept his eyes on his plate when Brandy had mentioned the men crippled in the war. He thought of John, and his brow furrowed. From what he'd heard, Laura Lee didn't think any the less of a man for his war injuries. Would she change her mind when she found herself married to a man in a wheelchair? Would John's not being a decorated war hero make a difference to her?

Perhaps it would.

Then again, he thought, she knew that shiploads of food had been donated to the Confederacy by the Wynthrops, not to mention horses and cattle. The Union blockade of the Southern ports had gradually choked off the Confederate supply lines, and railroad transportation had become impossible after the capture of Chattanooga. The Confederacy had had to resort to using wagons, which were slower, more cumbersome and more likely to be intercepted en route. In such desperate circumstances, the Southerners who had gone to Texas to raise food and other supplies for the Confederate armies had been indispensable to the Cause.

Like the other transplanted Southerners in Texas, the Wynthrops were unsung heroes. They'd honored their commitment until the Mississippi River and all the Confederate seaports were in the hands of the Union armies. Not until then had they begun carving out an empire for themselves.

Tad cleared his throat, drawing the attention of both adults. "I promise, sis, I'm gonna stay here till Blythewood is just like it used to be." He reached over to pat his sister's hand. "Right now I'm going to go out and pull weeds in the vegetable garden. Can I be excused?"

Touched, Laura Lee could only nod. The small piece of candied yam in her mouth tasted like a wad of flour paste. Her eyes gleamed with pride as she watched Tad march through the kitchen and out the back door.

J.B. wiped his mustache, raised his water goblet and said, "My compliments. He'd make a fine rancher."

"He'll make a better planter. It's in his blood." Laura Lee flung her napkin down on the table. "Don't you dare say another word about him going to Texas. Why don't you jingle those spurs of yours in Brandy's direction and leave Tad and me in peace?"

"Ah, so that's why you were heaping praise so lavishly on Brandy. You think you can toss in a ringer."

"This isn't a game, Mr. Wynthrop. There's a great deal at stake here."

She had no idea what an understatement that was, he thought dryly. "You talk about honor and perseverance—for others. But what about you, Miss Shannon? Don't you practice what you preach?"

"I am not going to sit here and be insulted by you. There's something wrong with a man who wants his brother to marry a woman he considers dishonorable and—" She started to scoot her chair back. It wouldn't move. J.B. had stuck his foot behind the front leg of the chair.

"And stubborn?"

"You're asking to have your shin kicked. You're the one being stubborn."

"Why? Because I won't agree to sell one square inch of the Rocking W Ranch? Because I won't come back and help rebuild the glorious South?" He bent toward her. "Listen carefully. I won't repeat myself again. In exactly three days you're going west. In the meantime, I'm going to make arrangements to sell what remains of Heavenly Acres. I'm going to see to Blythewood by locating a manager to take over your responsibilities here. And I'm going to buy seed and hire help to get a crop in the ground. In return for my benevolence, my lovely hoyden, you are going to write personal invitations to your farewell party, pack a minimal amount of belongings and prepare to leave for Texas. Do you understand?"

Laura Lee rocked backward to free the front legs of the chair. J.B.'s toe caught the rung, bringing the chair back down on the hardwood floor with a sharp thud. Long-forgotten curses that she'd heard Beau use were on the tip of her tongue. Only the dangerous look in J.B.'s black eyes kept her from giving him the tongue-lashing he so richly deserved.

She tapped her forefinger against her temple. "You're mad. Stark raving mad!"

Grinning, J.B. softly replied, "I couldn't agree more."

He had to be out of his mind to think he could get to Texas without touching her . . . one way or another.

Chapter Seven

"Who does he think he is?" Laura Lee muttered, pouring the water she'd heated into the sink and throwing a bar of lye soap in after it. "Sherman? Grant?"

"No, just Wynthrop." J.B. said teasingly, coming into the kitchen with a pile of dirty plates. He stacked the plates on the counter beside her. The thin white line circling her pressed lips warned him to be wary. "I could use your help, you know. John recommended a few people who'd be good managers, but I'd like your opinions."

Her head popped up, and she glared at him. "Am I supposed to be flattered that you're consulting me?"

"It would be to Blythewood's benefit."

Laura Lee rolled her eyes in disgust and devoted her attention to cleaning the plates that she'd submerged in the soapy water. "You can give orders, but I don't have to take them." Or follow them, she tacked on silently. Why didn't he just leave her alone? He didn't belong in her kitchen, helping with the dishes. This was women's work. "I'll do the dishes."

"Cowpunchers give the trail cook a helping hand."

She glanced at his large hands and decided they were better suited for punching cows than for handling irreplaceable china.

An unwelcome smile twitched the corner of her lips. Cowpuncher. Did cowboys really smack cattle with their fists?

J.B. strode back into the dining room, wondering what had caused the faint flicker of a smile he'd witnessed. He returned carrying glassware.

"Don't you think it's a bit nervy of you to ask for my advice?" Laura Lee asked.

"It's your family's land."

He deposited the glasses on the counter.

The plate she scrubbed was so clean it squeaked, but she continued washing it. She dared not risk looking up into his face. His ebony eyes had an unsettling effect on her nerves.

"You know who to trust around here. Who left? Who stayed? Who knows how to tend the land? I'd think you'd want to help."

She did. She gripped the plate in both hands as she silently wrestled with the temptation to bounce it off the back of his head.

"Don't do that," he said suddenly. "The plate will break. My head won't."

"That's for certain," she muttered, carefully setting the plate in the rinse water. Who better than herself to choose someone competent to run Blythewood? He had put his finger on one of the things that were nearest and dearest to her—Blythewood—and he was applying pressure. She could stubbornly refuse to be of help, which would be detrimental to Blythewood, or she could volunteer the name of a man who had the experience to make the land productive.

"And then there's Tad to consider. I'd think you'd want someone he could look up to for your overseer."

"Quit pushing me!"

From halfway across the kitchen he replied, "I haven't touched you."

Much to his dismay, he found himself wanting to touch her. Wouldn't this discussion be easier if she were sitting on his lap, with her arm draped over his shoulders and her head resting on his chest? He inched toward her.

Silently she cursed his astuteness. She might be able to rationalize keeping mum on the subject of a manager for the plantation, but nothing could be left to chance when it came to Tad. Through clenched teeth she murmured the name of the man who could care for both the land and Tad: "Bill Carpenter."

"The man I met at the bank?"

Laura Lee swallowed her stubborn pride and replied, "Yes. He's a good father, and he loves the land."

She turned her head to gauge his reaction as she raked the silverware through the soapy water. Her fingertips tingled, but it wasn't until J.B. caught her wrist and raised her hand that she realized she'd nicked her fingertip on the carving knife.

"Did you hurt yourself?"

"It's nothing," she whispered, mesmerized by the concern she saw in his ebony eyes.

Her heart lodged in her throat when he lightly dropped a kiss on the tips of her fingers and she felt the tickle of his mustache. His thumb moved to the fleshy mound beneath her thumb; automatically her fingers curled around it. A shiver of anticipation ran up her spine.

"You've got to be careful." His fingers closed around the back of her hand. Heedless of the consequences, he lifted her knuckles to his lips. He lightly kissed each joint, one by one. From somewhere deep in the recesses of his mind the voice of sanity urged caution.

You're only the escort—it said—not the future bridegroom. She's going to be your brother's wife!

The small voice fell on deaf ears.

Laura Lee couldn't speak; her mouth was parched. Looking into the black centers of his eyes made her feel as if she were standing at the edge of the swirling, muddy waters of the Mississippi, ready to plunge in headfirst without knowing how deep the water was. She knew that if his lips closed over hers she could easily drown in the liquid heat of his mouth. Her eyelids fluttered shut.

J.B.'s conscience was still raging at him. *Stop. Don't kiss her! She's betrothed to John.*

He dropped her hand and strode swiftly to the back door. He had no right to touch her, much less kiss her hand. Not wanting her to feel guilty about what had just taken place, he mumbled, "Thank you for suggesting someone."

She heard the back door latch click, and her eyes flew open. The hand he'd been holding moved over her heart. Had she imagined the look of longing in his eyes? She rubbed her knuckles over the soft curve of her cheek to reassure herself that she wasn't the only one who'd been affected by their nearness.

A sensible woman, she'd known in the library that they were moving into dangerous territory. What was there about J.B. Wynthrop that kept drawing her closer and closer?

She shook her head violently, clenching her hand into a fist. He infuriated her by taking command of every situation and consistently doing as he damn well pleased. Just thinking of him in this way was abominable! He was everything she hated in a man: domineering, obstinate, cocky.

But, she silently mused, when his dark eyes had beckoned her to come closer, her knees had gone weak and she'd felt light-headed. She'd wanted . . .

"You can't have everything you want!" she said aloud. And she thought, You can't have *anything* you want! Not Blythewood. Not Tad. And certainly not J. B. Wynthrop! He's going to be your brother-in-law, for heaven's sake!

Curious about where he'd gone, she crossed to the window and saw him standing beside the vegetable patch, talking to Tad. He dropped down on his hands and knees beside Tad. She couldn't help but notice how the fabric of his trousers strained against his muscular thighs. Her brother pointed and pulled, then held up a weed, chattering all the while. J.B. listened, inspected the plant and followed the young boy's lead.

His shirt stretched across the width of his massive shoulders with each yanking motion. He stopped long enough to unbutton his cuffs and roll his sleeves up above his elbows. He glanced at the afternoon sun, unbuttoned his shirt as far as his wide belt buckle and tugged his shirttail from his pants.

Laura Lee became aware that she was gawking at the ripple of his shoulder muscles as he shrugged off his shirt. He swiveled at the waist to throw a rock that his fingers had uncovered and she caught a glimpse of a thick smattering of masculine hair that was the same sandy color as his mustache.

Watching him work set her stomach to fluttering. Her mouth felt as dry as cotton as she stomped back to the sink. "No sense of decency," she muttered to herself, resorting to indignation to smother her response. Her mouth quivered, then broke into a wide grin. "Who? Him or you? You're the one getting an eyeful."

* * *

But later that night, as she lay on her bed and stared into the darkness, she found herself visualizing him bare to the waist, working beside her in the garden. I'd be so distracted by him, she mused dryly, I'd probably be pulling up vegetables instead of weeds.

Her hand grazed over her nightgown from her ribs to her waist and settled on her flat stomach. The fluttering feeling that had begun in her father's office hadn't subsided throughout the day. She raised her hand to her forehead, checking for a fever. Her brow was cool, but she felt as if she were afire.

The door to the gallery squeaked. Laura Lee was suddenly alert. Maybe Luke Reynolds hadn't given up as easily as J.B. thought.

"Who's there?" she whispered, scared, sitting up and reaching for her drawstring purse. "I've got a gun."

"Don't shoot!"

J.B. slipped through the narrow opening.

The moonlight coming from behind him silhouetted him against the door. The bulky wad of cloth he held at waist level told Laura Lee the purpose of his nocturnal visit. He'd brought a blanket.

"You aren't sleeping in here on the floor tonight." Relief mingled with indignation. He was better than Luke Reynolds, but after what had happened in the library and in the kitchen she knew she'd be tempting fate if she allowed him into the dark seclusion of her bedroom. "Blast your stinking hide, get out of here!"

Sniffing, J.B. said teasingly, "My hide is clean. I took a bath in the creek."

When he began to spread the blanket on the floor, Laura Lee whipped back the bedclothes. She moved soundlessly in her bare feet to the blanket and kicked it into a heap.

One hand on her hip, she shook her finger at him. "You are *not* sleeping in here."

"I am."

"Why?"

He'd asked himself the same question and come up with the same flimsy answer he gave her. "You'll run away."

"I won't. I told you after dinner that I'd live up to my father's agreement. Dammit, I'm going to marry John! What more do you want?"

That was another question he'd struggled with. He'd excused his randiness by telling himself it was a long time since he'd been with a woman. The little hoyden who was standing in front of him, who had just threatened to shoot him, couldn't possibly be the reason he'd felt compelled to hold his hat below his belt buckle.

Even his hourly reminder to himself that she belonged to John failed to curtail his lustful thoughts. He shoved his hands in his pockets and blurted out, "You're lucky you're going to marry John. With me you'd be the mother of half a dozen children. I'd take you to bed morning, noon and night."

Laura Lee was stunned. Her jaw dropped, and her hand swung limply to her side for a moment. Then, suddenly, it was propelled upward. The sound of her open palm striking his face surprised her more than it did J.B. Before she realized what she'd done, her left hand arched toward the other side of his square jaw.

J.B. caught her wrist and looped his arms around her shoulders to prevent her from striking him again. "What the hell—? You've made it as plain as the nose on your face that you hate my guts. You're driving me crazy, but I'd never cuckold my own brother."

Her face was pressed against his chest. "Do you think I'd let you . . . cuckold your brother? You are crazy! You . . . you . . ."

He muffled the threatened torrent of abusive names by shoving his hand into her curly hair and glaring deep into her blue eyes. Desire ramroded through him as her lips parted. Her hot, moist breath penetrated his shirt.

He had to let her go; he couldn't continue holding her.

Laura Lee lifted her foot and came down hard with her heel on his instep. ". . . scoundrel!"

It didn't really hurt, but it did give him the excuse he needed to drop his hands and move away from her.

"Stop making so much noise!" she whispered. "I don't want Brandy and Tad in here."

"Back off, then. I think you may have permanently crippled me."

J.B. limped to her bed, pretending to be grievously injured. The second his backside sank into the goose-down mattress he knew he'd made a mistake. And when she crossed the room and climbed into the bed he knew that his mistake was more serious than he'd anticipated. All he had to do was tilt forward and she'd be flat on her back underneath him.

She'd caught him watching her several times during the evening. She didn't know the reason behind the peculiar sensations he caused low in her belly, but she knew intuitively that she wasn't the only one in the room who felt them. She plucked nervously at the lace edge of her long-sleeved nightgown.

Finally she worked up the courage to ask, "What's happening between you and me?"

"Nothing," he said in a strangled voice. "You've going to be my sister-in-law."

"It won't bother you to know I'll be sharing John's bed—and possibly having his children?"

The darkness hid her flaming cheeks. She silently told herself that she was a brazen hussy. She was fully aware that a lady should never even hint at those mysterious things that took place between a man and a woman.

Why don't you just come right out and spill the contents of your daydreams across the counterpane? Why don't you tell him how your heart pounds when he grins at you? Or how your stomach has been acting up all day? Or how his face seems painted on the inside of your eyelids?

J.B. rolled onto his side, wishing he'd lit the bedside candle so that he could see her face. He knew that eventually he'd have to tell her she wouldn't be sharing John's bed or having his children. And he knew what the consequences would be. Although she'd told him earlier that she didn't want John's children, she wouldn't likely take kindly to knowing that she'd be as much a virgin ten years from now as she was tonight.

He'd been around enough dance-hall girls to know that a woman could want a man as desperately as he needed Laura Lee at this very moment. And Laura Lee had been shockingly forthright on several occasions. Did he dare think that was what she'd meant by her last question?

Good God, man, she is driving you loco! She doesn't want to make love with you! This is all just wishful thinking on your part!

"J.B.?"

"Jack. My friends call me Jack."

She tried the name and decided she liked the feel of it.

"You didn't answer my question . . . Jack."

"I'm thinking." Lusting! his conscience corrected. Tempted beyond measure to at least taste her lips, he propped himself up on an elbow.

Mere inches separated their mouths.

"You'd better leave my room," she said, dismayed by his reluctance to answer her. Did he think her a slut for asking it? "Your being in here when you won't ever be my husband is inexcusable."

Her sweet breath washed warmly over his face; it smelled of the peppermint tea they'd had with dinner.

His mouth was watering.

Hers had gone dry.

Before he realized what he was doing, he cupped her face with his hand.

Did she lean forward? Or did his fingers draw her lips toward his?

Laura Lee sighed. "No..."

His forehead touched hers.

"John," he whispered.

Her heart thudded. "Why are you calling your brother?"

"Because I needed an insurmountable barrier between us," he admitted candidly. "John is more to me than a brother. He's risked his life for me more than once. He's the best friend a man could have."

Her scalp tingled from the feel of his fingers tunneling through her hair. Curiosity made her own fingers audacious. She let her forefinger trail over his mustache as her thumb followed the curve of his full lower lip. Both were softer, more enticing, than she'd anticipated.

An achy sensation gnawed at Jack's stomach. Passion and desire clawed at his self-control.

"Don't."

"Don't touch you?"

"Don't tempt me."

"Then go."

Her fingers had an erotic effect on his mouth. He opened his lips, fanning his hot breath across her knuckles.

Laura Lee quivered beneath his hand. He gently massaged the growing tension at the base of her neck. He gazed at her helplessly, caught between desire and honor. "You won't run away?"

"You'll have to take that risk. You can't stay...not now."

"I'd hunt you down and bring you back. Laura Lee, give me your word that you'll stay here and go to sleep."

Her shoulders slumped. Her thoughts scattered like seeds in a violent wind. John...the man her father had probably intended her to marry... J.B... Jack... Oh, mercy, mercy, mercy...had she fallen in love with him? What a time to discover that the peculiar feelings she'd been experiencing were the first pangs of love.

Jack had said he needed a barrier; she needed a castle, a moat and a fierce dragon to imprison her willful heart.

"I won't sleep, but I won't run away, either."

He untangled his fingers from her hair, but one strand tenaciously clung to his ring finger, like a strand of pure gold binding them together permanently.

"I won't dishonor myself by cuckolding my brother."

Hearing the reluctance in his voice, feeling his strong hand tremble on her shoulder, Laura Lee smiled. "It's a long, long trip, Jack. There may be some surprises you haven't planned for along the way."

Jack kissed her fingertips, then rose from the bed.

Aside from John, there was something else he could depend on to keep them safely apart. He grinned his cocky grin to reassure himself that her prickly temper would provide him with the ammunition he needed to keep her at a safe distance. They were both safer with her hating him. "I got what I came for tonight. You can pull every trick in the book, but you can't trick a trickster. When I need a woman, all I have to remember is that all she-cats are gray in the dark. Any woman will do nicely."

He heard her pillow thud against the door after he closed it. He wasn't proud of making what had passed between them seem like a passing whim on his part. But he had to content himself with knowing that he'd done the honorable thing.

Laura Lee grabbed the other pillow, pulled it over her head and screamed bloody murder.

He'd played her like a master fiddler. First he'd warmed up, letting his eyes work their magic. Then he'd flattered her, tugging at her heartstrings. And finally, when she'd sung to his tune, he'd made a fool of her.

"Fool! Fool! You slapped him. He made a fool of you. You're even."

They weren't even. He was way ahead of her.

Or was he?

He might be a master fiddler, but there were flaws in his performance. There were some things a man couldn't hide or fake.

She'd tried to repulse him with the sharp side of her tongue; she wondered what would happen if she tormented him with the sweet, beguiling side of her tongue. Would he be plucking a sweeter tune on that fiddle of his?

Laura Lee grinned. "A duet? With close two-part harmony?" Clinging to that thought, she shimmied between the muslin sheets and closed her eyes.

Visions of the lawn parties held at Blythewood before the war danced in her head, but with subtle differences. The wide-eyed child dressed in a ruffled gown with a blue satin sash, romping through the oak grove, playing hide-and-seek, catching Beau kissing a pretty girl and teasing him mercilessly, was replaced by an older version of the same little minx.

In a pleasant, swirling, hazy mist, she dreamed of Jack being unable to keep himself from falling in love with her.

* * *

Two days later Laura Lee felt wildly exhilarated as she stood beside Jack and introduced him to their guests. Jack's polite excuse—business concerns—couldn't be used to avoid her today. In the flurry of activity in preparation for the festivities and their departure for Texas, she'd been equally busy, supervising the help he'd hired.

The money from his saddlebags had had the same effect as a magical wand being waved over Blythewood.

Inside, brooms swept everything from the heart-of-pine floors to the nooks and crannies in the plastered ceilings. Bucketfuls of well water and lye soap removed years of accumulated grit and grime. The sweet fragrance of the lemon oil and beeswax used by crews of jovial women to polish the furniture permeated the air everywhere except in the kitchen where the odors of meat, spices and yeast breads were thick.

Outside, vines were snipped, bushes were trimmed and the lawn was raked free of fallen debris. Jack, with Tad's help, personally replaced the splintered wooden steps at the back of the house. The house still badly needed a fresh coat of paint, but she'd heard Jack talking to Bill Carpenter and knew that that chore was near the top of the list of priorities. Blythewood fairly sparkled in comparison to the way it had looked only a week before.

Laura Lee sparkled, too.

Pride and joy and excitement coursed through her veins. Her new pale blue dress, with its deep neckline, its snug bodice, its puff sleeves and its perky bow at the back of the waist, made her feel deliciously feminine. Brandy had ingeniously piled her unruly hair high on her head, with tendrils wisping capriciously along her hairline. Her brother's lavish compliments—and the steady heat radiating from Jack's eyes—contributed to her sense of well-being.

Now, arm in arm, Laura Lee and Jack mingled with the growing crowd of well-wishers who'd been invited to her farewell party.

"I think someone spiked the lemonade," she whispered, smiling. Nodding in the direction of the tables spread with food, she added, "I've been watching Doc Wainwright. He has been known to prescribe Kentucky's finest bourbon—strictly for medicinal purposes, of course."

"From the looks of the group over there, I'd say that some at least are well healed," Jack said. He led her toward the little knot of men. "Maybe I'd better talk to them alone."

"Not on your life, Jack Wynthrop. Those men have known me all my life. With liquor under their belts there's no telling what secrets they'll tell."

Doc Wainwright stuck his elbow in Claude Farrington's ribs and made a shushing noise.

"Yep, it's true," Claude said. "My wife said there was chunks of cake everywhere. You didn't hear that wild story Luke told to explain the bruises, did you, Doc? Seems to me he'd've had more scratches and fewer bruises if he'd've fallen off his horse into a blackberry bush like he said."

Engrossed in Claude's gossip, Jess Long hadn't noticed that Laura Lee and Jack were standing right behind him.

Doc Wainwright cleared his throat with a lengthy "Hrrrmph!"

"Serves him right, if'n you asked me," Jess agreed with a snaggle-toothed grin. "I jist hope goin' to Texas is fer enough away to keep from hurtin' her. Luke Reynolds don't take kindly to havin' the whole town laughing at him behind his back."

"Hrrrmph!" Doc Wainwright pointed surreptitiously in the direction behind the two men's backs. "You've met Jack Wynthrop, haven't you, fellas?"

Laura Lee felt her face turn a brighter pink than the camellias decorating the banquet table as Jess and Claude wheeled around. "Pardon me, gentlemen...I, uh..." Her mind fumbled for an excuse to make a hasty departure.

"What about that little chat we need to have?" Doc Wainwright said, taking her arm. "Claude, Jess, you've met Jack Wynthrop from Heavenly Acres, haven't you?"

"Shore 'nuff," Jess blustered, pumping Jack's hand like a rusty pump. "He brought Foxfire over to the livery stable for new shoes."

"He's almost emptied my store for this shindig," Claude added with a sound thump on Jack's shoulders. "You two go ahead. We'll just get Jack a cup of this fine lemonade."

Laura Lee didn't miss the sly wink Claude cast in Jack's direction. To let them know what she suspected, she recovered her composure enough to say, "I'll have another punch bowl brought out for the ladies."

After they'd moved out of earshot, Doc Wainwright patted her hand and said, "Why don't we go around to the back steps, where we won't be interrupted? Since your mother, bless her soul, isn't here to advise you, I feel responsible for letting you know what's going to happen on your wedding night."

She'd expected an apology for the lemonade's having been laced with liquor, not a mother-daughter chat—and certainly nothing about a wife's conjugal duties. She knew who would be the more flustered of the two of them: Doc Wainwright.

He dusted off the third step with his handkerchief, then spread the handkerchief and gestured for her to sit down. She did, leaving room for him to sit beside her.

"I can imagine what silly things you've heard," he began as he eased himself down on the step. "All claptrap. Don't believe a word of it."

In actuality, Laura Lee felt as well-informed as any modest young woman who'd been raised on the land. Her father hadn't purposely bred the horses that had filled the stable, but there had been new foals every year up until the war. She had a fairly good idea of what took place between a man and a woman.

"Men and women were put on this earth to procreate. To make babies." Doc reached into his breast pocket for his handkerchief to wipe the beads of perspiration that had begun to dot his upper lip. When he realized that Laura Lee was sitting on it, he used his forefinger to wipe his mouth politely. "Of course, a man and a woman have to be married first. I mean, well, there are people who do it before they get married, but—"

"Why?"

She'd fully intended to keep her mouth firmly closed and listen without commenting, but she blurted out the question before she could stop it. She wished she could stuff the word back in her mouth when she saw the scalp beneath Doc's thinning gray hair turn pink.

"Why? Why do men and women do it before they get married?" he asked.

Laura Lee nodded; her lips sealed.

"Good question." Doc cleared his throat. "Well, uh . . . yes, indeed, that's a mighty good question. You see, Laura Lee, there are good women and bad women."

"And good men and bad men?"

"No, not exactly. Men get an uncontrollable urge—sort of like an itch they have to scratch."

"But good women don't get this itch until after they're married," Laura Lee concluded logically. No one had explained this to her. Her curiosity about bad women compelled her to ask, "When do bad women get the itch?"

"They're born with it. That's why men don't marry bad women."

She raised a questioning eyebrow. Did the mysterious churning of her insides when she was within sight of Jack Wynthrop qualify as this unseemly "itch"? Jack did make her feel as though her skin had turned inside out. But she didn't itch; she ached.

Doc Wainwright dabbed his forehead with his sleeve to curtail the sweat dripping down his cheek. The puzzled expression on her face demanded a clearer explanation. He picked up a small twig and drew a straight line, then a circle.

"Some men itch every night. It's a woman's wifely duty to, uh, scratch their itch . . . to make babies. That—" he pointed to the line "—is like a man's baby-making tool. He hides it in his britches." The blunt end of the twig moved to the circle. "Women hide theirs under their skirts. After you're married, your husband will use his tool to plant a baby seed inside of you." He hastily drew an arrow from the line to the circle, then tossed the stick into the bushes. With the toe of his boot he erased the marks he'd made in the dirt. "Got the picture?"

One blink of the eyes and I'd have missed it, she mused.

"Your husband will know what to do if you forget." His difficult task completed, he rose slowly and offered his hand to Laura Lee. There was more to tell, lots more, but he'd fulfilled his responsibility. He retrieved his linen hankie and mopped his face. "You're a smart young lady. A bit narrow between the hip bones, but you'll be blessed with lots of fine sons and daughters."

"I appreciate your kindness, Doc." She lightly kissed his cheek. "I'm going to miss you."

"The whole town is going to miss you. We're liable to sink into a deep sleep like Rip van Winkle without you to keep things lively." His eyes danced with merriment as he took her arm and escorted her around the corner of the house. "I've kept you from socializing with your other guests. Why don't you run along while I help myself to a piece of cake and another cup of lemonade?"

She followed him with her eyes as he walked away; bobbed in greeting as he strode past Luke Reynolds and Betsy Mae.

The Reynoldses had been invited, but the townspeople had snubbed them. Laura Lee had noticed that each time they had tried to join one of the tight little clusters of Southerners the group dispersed within minutes.

She didn't realize she was staring at Luke until their eyes met. He sneered at her and imitated a gunslinger, slapping his thigh, pointing his finger, pulling an imaginary trigger, then blowing at the tip of his forefinger.

The blood drained from her face.

Luke's finger hadn't pointed toward her; it had been aimed at the center of Jack's back!

Terrified for Jack, she walked toward Luke, not knowing what she'd do when she confronted him. Why, oh, why, hadn't she told Jack that Luke was the kind of man who wouldn't do the dirty work of handling money or pulling a trigger. He was shrewd, and hired killers were cheap, just like bank tellers.

Betsy Mae fluttered her lace fan even more slowly than she batted her eyelashes. Her voice was sweeter than sugar and deadlier than poison as she cooed, "What a charming party, Laura Lee. I was just telling Luke that you must have hired someone to bake that cake. It's so much prettier than the one you wanted me to serve Luke."

"You hired someone, didn't you?" Laura Lee said accusingly, unwilling to play games with her.

"Sure did," Luke said. The finger he'd pointed at Jack's back touched her under the chin. "Did you think you and Bill Carpenter couldn't be replaced?"

"We're glad you quit," Betsy Mae said smugly. She jerked on her husband's arm, hard enough to make him retract his finger. "I know you tried to seduce him. It didn't work. You can't break up a happy marriage."

Slicing her a sharp glance, Laura Lee said, "Hush up, Betsy Mae. This is between Luke and me."

Betsy Mae rapped Luke's forearm with her fan. "Are you going to let this strumpet tell me to shut up?"

Chuckling, Luke hugged his wife. His gaze lingered on the bodice of Laura Lee's gown, then shifted to Jack. "Now, now, sweetling, you don't have to worry your pretty little head about her. By tomorrow she'll be out of your hair. Forever."

He didn't have to draw Laura Lee a picture. Dead. That was what he was implying. And she didn't like the looks he was giving Jack, either.

"I'm the one who baked the cake, Luke. Leave Jack Wynthrop out of our private feud."

"Me? Harm him? Why, Laura Lee, I wouldn't do anything dastardly. Why would I, when I'm considering making an offer on Heavenly Acres."

"Don't play innocent. I saw where you aimed your finger."

"You must be hallucinating. I thought you were looking for him. I merely pointed out where you could find him."

Laura Lee saw his gaze flicker slightly. She glanced over her shoulder and saw Jack striding toward them.

"Now that you've finally found a man who'll marry you, why don't you leave my husband alone?" Betsy Mae snarled. She looked as if she'd held her tongue so long that she was ready to burst at the seams. "You may think you've convinced everybody that you're as pure as the driven snow, but I know you for what you really are, missy—poor white trash. C'mon, Luke. You can take me home now. I don't care to associate with her kind."

"Wise decision," Jack said. He looped a protective arm around Laura Lee's rigid shoulders and looked at Luke, his eyes narrowed dangerously. "Otherwise, while I mow the lawn with your teeth, my future sister-in-law can have the pleasure of escorting Betsy Mae into the kitchen and washing her foul mouth out with soap."

Luke paled visibly, but he managed a cordial smile. He stuck his hand out and said loudly, drawing the attention of several couples nearby, "Your brother is a lucky man, Mr. Wynthrop. May you and he and Laura Lee live long, happy, prosperous lives."

Jack clasped his hand, squashing his knuckles in a way that was meant to show the banker that he'd break him, bone by bone, if he tried anything.

Once the Reynoldses were out of sight Laura Lee whispered, "He's hired someone to kill you."

"Or you."

"Or both of us."

Jack smiled grimly. "Don't worry. I'll be watching our backs and sleeping with one eye open."

Chapter Eight

I wanted to give you something extra-special," Tad said. Choking back his tears had made him hoarse. "I know you're gonna be kinda lonely. Homesick. So . . . I want you to take Captain Bligh with you."

Touched beyond measure that Tad would part with his bird, Laura Lee pulled her brother close. He wound his arms around her neck. The wetness of his tears and his heaving chest were almost her undoing. She raised her own damp eyes to Brandy, who wasn't trying to hide her tears.

Earlier, when she'd climbed in the carriage Jack had borrowed from Bill Carpenter, she'd had to clench her fists and bite her lip to keep from sobbing. Despite the moon-shaped impressions her fingernails had made in her palms, the tender spot inside her cheek and the lump of unshed tears lodged in her throat, no one else knew of her desolation.

"I taught him to whistle the first few notes of 'Dixie,'" Tad whispered. He burrowed his nose against her nape. "And I taught him to say something special, just so you'll think of me and Blythewood and how much we miss you. Wanna hear him?"

"Yes." As Tad turned to pick up the cage, she caught sight of Jack from the corner of her eye as he walked down the plank from the paddle wheeler to the dock. She tried to focus her attention on Tad and the bird, but she was keenly aware of every footstep Jack took as he came closer.

Tad raised the cloth cover on the bird's cage.

"Prrr-e-tty lady!" the Captain squawked. Then he whistled shrilly.

Smart bird, Jack thought, avidly watching the interaction between the tiny woman and the young boy.

"No, Captain!" Tad patiently mouthed the words he'd taught the bird. "C'mon. Say 'em!"

"Awwwk! I love you!"

"He did it! Did you hear him, Jack?"

Laura Lee felt her cheeks warm under the heat of Jack's intense black eyes. His loose-fitting plaid shirt and dark trousers emphasized his size. The wind ruffled his hair playfully. She fought an impulse to prompt him to say the same words to her.

Mesmerized, she barely felt Tad tug on the sleeve of her dove-gray travel dress. "When Captain Bligh says it, you'll think of me, won't you?"

"You'll always be in my thoughts, Tad." She could barely see through the tears swimming in her eyes. "You take care of yourself and mind Brandy."

Brandy spread her arms, one around Tad's shoulders and the other around Laura Lee's waist. "Now I know what you were doing the past couple of days while I was turning blue in the face from calling you."

Uneasy laughter twittered through the little group. Her heart pounding, Laura Lee dared to take a second glance at Jack. She'd have to be pretty dizzy to believe he cared for her, wouldn't she?

A horn sounded from the top deck. The captain shouted, "All aboard!"

Laura Lee swiftly kissed Tad and Brandy. "I love you both. Take care!"

All too soon she was leaning over the railing, waving her hankie at her loved ones until they were no longer visible. She stood rigid, staring at the bank of the rain-swollen river as though it could somehow give her solace.

With each blink of her eyelashes a tear slid unnoticed down the soft curve of her cheek.

The sorrow she felt went deeper than leaving her family. Deep in her bones she knew that Blythewood would never be her home again. Soon she'd be Mrs. John Wynthrop of the Rocking W Ranch.

A small shudder accompanied that realization.

Jack glanced around the empty deck. The recent rains must have discouraged others from traveling down the Mississippi, he mused, welcoming this moment of privacy that Laura Lee needed to regain her composure.

"Bill will take care of them and Blythewood," Jack said, longing to let her lean against him and weep until the sadness had left her eyes. But he couldn't risk holding her, given the way he reacted to having her in his arms. "Workers are straggling in two by two. Once the seed I ordered arrives, Bill will have the weeds cleared and they can start planting."

"He'll have his hands full," she murmured stiffly. Her mind veered from the path leading toward self-pity and turned down a familiar one: Blythewood's problems. Her gloved hand swept at the moisture on her face. Her slumped shoulders slowly straightened. "Neither your money nor Bill can solve all the problems."

"Such as?"

"Transportation. You ordered the seed from New Orleans, right?"

Relieved to hear her voice growing steadily stronger, he nodded. He'd have agreed to anything she said.

"How's it going to be delivered? There are only sixty miles of railroad track in the entire state of Louisiana. The levees on the Mississippi weren't maintained, so barge traffic is restricted. The river road is hardly more than a muddy trail, impassable for heavily loaded wagons. The seed you ordered may never arrive."

"It'll get there," Jack promised her.

Sighing, she sadly shook her head. "Those aren't the only problems facing Bill and other planters like him. Money can't cure yellow fever. Or get the Union forces out of the South. Or convince the men who returned from fighting to sign the allegiance pledge. They've lost their right to vote, to make laws, to hold office. Can you do something magical to alleviate those problems?"

"Time, my dear. Nothing is impossible, not if you believe in it and work to get it." His hand reached for her shoulder, but it stopped in midair and dropped to the rail beside hers. "You sound as though you're ready to wave the white flag of surrender."

Her head snapped up.

"Never. I just don't want you to think reviving Blythewood is going to be like organizing a cake sale at a church social."

Fire shot from her eyes. Little did she know how those flying blue sparks warmed Jack's heart. He turned toward the paddle wheel and smiled.

He had done his part to remove the South's burden from her shoulders by taking her to Texas. While they were in New Orleans he'd do his best to put the roses back in her cheeks. More than anything, he wanted those sky-blue eyes of hers to be lit with laughter.

His smile broadened. He'd tickled Tad's funny bone with tall tales he'd heard around the campfire on cattle drives. A Texas-size tall tale might be just what the doctor ordered. He turned to her again.

"The last church social I attended almost had me singing hymns at the pearly gates." Jack pushed the wide brim of his hat off his forehead as he waited for her curiosity to wade through her ebbing anger. He'd lie through his teeth to distract her from her melancholy thoughts. He snaked his hand toward her. "On the way home I met up with a timber rattler. Forty feet long, and thick as my thigh. It scared more hell-raisin' out of me than the preacher's fire-and-brimstone sermon."

At once horrified and fascinated, Laura Lee glanced away from the riverbank and saw his determinedly sober expression. Only the sunshine captured in his dark eyes and the slight upward tilt of his mustache belied his deadly-serious pose.

"Is this the same snake Tad told me about?" she asked, unable to resist the tall tale. "The one that curled up so fast it caused a whirlwind that stopped a stampeding herd of cattle from galloping off a cliff?"

"Now that you mention it, I guess they could've been first cousins." Jack lowered one eyelid and grinned. "Both of 'em were cross-eyed."

"What'd you do? Pull out your trusty six-shooter and pepper it with bullets?"

"Nope."

"You wrestled it? The way you wrestled the grizzly bear you told Tad about?"

"Nope."

"It bit you," she guessed, a wide grin parting her lips. "That's why you're meaner than a snake shedding its winter skin."

Jack chuckled and said, "You're getting closer. It was wintertime. Snowflakes bigger than pie plates were falling from the sky. The wind was blowing through the canyon so hard I could barely hear that snake snoring."

"A cross-eyed, forty foot, snoring snake?" Laura Lee made a *tsking* sound with her tongue. "What did you do?"

"At first I didn't see him. I seem to recollect that a pebble had worked its way into my boot and was rubbing a blister on the tip of my big toe."

Laura Lee raised one hand to stop him. "Stop right there. I know what you did. The pebble was the size of a boulder, right? You squashed the snake when you dumped the boulder out of your boot."

"Wrong. I didn't realize it was a snake. I thought it was a log, so I dismounted and sat down on it while I took off my boot to get rid of that bothersome pebble."

Wrinkling her nose in delight, she said, "You sat down on a snoring log?"

"The wind was howling, remember? Once I'd removed the pebble I realized I was sitting smack-dab on a hibernating timber rattler. Between snores I rolled him up, stuck him in my saddlebag and rode on home. Before that ol' snake knew what had happened to him I'd skinned him and Cookie had made enough rattlesnake stew to feed the ranch hands for a month."

"Rattlesnake stew?"

"Yep. Tastes like chicken." The corners of his eyes crinkled with restrained laughter at the disbelief that was plainly visible on her face. "You don't believe me, do you?"

"Frankly? No."

"You'll have to wait until you get to the ranch to taste rattler stew, but I can prove the snake story." He pointed to his belt. "Snakeskin."

Her eyes dropped to his trim waist and his flat belly. His hips were thrust forward. Impulsively she removed her gloves and reached forward to touch the belt.

"Really?"

His stomach muscles contracted as though he expected a roundhouse punch. He gritted his teeth to control his physical response to her knuckles pressing against his shirt as she examined his belt. His imagination soared to new heights—to thoughts of her unbuckling the narrow band of genuine cow hide.

"It doesn't look or feel like snakeskin," she said challengingly.

Since he'd tricked her, she expected to see his devilish eyes filled with laughter when she lifted her face to his. They were closed. A muscle beneath one of his high cheekbones pulsed. Her fingers released their hold on his belt as if the imaginary snake had come to life. The moment she was no longer touching him his eyes flew open.

"I lied," he whispered. His voice almost failed him. Silently cursing his weakness, he considered throwing himself overboard in an attempt to regain some measure of control.

Though she was dazzled by the brilliance in his eyes, she knew intuitively that he wasn't referring to his tall tale. "When?"

"The night I came to your room." He turned to the rail, gripped it and stared blindly down at the swirling water.

"When you said women were like cats? That they all looked alike in the dark?"

"You aren't a gray cat any more than my belt is made of snakeskin." His forefinger tapped his temple. "My mind knows you're promised to my brother, but I can't seem to convince my body. So I have to keep you at arm's length."

His doubts fueled her hopes. She laid her hand over his heart. "Is it possible that some promises aren't meant to be kept? Tell me what your heart is saying to you."

Jack glanced around the empty deck to ensure their solitude before he cupped her face in his hands. Only Captain Bligh, whose cage was on the deck beside Laura Lee's feet, watched, and without comment. Jack reflected that the parrot's tongue was more agile than his. Compliments came hard for a man who'd spent more time with heifers than with women.

"I want to kiss you, Laura Lee. I've wanted to kiss you from the moment that ridiculous hat fell off your head. As much as I've moaned and groaned about that sharp tongue of yours, I admire your spunk."

A faint hint of a smile and her hands moving to his wrists encouraged him to slant his head, then lazily lower his lips to hers. She was so tiny, so fragile, he dared not crush her by pulling her into his arms. He rested his lips on hers, letting her get the feel of him, getting the feel of her mouth beneath his, until at last her lips parted.

Her breath shuddered faintly against his lips. She wilted against him; her knees trembled until her legs could no longer support her weight. She held on to his wrists as if for dear life.

A slow hunger began filling the pit of her stomach. She wanted more than a sweet kiss, but she didn't know how to get it. Womanly instincts that had been buried under tons of responsibility slowly surfaced. Her hands wandered up the front of his shirt. One rested over his heart, and the other continued its trek until she felt the longish hair at his nape.

"You smiled," he whispered, the tip of his tongue tracing her lower lip.

"Your mustache is as silky as your hair."

PEEK-A-BOO!

Free Gifts For You!

Look inside—Right Now! We've got something special just for you!

GALORE Behind These Doors!

SEE WHAT'S FREE!

Open all four doors to find out what gifts are yours for the asking from the Harlequin Reader Service.

Just peel off the four "door" stickers.

YES, I have removed all four stickers. Please send me the free gifts revealed beneath the doors. I understand that under the terms explained on the facing page no purchase is necessary and I may cancel at any time.

NAME ______________________________
(PLEASE PRINT)

ADDRESS ______________________________ APT. ______

CITY ______________________________

STATE ______________ ZIP CODE ______________

246 CIH YA3Y
(U-H-H-10/90)

"Your lips are as soft as I knew they'd be. Open them for me."

Why? she wondered, unable to imagine anything sweeter than what they'd shared.

In answer to her unspoken question, his tongue swept inside her mouth. It tasted hot and enticing, and it dared her to taste him. Her tongue darted between his lips, touching the serrated edges of his teeth, contrasting the feel with the rasping velvet texture of his tongue.

His arms closed around her waist and lifted her until her fingers tunneled through his hair and her arms wound around his neck. She felt lighter than air. Her breasts flattened against his chest; her nipples tightened into hard, aching buds. Instinctively she brushed the tips against him.

Love, set afire by a frenzy of desire, glowed behind her long lashes where her lips separated from his. Short, quick breaths soothed the burning sensation in her lungs.

He was unable to resist the hunger he saw in her eyes. His hand inched along her ribs until it covered her breast, slowly rotating her taut nipple in the center of his hand. He yearned to draw the peak into his mouth and savor its flavor as thoroughly as he'd tasted the dark, hot secrets of her mouth. He imagined kissing her breast, drawing the nipple deep inside his mouth, sucking, nibbling, licking the rosy crest until her legs parted as naturally as her lips had opened for him.

His imagination suffocated the small but insistent sounds coming from his conscience. Or were those tiny sounds coming from the back of her throat?

For half a second her spine went rigid at the shock of his intimate touch. Then she collapsed helplessly against him, crushing her mouth to his.

That momentary pause of hers allowed a flash of sanity to permeate the red haze of passion blanketing his mind.

One of them had to regain control. He was the man . . . the one with experience, and yet when she moved against him he felt as virginal as he'd been the night his father had liquored him up, dumped him in the parlor of a whorehouse and flipped a gold coin in the madam's direction.

Youth would no longer serve as an excuse.

He had to be the one to stop.

Her fingers pressed against the back of his head as he began to withdraw. Why was he denying them what they both so fervently wanted? All her life the promise of happiness had been snatched from her open arms. First she had lost her loved ones, and then her land. Deprivation during the war had taught her to take what she needed to survive. Now she felt as though she'd wither into nothingness if she denied herself this fragile moment of intimacy.

"No, Jack," she panted. "Please don't . . . stop."

He heard her. She wanted him to stop.

He peppered tiny kisses below her ear, along her throat, as his good intentions waged war with his masculinity. He knew he shouldn't, but he couldn't refrain from taking one more kiss.

Just one more kiss, he silently promised himself.

Intent on the sweet imprint of her body pressed against his, he swiftly turned her back to the rail and wedged them closer together. His toe nudged the bird cage.

Captain Bligh squawked as his perch swayed.

A sharp cracking sound pierced the air.

Jack pitched forward. Off balance and in danger of knocking Laura Lee overboard, he grabbed her by the waist and fell backward until his left shoulder jarred against the bulkhead. The back of his head struck the wood soundly.

Everything was happening too fast for Laura Lee to grasp. "Jack! Jack?" she cried frantically, still hazy with passion.

"Arrrrrrk!"

Pain blinded him. He opened his eyes and struggled to focus them on Laura Lee. Her face was white as a sheet, and her hand trembled as she ripped his shirtsleeve. A circle of pain seemed to be tightening around his head. Embarrassed by his clumsiness and concerned for her, he quickly asked, "Are you all right?"

"You're the one who's hurt."

Certain that his male prowess had suffered worse injury than his arm, he said, "I've been thrown off broncos and landed easier. How'd that happen?"

"You tell me."

Her voice was shaking. The sight of the blood oozing from his wound made her stomach roll. She'd seen wounds like this before—gunshot wounds. She scanned left and right, then looked up. The man who had pulled the trigger must have been on the top deck; there had been no one on level with them. She hunched low over Jack in the hope of protecting him.

Was someone hiding up there? Waiting for them to make the wrong move? Swearing silently, she reached for the gun strapped to Jack's hip.

Jack brushed her hands away and took a closer look at his arm. What he saw raised the hair on the back of his neck. He pulled Laura Lee against him with his good arm and shifted her until she fitted snugly against the wall. Cautiously, listening for footsteps overhead, he unholstered his gun and inched backward.

"Get back here," Laura Lee whispered, grabbing the front of his shirt. His arm deflected her hands. "What are you trying to do, get your head blown off!"

"Shhh." The thought of someone taking a potshot at him while he was kissing a woman made him damn angry, but he wasn't about to let his anger distract him from the task at hand. All his senses were on alert. Acidity coated the sweet taste on his tongue.

The upper deck was empty. "Whoever bushwhacked me isn't sticking around. You stay here. I'm going to check the stairs."

"Like hell! You aren't going anywhere without me."

"Jesus, woman! You want to argue when someone just took a shot at you?"

"Me?" An image of Luke Reynolds's finger pointed at the center of Jack's back rose in her mind. Without thinking, she blurted out, "You're the one he's after. Luke must know that killing you is the worst thing that could happen to me."

Fairly certain now that they were safe—at least temporarily—Jack lowered his eyes to hers. What he saw compelled him to holster his weapon and take her in his arms. "Don't cry, sweetheart."

"I never cry." Despite her calm, tears spurted from her eyes. Muffled against his chest, she muttered, "I hate being a crybaby. I should be tending to your arm—" she was sniffling now "—or going after the man who shot you."

"You aren't a crybaby, and you certainly aren't going after a gunslinger." His fingers soothed the tension from her spine. "The bullet only nicked my arm. It's stopped bleeding."

Precious, he thought, so damn precious. The women he'd known cried when they were hurt or angry. He'd seen the look in her shimmering eyes. It was the same expression that had been there when the boat had pulled away from the dock. The tears wetting the front of his shirt were precious tears of love.

"But, Jack, someone tried to kill you!" she said, her voice choked.

He nodded. He would let her think the bullet had been intended for him, though he knew differently. If he hadn't swung her around, if the parrot hadn't squawked, she'd be dead in his arms now. The thought made his blood run cold.

He'd misjudged Luke Reynolds, taken him for a weakling who valued money more than pride. He wouldn't make that mistake again.

"I'm going to take you inside, where you'll be safe, and then I'm going to have a look around." Jack bent at the waist and stuck his fingers through the hook atop the bird cage. He raised the cage to eye level. "Keep an eye on her, Captain. You're one helluva bodyguard."

Chapter Nine

The earliest departure for Galveston?" The ticket agent peered over the top of his wire-framed spectacles. "One cabin for you and the missus?"

"Two cabins—side by side," Jack replied, glancing over his shoulder at Laura Lee.

She'd scarcely spoken a word since they'd disembarked at the Canal Street wharf. Only her face gave any clues to her private thoughts. Her eyes narrowed as they searched the faces of other pedestrians and widened with obvious interest as she peered into shop windows. Union soldiers loitering on a streetcorner pleated her brow with apparent dismay; her nose had a decidedly upward tilt as she passed them.

New Orleans, an occupied city, must remind her vividly of a past she'd rather forget, he decided. But the only comment she'd made was that this wasn't the city she remembered visiting with her family before the war.

He'd kept an eye out for a suspicious-looking character who might be the hired gun who'd shot at them.

The ticket agent raised a dark eyebrow, licked his thumb and turned the page of the departure ledger. His gnarled finger skimmed downward. "Mmm-hmm. Nothing available today or tomorrow. The *Matadora* departs at noon

Wednesday. Two cabins available, but they aren't next to each other. How does that suit you?''

Two nights, Jack thought uneasily. He had misgivings about staying so long in New Orleans, but he knew he'd rather face Luke Reynolds's gunslinger than hand Laura Lee over to his brother. ''Book passage on the *Matadora*.''

Two days, Laura Lee mused. She, too, had mixed feelings about this temporary reprieve. It worried her to be in the same city as the would-be assassin, but it delighted her to have two days alone with Jack.

Jack paid the man for their tickets and went to her side. He took the bird cage in one hand and her carpetbag in the other. ''See anybody familiar?''

''No one from Blytheville.''

''Arrrk!'' Captain Bligh batted his wings as though he were preparing for flight. ''Cracker! Arrrk!''

''We'll feed you when we get to the hotel,'' Jack told him.

''Watch out, Jack.'' She grinned and took the cage from him. ''Gratitude isn't the Captain's middle name. He bites the hand that feeds him.''

''It won't be the first time on this trip I've been bitten,'' he said as he held the door open for her. ''I don't know about you, but the Captain isn't the only one around here who's hungry. Is the St. Charles Hotel agreeable with you?''

''It's frightfully expensive.''

She'd guarded her pennies too long to be extravagant. For the three dollars it cost to stay there for a night she could buy several bags of seed. But at least they wouldn't have to pay extra for meals; they were included. Automatically she tightened the strings of her purse.

"Don't worry about money, Laura Lee." He smiled down at her and winked lazily. "No more sleeping on your bedroom floor for me."

Laura Lee returned his smile and said lightly, "You aren't worried about me running off in the middle of the night?"

"No. Should I be?"

He wasn't worried about her vanishing; he was worried about delivering her to John . . . with her virginity intact. Twice he'd come close to breaking his solemn promise. Hot tentacles of desire had tightened the muscles around his heart until he'd felt as though it would burst. No, he wasn't worried about her running away; he was worried about keeping her at a safe distance.

"I gave you my word I wouldn't go anywhere without you." She looked him straight in the eye and added provocatively, "We've gone too far to turn back."

Sister-in-law. Jack had silently reminded himself of his future relationship with Laura Lee while he'd shown her around their elegant suite of rooms, and while they'd eaten a leisurely dinner, and he did so again now, as they strolled arm-in-arm down Charles Street, peering in the windows of the fashionable *modistes*. But when they were alone, without the possibility of Tad barging in or Brandy showing up at an inopportune moment or John knowing what was happening, the reminder was as ineffectual as giving a thimbleful of liquid to a man stranded in West Texas and dying of thirst.

The closer they came to the hotel, the slower he walked.

"Jack," Laura Lee whispered, clutching his sleeve and glancing over her shoulder, "I think someone is following us."

"Keep walking naturally." Out of habit, he brushed his upper thigh with his fingertips. He cursed silently. He should have known better than to leave the hotel unarmed. "Did you see him?"

"No, but I heard footsteps echoing behind us."

Her fingers trembling, she reached for her purse. The small derringer at the bottom would afford them some protection. Swearing to herself she picked at a knot in the drawstring.

Fully alert now, Jack turned his head. His skin crawled at the thought of Laura Lee being in danger. Street lamps cast wide circles of light in front of them and behind them. Dark shadows concealed the next storefront. "Walk closer to the buildings."

"I can't get my purse untied!"

"Dammit, Laura Lee! Are you packing a pistol?"

Her head snapped. "You couldn't get into a restaurant wearing yours strapped to your hip, so I brought mine."

The prospect of her defending him struck hard at his masculine ego. He was infuriated. He wasn't the sort of man who would willingly hide behind a woman's skirts.

"Give it to me."

"I would if I could get the knot out of these damn strings."

Jack steered her into a shallow doorway, pivoted and looked back down the sidewalk. "I don't see anyone other than a man and woman on the other side of the street."

"Maybe he ducked into a doorway." She started to poke her head around the corner.

Jack blocked her by raising his arm. "For heaven's sake, stay put. Swoon or faint, would you? You're gonna get your head blown off."

"You're the one he shot! Your name is on the bullet, not mine!" The recalcitrant strings loosened. She dug her hand into her purse and pulled out the gun. Irked by his remark about swooning, she dodged under the arm he'd stretched out, shouting defiantly, "Come on out, you lily-livered sneak!"

Groaning at her foolhardiness, Jack slung his arm around her waist and hauled her back into the doorway. "Are you crazy?"

"I may be hearing things, but I'm not crazy." Mashed against his chest, her feet dangled off the ground, she felt light-headed. She squirmed against him. "I must've scared him off."

The groan Jack bit off with his teeth had nothing to do with what she'd done; it was caused by his physical reaction to her wiggling bottom. He dropped her to her feet, none too gently.

Anger concealed his chagrin. "A pint-size woman waving a firecracker? He's probably dying of laughter."

For a second Laura Lee considered kicking him in the shins and crowning him with her purse. Why was he deliberately goading her when she'd saved his skin? But insight kept her feet on the sidewalk and her hands on her hips. Male pride had prompted his wisecrack; but still, Shannon pride stopped her from apologizing for her behavior.

"I'm unaccustomed to having anyone other than Tad defend me." The closest she could come to offering him an apology was to hand him the little pistol.

With a curt bob of his head, Jack stepped away from the door. "Wait here a minute. I want to make certain we aren't going to be ambushed."

He strode back up the street, feeling small enough to slip between the street's flagstones. He was completely in the wrong; he had to be man enough to admit his mistakes, to try and make amends. But how? He'd never been faced with the problem of being attracted to a woman who didn't need his protection.

Laura Lee stared vacantly into the window of the milliner's shop. Would she ever learn to curb her streak of impetuosity? What man would want a woman who acted like a demented sharpshooter? A man's man, a man like Jack, would want someone soft and feminine to complement his masculinity.

"I'm sorry I snapped at you." He couldn't look her in the face; he stared blindly at the hats displayed in the shop window. He wondered what he could do to make up for his churlish behavior. "You've got more guts than most men twice your size."

His apology compounded her guilt feelings. She certainly did not want him comparing her to a man!

Clutching at straws, she followed his gaze to a wide-brimmed straw hat decorated with clusters of silk magnolias and murmured, "I like that one, too."

"You'd look beautiful wearing it," he replied, focusing on what was behind the glass. A flicker of light shone from the back of the shop. "You're brave and beautiful. It's a rare combination."

"Thank you." Brandy would be proud of me for accepting the compliment graciously, she thought, a shy smile curving her lips. "We'd better be getting back to the hotel."

"Whoa there." He rapped on the window with his knuckles. "I think someone must be in there."

She tugged on his sleeve. "Jack, the shop is closed. And anyway, I can't let you buy me a hat. Ladies don't accept personal gifts from gentlemen."

"You can't stop me this time. I've got the gun and the money. Don't argue." The light from the back room spilled into the showroom as a figure parted the curtains. He rapped harder. "Open up."

Her heart skipped a beat when he turned, put his finger on her lips and dropped a playful kiss on her forehead. Even when he bullies me, she though, he's irresistible!

"Only a woman with feathers for brains refuses a new bonnet. Write me an IOU if it makes you feel better, but I'm going to buy that hat."

A middle-aged woman with wiry silver hair, lively gray eyes and a mouthful of pins opened the door. "Must a mecond," she mumbled, plucking the hatpins from her mouth and jabbing them into the little cushion tied to her wrist. "Ah. There. I must have looked like a pincushion with feet. The shop is closed, but—"

"My lady is interested in the hat in the window," Jack said before she could politely refuse to conduct business. "I'm willing to pay extra for your inconvenience."

"Aren't you . . . ?" the older woman squinted at Laura Lee, searching her memory.

"Laura Lee Shannon. My mother used to shop here."

"Of course!" Pleased to recognize the daughter of a former customer, she exclaimed, "I never forget a face! Martha Howard . . . remember me? No, no, of course you don't. You were wearing short dresses the last time you were here with your mother." She saw the flash of pain in the young woman's eyes and decided not to inquire about her mother. She turned toward the giant man grinning down at her. "Young man, your good taste in the latest in millinery fashion is only exceeded by your choice of companions."

Blushing at being the object of such effuse compliments, Laura Lee turned and pretended to study the bolts of fabric lining the wall as Jack introduced himself and Martha bustled to the show window to retrieve the hat.

In a jiffy Martha had her customer seated in front of a mirror and had the feminine confection in place, its forest-green ribbon to one side of Laura Lee's face.

"Utterly charming, m'dear. I must have had your heart-shaped face in mind when I designed it."

Her eyes like saucers, Laura Lee gazed at her reflection in the mirror. She had been transformed. The brim of the hat cast mysterious shadows beneath her cheekbones, making delicate hollows that accentuated her eyes, the perfect bow of her lips, and her cameo features. The size and color of the bow made her slender neck appear fragile, her hair lustrous.

In the mirror, Jack's eyes met hers.

From ragtag urchin to a lady of refined elegance, Jack mused, his eyes bright with discovery. Tiny but perfect. He wished John were here to paint a miniature of her for him to carry in his breast pocket, next to his heart.

"She'll take it," Jack said, his voice uncommonly gravelly. His hands settled on her shoulders. "Choose a bolt of cloth. Something pretty. Pink?"

"I have just what you're looking for over here." Martha went over to a row of bolts and selected fabric of the palest pink that perfectly matched the hint of pink in the magnolia blossoms decorating the hat. "Isn't this a lovely piece?"

"Perfect," Jack said.

Her fingers stiff, Laura Lee fumbled with the bow. It had been ages since she'd had anything new. She wanted the hat and the fabric, but she couldn't accept his generosity.

"It's lovely, Martha, but—"

"Nonsense. We'll take them both. Any chance of your contacting a dressmaker and having a gown made in the next couple of days?"

Martha, caught between Jack's definite yes, Laura Lee's wistful no and her own need to provide for her orphaned grandson, sided with the handsome stranger. She swiftly brushed Laura Lee's fingers aside. As the lengths of long ribbon whispered against each other, her gray eyes begged the young woman not to refuse.

"Certainly. Early tomorrow morning Miss Shannon could come for a fitting with the seamstress. Rose Buchanan and her daughters can have it made in nothing flat." She leaned over Laura Lee's shoulder and asked softly, "Do you remember the Buchanans, from up near Bayou Goula?"

Laura Lee nodded. She understood the silent message in Martha's eyes. Before the war the Buchanans had been customers, too. Tragedy must have hit them hard for the women to be sewing for Martha.

Poor, but too proud to accept charity, she thought sympathetically. Martha needed the sale, the Buchanan women needed the work, and most of the clothes she'd packed were threadbare.

She rose from the chair and put her hand on the hard line of Jack's jaw. Her thumb traced the curve of his mustache. "Thank you, Jack. I'd love to have the hat and gown."

Grinning, Martha excused herself to get a hatbox.

Jack felt his chest tighten. He'd been about to try to make her give in by saying that he wanted to buy her something for her trousseau. Misplaced altruism, he thought, an aching lump in his throat. He'd bought other hats for other women for less honorable reasons, but no woman had tugged on his heartstrings the way Laura Lee did.

His hand closed over the back of hers. He placed a kiss in her palm and folded her fingers over it.

"Mr. Wynthrop..." Martha pushed the curtain aside, unaware of her bad timing until she saw the look on his face. She knew love when she saw it; her husband had cherished her until the day he'd died in her arms. "Oh . . . uh . . . I put an extra silk magnolia in the hatbox."

As if on cue, Jack turned to the counter and Laura Lee turned to the window. Awareness of what they'd just missed brought a shared sigh.

"With this cloth," Martha said, ducking her head and rummaging through a box of ribbons behind the counter, "a flower at the neckline or a ribbon would be chic."

Jack's eyes traveled hotly over Laura Lee's throat. "Lovely idea, Miz Howard."

Suddenly weak in the knees, Laura Lee braced herself against the front window. Jack had a devastating effect on her equilibrium, she thought. She was simmering, close to the boiling point. Frustration ripped through her savagely.

The moment was lost; it couldn't be recaptured.

Or could it?

"After the surrender at Appomattox—" Laura Lee was babbling nervously, unsettled by the direction her thoughts were running as they entered the suite "—any penniless Confederate soldier could stay here at the St. Charles Hotel for free."

Jack closed the door and leaned against it, carefully watching her every movement. Earlier that afternoon she'd been tongue-tied; now she was chattering like a windup toy. In ten minutes she'd told him everything there was to know about the hotel, about the fire that had burned down the original structure and about the politicians who'd argued the pros and cons of going to war in the huge rotunda on the main floor.

"Imagine the cost to the owners!" She tossed her purse on the brocade-covered sofa and whirled around. "You should see the mirrors in the ladies' parlor. Five of them. They're the largest ever imported into this country."

Lithely he pushed away from the door and closed the gap between them. "I've heard a completely different version of what to expect in New Orleans from the few cowhands who've been here," Jack said teasingly. "One fella told me he'd been here a week and soaked up enough liquor and sin to keep him in stories for the rest of his life."

Sin? Laura Lee flinched. Beneath her brittle chatter her thoughts were absolutely, undeniably sinful. Could he read her thoughts?

"Marble floors . . . bronze chandeliers . . ." She pointed to an ornately carved chair and hiccuped. "Walnut."

"It's late," Jack said quietly.

He caught her wrist and brought the back of her hand to his lips. The tip of her tongue darted between her dry lips as his mustache brushed sweetly against her skin. Her fingers curled around his, and her heart raced. Her eyelids grew heavier and heavier with each tiny kiss he placed on her knuckles.

I should be protesting, she mused dreamily. A long shudder ran the length of her arm as he tongued the tiny web between her fingers.

"Laura Lee?"

"Mmm?"

"Is the furniture in my room like yours?" he asked, his mouth dry.

There was no mistaking the meaning behind his thinly veiled question. He was inviting her into his bedroom. The dormant fires he'd previously ignited now rekindled, and the achy fire at the juncture of her legs flared.

"I don't know," she whispered, hesitating before willingly plunging into the fires of passion.

"Don't know or don't want to know?"

He guided her hand to his shoulder. Slowly, one by one, he withdrew the pins from her hair, until its soft fullness cascaded halfway down her back. His hands circled her throat; his thumbs followed the lacy edge of her high-necked dress. His dark eyes caressed her face.

"I told you we've come too far to turn back. I want to go anywhere you go."

"I want you, Laura Lee."

She struggled to lift her weighted eyelids. She stood on tiptoe, circled his neck with her arm and rested her face on his broad chest.

His arms circled her waist and laced together low on her back. "Will you make love with me?" he asked.

His breath caught in his throat as he waited for her to refuse him. He had no right to be holding her, wanting her, asking her to share his bed. But rights and wrongs were buried in his desire to make love to her.

He felt her head move fractionally up and down.

Had any woman he'd had before responded similarly he would have shed his clothing and quickly released the tension building in his body. But Laura Lee wasn't some wanton, feverish woman who resided above a saloon. He didn't want her first time with him with his pants around his knees. He couldn't treat her as though she were some cheap dance hall girl he'd bought with a few rounds of whiskey and a couple of gold coins. Never. She was *his* woman—for now. However temporary these fleeting moments would be, he knew he'd be creating memories that would fill a lifetime of dreams.

He'd carry enough guilt on his shoulders without the additional shame of knowing he'd frightened or hurt her. So, instead of hastily shucking his trousers and pushing his turgid flesh into her, he lifted her into his arms and carried her into his room.

Once there, he was stymied. Should he put her on the bed and undress her? Cumbersome, he decided, lowering his arm until her feet touched the floor. Should he take her clothes off, then remove his, or vice versa? One of them would be buck naked and damned uncomfortable while the other disrobed.

"I feel as if this were my first time," he confessed. "You'll have to tell me..."

She guessed that dispensing with their clothing was the problem. Her cheeks felt as though they were on fire, and yet she found the courage to say, "Would you get my robe while I undress behind the screen?"

Reluctant to leave her, he dropped a searing kiss on her parted lips. His tongue sought and found the inner sweetness of her mouth.

In her mind the hands of time turned backward with each thrust of his tongue. The hours between the mind-drugging kisses they'd shared on the boat and the one taking place now vanished. She responded with the same passion he'd evoked earlier.

The barriers of cloth between them were dispensed with as easily as the major problems that Jack had removed from her life. There was no awkwardness. Between fervent kisses he unbuttoned her dress and she undid his shirt. His jacket and shirt were flung on a chair, and her gown landed on top of them. He unlaced her corset; she unbuckled his belt. Her petticoats and his trousers hit the floor simultaneously. Who removed what was no longer of any importance.

Modesty and inhibition be damned.

She was too eager to explore him to worry about silly bedroom protocol.

If she was wanton, she decided, then so be it.

Her eagerness was hotly reciprocated.

Each layer of clothing removed only heightened his anticipation, his need to touch her secret places. As he undressed her she shivered with desire beneath his hands; he gasped with pleasure as her inquisitive fingers discovered the basic differences between a man and a woman.

Her eyes lingered on his backside while he pushed down the covers and pulled the top sheet back. Just as she'd marveled at the play of muscles across his broad shoulders when he'd helped in the vegetable garden, so she was mesmerized by the elongated thickness of the muscles on his thighs and calves.

"Laura Lee..." He'd crawled across the width of the bed, and he waited for her now, arms open, eyes burning with passion. "Come to me, love."

"Anywhere," she whispered, moving into his arms.

For a long moment he simply held her, rocking her back and forth, while she absorbed the feel, the scent, the taste of him. A sensuous feast, she thought, her hands following the sleek contours of his arms as she burrowed her nose in the thick mat of hair covering his chest, filling her senses with his fragrance, a pleasant blend of soap and his own scent. Her fingers fanned over his chest. His chest hairs were only slightly darker than his mustache in color, but they were coarser, wirier. They tickled her nose. She darted her tongue, and it rasped against his hard chest muscles. Salty...sweet... She heard him catch his breath, then felt her shoulders pressed into the enveloping softness of the feather pillow.

Her eyes followed the trail of his fingers as they made a lazy loop around the deep dimple below her rib cage. She sucked her stomach flat. A flood of heat sprinted downward. Her legs bent reflexively, and her knees clenched together. A tiny, broken sound stuck in her throat when his hand moved upward to the rosy crest of her breast.

"You're beautiful," he said, his voice filled with awe. He cupped the weight of her breast in his palm; his thumb circled the turgid tip until it stood erect, begging for more. "Perfect."

Helplessly she watched as his head followed the trail his fingers had blazed. His mouth opened; his hot breath and the sight of his tongue teasing her heated flesh sent shivers straight to her curled toes. He tongued the deep dimple, and she cried out in surprise. Her back arched in pleasure and her fingers clenched the sheet as shafts of pleasure rippled through her.

He raised his head. His ebony eyes had a polished sheen as they met her brilliant ones. His mouth moved from side to side, his tongue laving the delicate tip of her breast, molding it, before his eyes closed and he opened his mouth to pull it deep inside him.

She could no longer stifle the whimpering cries behind her lips. Each tugging sip coiled a knot in her stomach. When his fingers rubbed through the warm hair between her legs, seeking and finding the key that could unlock her passion, she gasped in a voice thick with desire, "Jack...Jack...what are you doing to me? I feel as though I were melting."

"Loving you. It's all right. Relax, love," he murmured, peppering the breast he'd been neglecting with moist kisses. "For days I've thought of little but how much I wanted to kiss you...all of you. You're delectable...spicy, sweet...roses and champagne."

He paused to lave the pinkish-brown circle, and his mustache teased the pouty tip. All the while, his fingers were touching her, preparing her for him. The heel of his hand was snuggled against her. His fingers tantalized the sensitive skin of her inner thighs until they gave him access to the very core of her womanhood. "I'll only pleasure you."

"Such pleasure," she moaned, her narrow hips arching against his hand. Soul-stirring sensations singed her. Ecstasy rippled beneath his clever fingers, but some instinct made her whisper, "I want to give you pleasure, too."

"Touch me. Here."

Lightly he tugged at her hand until it was below his waist. Her eyes widened in astonishment, but her fingers closed around him. He wondered if he was making the worst mistake of his life. His control slipped to a treacherous new low. Her fingers, circling him, sliding down his length to the root of his passion, brought a ragged groan through his clenched teeth.

Her touch was agony... it was ecstasy... a paradox of heaven and hell... paradise.

She'd thought from seeing it that it would be hard, like a broomhandle or a doorknob, but his turgid flesh reminded her of the feel of a baby's skin. Her thumb circled it, imitating the way he'd touched her nipples.

"It's... not like I thought it would be."

Jack's grin resembled a grimace.

"Am I hurting you?"

"No."

His heart pounded as her small hand explored him curiously. No woman had ever touched him with such loving tenderness. Others, more experienced than Laura Lee, had taken one look and smiled a knowing smile. They had seen that he was built like a young stallion, and they had known from previous encounters that he was capable of taking them to unknown heights of rapture. Those women had known what to do, how to stroke the long shaft of his manhood until it reached its zenith. Laura Lee lacked their knowledge, and yet her tentative fumbling excited him far beyond anything he had ever experienced.

Fearing he'd explode prematurely, he groaned, "Stop."

"Stop? Now? What'd I do wrong?" Confused, she clasped him harder. His eyes were closed; his face was contorted as though he were in pain. She let go of him and babbled, "I'm sorry. I didn't mean to hurt you!"

His eyes sprang open. A lusty smile tilted his mouth. He moved her hand to his chest.

"You didn't. Just touch me somewhere else for a second or two."

"The way you touched me?"

He nodded and shifted her on top of him. Her fingers trailed across his chest. Then lips followed fingers, licking, mimicking the way he'd touched her. She found the flat, smooth circle of his nipple and bathed it with the silken moisture of her tongue until she felt his chest rumble with a low moan of pleasure.

Her waist-long hair caressed his shoulders, and he blanketed himself with its softness. He made a silken manacle around his wrists, tugging on it when her teeth abraded his nipple.

In the steamy process of learning the contours of his muscular body she slid closer and closer, until her hips were cradled against him. Jack smoothed his hand over her rounded buttocks and pulled her closer. He traced her spine with his thumb and huskily whispered words he had never spoken to any woman: "I love you, Laura Lee."

Her mouth opened in a gasp of pleasure. He covered it, kissing her with all the love and tenderness he possessed. Her tongue twined against his. Silently, with the thrust of her tongue, with the arch of her hips, with her fingers weaving erotic patterns on his chest, she communicated her love for him.

His hand crushed their hips together. Then he moved over her, between her thighs. His finger synchronized with his tongue as he dipped inside her. Shallowly at first, then slowly, he slipped deeper and deeper into her.

She twisted and turned against him, her breath catching in her throat. Her mind had gone blank; she was unaware of anything but a sensation of drowning, so she hardly noticed when he nudged her onto her back.

In one powerful movement, as her hips arched upward, he pushed slowly into her.

The torment she'd seen on his face earlier was nothing compared to his expression as he fought to control himself. Inch by inch he thrust into her, prolonging the exquisite agony they both felt until he was completely submerged in the heat radiating around his manhood.

So hot. So tight. So perfect. God help me! I've got to hold back! he cried soundlessly.

He felt the fragile barrier of her virginity; it touched him clear to his soul. Before he could pull back, she wrapped her legs around him, impaling herself on him.

Laura Lee thought he'd turned to stone. She'd felt the building pressure inside her, a slight twinge of pain, and then he'd stopped. "No. No. More," she cried as she arched higher.

"I'm afraid I'll hurt you," he panted. "Don't . . . let . . . me . . . hurt . . . you!"

His words punctuated each hard thrust of his pelvis. Her hips moved instinctively in a circle, seeking divine pleasure from him. She was spiraling up a mountain peak. She called out frantically to him to help her climb higher. She dug her nails into his hips, his buttocks, demanding to be taken to the height of rapture.

Awed and pleased beyond measure by her wantonness, Jack released the tight reins he'd held on his self-control and rode her hard. Perspiration dotted his forehead; a sheen of moisture coated his skin. His breathing became increasingly labored.

Shimmering waves of ecstasy were on the horizon.

She reached for the burning white heat of rapture.

He exploded, hotter than the sun, at the supreme moment when he felt her insides contract spasmodically. His skin, wet and feverish, felt as though her heat had burned and melted him.

"Jack—? Oh, Jack . . . are you all right?"

"I think I died . . . a little." He lifted his head from her shoulder. Humbled by her unfettered lovemaking, he asked, "Did you like it?"

A small, satiated smile raised one corner of her love-swollen lips. She nodded in response to his question. He moved to her side, and she cuddled against him. "Doc Wainwright told me about making love, but he left out the good part. Now I think I know why nobody talks about it."

"Why?"

He bent his elbow, propped his head on his hand and stared into her eyes. Bluebonnets. Her eyes had the same intense blue coloring as his favorite Texas wildflower.

"Because if all the good women were told how magnificent making love is there wouldn't be any good women. We'd all be bad, bad, bad!"

Jack tossed back his head and gave a hoot of laughter. "Only an irrepressible, lovable hoyden like you would think like that, much less say it."

"It's true," she retorted smugly. She brushed his damp forelock off his forehead and made a cross over her heart with one finger. "Honest Injun."

"It hasn't taken long for you to pick up the Texas slang, has it?" he said. His heart felt lighter than it had been in years. "Wildflower eyes and shoot-from-the-hip honesty."

She tweaked the short hairs on his chest. Tongue in cheek, she asked, "What happened to the sweet, innocent Southern belle you came looking for in Louisiana?"

"I wouldn't know about her." He slapped her fanny lightly, then smoothed it with the palm of his hand. "I've never met her."

She let the gibe pass; she felt too glorious to pick a fight with him. Then she recalled something. "Jack," she asked, "why did you look as though you were in pain?"

His fingers scampered over her ribs, and she emitted a husky chuckle.

"You weren't supposed to be peeking . . . just feeling."

That made little sense to her. "You're not supposed to keep your eyes open?"

"Uh-uh."

"Seems like a shame to me." She ran her finger along the thick muscles of his chest, then glanced down at the smooth skin on her breasts. "You're so different from me."

"Yeah. And you recover faster than I do."

"I wonder—" She bit her lower lip. They'd shared the most intimate act possible between a man and a woman, but she knew that her curiosity still wasn't ladylike. She squirmed, wanting to ask but knowing she shouldn't.

"What do you wonder? Ask."

"Well . . ."

Jack chuckled. "Shy? Now?"

"No, but . . . it's sort of a . . . an impudent question."

"My favorite kind. Fire away."

"Who enjoys doing it most? A man? Or a woman?"

He tried not to laugh. She was such a joy. Her uninhibited tongue was as delightful to him as her uninhibited lovemaking.

"That's the damnedest question I've ever heard. Frankly, I don't know who enjoys it most."

Grinning, Laura Lee gave him a peck on the lips. "I think I know."

"Okay." He nibbled the lobe of her ear. "I'll bite. Who?"

"Well, if my ear itches and I put my finger in my ear to scratch it, which feels better? My finger or my ear?"

Her logical deduction amused and amazed him. It also made him feel ten feet tall and as strong as a bull to know that she believed a woman enjoyed making love more than a man.

"You're priceless," he told her, gloating inwardly.

"Are you ready for the next question?"

"Probably not, but fire away."

She changed her position by stretching out until she lay flat on top of him. "How long?"

"Good gracious, woman! I think I've unleashed a monster! Do you mean inches?"

"I'm not blind. I kept my eyes open, remember? *Minutes!* How long do I have to wait for you to 'recover'?"

Jack grinned. "Far be it from me to keep a lady waiting."

For long, lovely hours they made love, slept, awakened and made love again, until they were too exhausted to do more than sleep, entwined intimately, with their hearts beating as one.

Chapter Ten

Wednesday morning came too soon to suit Laura Lee.

As she lay snuggled against Jack, who slept soundly on the wide feather bed they'd shared for two nights, pangs of anxiety swept through her at the thought of boarding the *Matadora* at noon.

He'd come to Blythewood seeking his brother's fiancée, she mused. He'd found her and made her his lover. What would he do now? She hadn't an inkling of his plans.

Sure, they'd talked seriously about the plantations and the ranch, and he'd spun wild tales that had had her giggling with delight, but not once had he broached the subject of her planned marriage to John.

Her worried eyes slanted upward to his face. Asleep, he looked vulnerable. Laura Lee knew better. Every time they left the room he packed his side arm, ready for any unforeseen event. He'd been caught off guard once; he wouldn't let that happen again. The wound on his arm was a constant reminder of the danger.

Handsome, funny, muleheaded, she thought, longing to reach up and feather the hair back from his forehead with her fingers. *Muleheaded.* It was the last trait that bothered her. Once he'd set his feet on a certain path, there was no altering the final destination.

She was unaware that her arm had tightened on his chest and wakened him, so when his hand began caressing her waist and hip it startled her.

"G'morning, love," he said, dropping a kiss on the crown of her head and giving her a drowsy grin. "Sweet dreams last night?"

"Who had time to dream?" She tried to inject lightness into her tone, but the laughing lilt came out flat.

His hand moved lazily over her ribs to the trio of dimples at the small of her back. The closeness they'd shared had gone beyond the physical to an almost-perfect mental meshing. "You're thinking about sailing out of here, aren't you?"

"Umm-hmm. Dreading it."

"Why?"

She lifted her face and met his eyes. "John."

She had hoped he would discuss the matter with her, but he turned away silently. Pulling back the coverlet, he rose to his feet, grabbed his trousers from the bedside chair and tugged them into place.

"I can't marry him."

Her eyes widened as Jack wordlessly strode to the window, which overlooked Chartres Street. Primly she pulled the sheet beneath her arms and pushed herself up until her back rested against the headboard.

Jack pushed aside the drapes and stared down at the street as he carefully searched for a way to make Laura Lee understand his dilemma. Until he found a way to tell her of John's paralysis, he couldn't even start to communicate the guilt he felt over being the cause of the accident. Nor could he tell her that he saw his role in arranging her marriage to John as some small reparation for the accident. He loved Laura Lee—he'd told her so repeatedly, all through the night—but he loved John, too.

Whose heart should he break? John's? Laura Lee's? They were both innocent of any wrongdoing. He was the villain.

He slowly pulled his hand through his hair. His scalp tingled from the self-inflicted punishment, but there wasn't enough pain to overshadow the tight feeling in his chest.

Laura Lee began to panic. She saw his shoulders and his hands tremble as he shoved them into his pockets. Whatever he was planning on telling her, she knew it wasn't what she wanted to hear. She wanted to hide, to dive under the blanket and cover her ears. Raw courage allowed her to remain stock-still.

"He'll know." She wanted to keep Jack from saying something unforgivable. "He'll know we slept together."

Jack shook his head. "No, he won't."

She watched him turn slowly. His black eyes were filled with self-loathing and misery.

"John is—" He gagged on the word *crippled*. His throat worked hard to keep his stomach from revolting.

"Understanding?" Laura Lee said, supplying a word.

No man is that damned understanding, Jack silently replied, shaking his head. Telling John he'd made love with Laura Lee would be as difficult as telling her John couldn't make love. Why, oh why, hadn't he kept his promise to John? Because he loved her. Because he couldn't help but love her.

He took a deep breath as though he were preparing to plunge into a bottomless pool. When he could hold it no longer, he slowly expelled the air he'd had locked in his lungs. "John's crippled, from the waist down. He was in an accident over six months ago."

Several seconds passed before Laura Lee could assimilate that piece of information and its ramifications.

"You should have told me."

"And have you tear the Wynthrop-Shannon agreement to shreds? " he snapped. His anger with himself spilled over onto her. "I already practically had to toss you in a gunnysack to get you this far."

"Is that why you made love to me?" Her fist pounded the pillow where his head had rested next to hers during the night. "To make damn certain I wouldn't leave your side?"

He considered replying affirmatively to her loathsome accusation. She'd hate him if he did. But wouldn't it make it easier for her to accept John as a husband? His hands knotted into hard fists in his pockets; his eyes dropped to the patterned carpet covering the floor. The thought of Laura Lee married to John was as repugnant to him as it was to her. He doubted he'd ever again shut his eyes without remembering making love with her. He couldn't debase that memory with a lie.

"No."

One look at his black eyes as he raised his head erased her anger. She scurried to the foot of the bed for her robe. She'd seen the same blank look in a soldier's eyes before the doctor had closed them and placed copper pennies on his eyelids.

She shoved her arms into the sleeves, knotted the belt and crossed the room until she stood directly in front of him.

"Talk to me, Jack. Make me understand," she pleaded.

Every instinct urged him to pull her into his arms and carry her away. His honor kept him motionless.

"I hated lying to you—not telling the whole truth—but I promised John I wouldn't tell you he was confined to a wheelchair."

"Why would you make such a promise? I had a right to know, didn't I?"

"It's my fault he's crippled."

His lips had barely moved as he'd said it. Laura Lee could see his agony. She wondered aloud, "How could you be responsible? Didn't you say John had an accident?"

"John came out to the branding pen to talk to me. A bull broke loose from his pen and charged me. My brother saved my life by waving his bandanna to distract the bull." He swallowed. "The bull gored him and tossed him against the fence rails."

"You'd have done the same for him. It was an accident, Jack. You can't take the blame for what happened."

"I can and do. He came out there to discuss his leaving Texas; we had argued about it repeatedly. I should have let him return to Heavenly Acres right after the war when he started badgering me. Then he wouldn't have been there to get hurt."

"That's hindsight!"

Jack shook his head, his hands closing over her shoulders. He glanced at the rumpled bed, and his eyes misted with self-recrimination. "My selfishness caused his accident, and it caused what happened between us. I've hurt you and John—the two people in the world I love. I'd say you'd be right to think of me as a lousy son of a bitch, but I'm selfish enough to hope you won't."

"Do you want me to marry John?"

"No," he replied honestly, "but you're better off married to him than to me. I'd only hurt you more."

All the love in her heart shone in her eyes as she said, "I'll take the risk of being hurt."

Jack shook his head; his hands swung to his sides. "I won't let you."

"You can't stop me," she told him. She raised herself up on her toes and kissed him lightly. "There. A vow sealed with a kiss is sacred."

* * *

Stomach heaving, Laura Lee clung to the rail at the bow of the steamship *Matadora*, bound for Galveston. Seasick, homesick and sick at heart, she thought, silently diagnosing her ills. The salt air teasing her hair and the salt spray mingling with her tears could cure only one of her illnesses.

Only Jack could miraculously heal her heartache and her homesickness. He held her heart in those large, callused hands of his. And he had cherished it by being kind, considerate, and gallant—the perfect brother-in-law.

Hard as she tried, she couldn't fault him. She fervently wanted to hate him; she loved him more fervently than ever. Jack Wynthrop was the living, breathing embodiment of her dreams: honorable, responsible, indescribably handsome. Without turning her head, she knew he was within ten paces of her, ready to protect her with his life if necessary.

"Awwwk! Ship ahoy, mates! Pirates!"

Laura Lee grinned and dabbed at her eyes with her handkerchief. Jack brought Captain Bligh up on deck every day, and with each passing day the bird's vocabulary grew saltier.

"Excuse him," Jack said, adding, "His beak needs to be clipped instead of his wings." His natural gait changed to a swagger as he rolled with the pitching of the deck and crossed to the rail. His black eyes swept over her, taking in her wan, pallid face and her white knuckles. "Feeling better?"

"I'll survive. I always do."

"Prrretttty girl! Awwwk!"

No, Jack thought. Not pretty. Beautiful. His heart tripped in his chest when Laura Lee smiled at him. He held up the cage. "I think our fine feathered friend here needs to spend a few years living with a priest in a monastery."

"The salt air seems to agree with him." She poked her finger through the bars and stroked the top of his head. "You're incorrigible, aren't you, fella?"

"That's putting it mildly. He's going to make my ranch hands blush."

"What about..." She'd meant to say "John." Instead, she said, "...my fiancé. Will he object to Captain Bligh?"

Sharper than a hat pin, deadlier than a rapier, her remark hit where she'd aimed—his heart.

"John'll love both of you," he replied in a low voice that could barely be heard above the sound of the waves. "You'll learn to love him, too," he continued, hating the thought.

Laura Lee felt his pain, or was it her own? Intentionally hurting Jack had the same effect as self-inflicted pain.

"How can I learn to love John when..." Her chin dropped to her chest. She shouldn't burden him with her love. His shoulders were stooped with his own burden of guilt.

"...he's paralyzed from the waist down?" Jack finished for her.

She nodded, hiding her love for Jack with a fringe of sooty dark lashes.

"There's a difference between love and lust."

Her raised eyebrow silently asked him how long it would take to recover from "lust"? She couldn't look at him without remembering the feel and taste of him. How long would it take? A month? A year? Deep in her heart, she knew the answer—an eternity.

"I've decided to build another cabin," he said. "One farther away from the big house, which is where you'll live with John."

"Where you live won't make a difference to me."

She turned her face seaward. Jack Wynthrop could live on a mountaintop, thousands of miles away from the Rocking W Ranch, and she'd still love him, still think of him, still want to be with him.

Jack watched the ocean breeze gently caress her blond hair, blowing it behind her shell-like ear. Just the thought of her living in John's house, caring for him, learning to love John platonically, made his heart beat erratically. He hadn't thought he had a jealous bone in his body until he'd lain in his bunk in the cabin below and envisioned John and Laura Lee together. On the spot he'd decided to move from the main house.

"Laura Lee?" His hand covered hers. For a long moment he was silent, collecting his thoughts. He'd done her a disservice by hiding the whole truth from her, just as she'd done him a disservice by not telling him what had happened to Heavenly Acres. What he had to tell her had to be said. "It isn't just lust that I feel for you."

Her head snapped toward him, but he stared sightlessly at the empty horizon.

"Lust is when a man wants a woman without caring what happens after they have sex. I do care."

His thumb stroked over hers to her wrist; he felt her pulse hammering beneath it.

"I . . . admire you," he continued. Admiration did not exactly describe his feelings, but it was better than admitting to love—real love, not the kind you murmured in the throes of passion, but the kind that lasted always and forever. "I admire your dedication to reviving Blythewood, and I admire you for valiantly providing for Tad and Brandy. I...respect you for having the gumption to boldly disguise yourself as a man and take risks. Other Southern women, in a similar situation, have helplessly buckled under and sold their heritage for whatever they could get. I...like your stubbornness, that willful streak in you that scoffs at failure."

He lifted the back of her hand to his mouth and dropped a kiss on her white skin. "And I like the color of your eyes and how your hair curls when it's damp. And how you laugh." And kiss, and smell, and taste, he added silently.

He lowered her hand to the pulse point on his neck. "And how you make me feel inside. Lust is a small part of...of what I feel for you."

Laura Lee felt her heart swell until she thought it would burst with love for him. "You can't let me be John's wife."

"I can. I have to."

"So what do you expect me to do? Pretend I don't love you? Pretend I love John?" Never once, during all the struggles of the past years, had she felt as completely defenseless and helpless as she did right now. "Do you really believe what your feeling—what I'm feeling—is something we can hide! John is crippled, not blind."

Captain Bligh restlessly flapped his wings against the cage. "Awwwk! I love you! Prrretttty girl! I love you!"

"I'm sorry, Laura lee. I have to keep my promise. There's nothing else I can do."

Jumping off his perch, the Captain blasted out, "Tarnation!"

Laura Lee couldn't have expressed it better. "Knowing what you've told me, I won't give up, Jack." She jerked her hand off his shirt and clamped it on one hip. "Well, to quote our fine feathered friend...tarnation! I love you, too!"

She spun around, her skirts whipping against his legs. Moving at almost a dead run, she nearly knocked down a whiskered, scar-faced man who'd been keenly observing them.

"Pardon me," she gasped.

The stranger's blunt fingers dug into her upper arms to prevent her from falling. "That's okay, missy. I'm used to havin' women knock me down."

The stale whiskey on his breath assaulted her nose. She wrenched free, shot Jack one last defiant look, then hurried below to her cabin.

"Jack may not be able to do anything—" she slammed the door "—but I can."

She drew a deep breath, linked her hands at her waist and paced the short length of her cabin. She didn't know precisely what she was going to do, but she'd think of something. She always had in the past.

It had been a frustrating two hours for Jack. He rarely smoked, but moments ago he'd begged a cheroot off a dandified gambler dressed in a silk shirt, a brocade vest and a broad-lapelled black linen suit. He'd offered to pay for it, but the gambler had refused, inviting him to join a friendly poker game after the dinner hour.

Since he'd appointed himself Laura Lee's personal bodyguard, he'd returned Captain Bligh to his cabin and assumed his post outside the passengers' only entry into the bowels of the ship.

For the past few hours he'd been watching the sun sinking into the Gulf. A quarter moon that looked as though the North Star had spilled from its curve lit the velvet darkness.

Dinner hour had come and gone. No Laura Lee. She'd sequestered herself in her cabin.

He bit the tip off the cheroot. You had to clear your conscience by telling her, didn't you? You just had to kiss her. You had to perch her on that damn rail and sample her special brand of sweetness, didn't you? And you had to make love with her, too. What did it get you?

He wiped the tobacco on his middle finger and flicked it overboard. He'd eased his conscience, but his trousers still felt as though they were three sizes too small.

He dug in his pocket for a match, then raked the end of it across the heel of his boot. The orange flame touched the end of the slender cigar. Smoke burned his eyes, and the tobacco burned his tongue. And yet he inhaled. Tobacco calmed a man's nerves—or so he'd been told. He exhaled. His thoughts were as capricious as the smoke curling from his mouth.

Laura Lee Shannon. Half child, from her mud-splattered disguise to her naive enjoyment of life's little pleasures. Half hoyden, from her smart mouth to her short temper. There were times when her stubbornness made him want to throttle her, and times when he wanted to love her, completely, without feelings of guilt gnawing at him.

Guilt had motivated him to fetch John his bride. His brother could have made the journey himself if he hadn't stepped in front of a charging bull, waving his red bandanna. Jack still had nightmares of John flying through the air like a rag doll, hitting the ground hard enough to bounce twice. Yeah, he owed his brother his life.

Right now, when he should have a feeling of accomplishment at having successfully discharged his moral debt, he felt like the lowest of snakes, with a forked tongue and no backbone.

Frustrated, he chewed on the end of the cheroot and inhaled.

He should have known when Laura Lee had sunk her sharp little teeth into his tough hide that he was a goner. And don't forget the damage she did with her elbow, he thought. Now there was a real indicator of things to come.

He swallowed a mouthful of smoke and coughed. "She's got me so muddled I can't even breathe in and out properly!" He pitched the cigar over the railing and watched the glowing ember arc, then fall out of sight.

Quit blaming her. You're the coward. Why don't you go to John and tell him face-to-face that you're in love with his future bride?

"I can't hurt him," he muttered despondently.

He'd caused John enough pain when he'd cost him the use of his legs. With Laura Lee taking up residence in the big house, how much help was he going to be? Wouldn't John be thrilled to see him mooning over his wife? And, worse, how was he going to like seeing Laura Lee follow his every footstep with those gorgeous blue eyes of hers?

You're a living, breathing bastard for doing this to the two people you care about most in this world. A self-made bastard. You can't blame this on your parents. The blame sits squarely on your shoulders!

"Waiting for me?" Laura Lee asked, stepping through the passageway. "Have I missed dinner?"

"Yes—to both questions."

His eyes were wide with uncertainty. He recognized the wide-brimmed straw hat with the floppy silk magnolias, and recognized, too, the pink taffeta gown she'd had made from the fabric he'd given her.

"Like it?"

She swirled in front of him, seeming to dance in the moonlight to a pagan melody that only she could hear. The pink-tinged taffeta was simply styled, with a neckline that dipped enticingly low to bare the generous swells of her breasts, and had the same pearly iridescence as the inside of a conch shell. The skirt lay flat against her stomach and pulled into a stiff bustle bow in the back. Pinned high in the crown of her hat, her long blond curls draped elegantly against her shoulders. A thin black velvet ribbon circled her slender neck; on the knot she'd pinned a tiny enameled shamrock. Her brilliant eyes danced as merrily as her white satin slippers.

"Enchanting." He blinked slowly. He wanted to capture her beauty in his warehouse of memories, for the tomboy hoyden had magically been transformed into a fairy tale princess.

Her breath caught in her throat when she saw his mustache lift on one side in the endearing lopsided smile she loved. Torrid heat stemmed from those black eyes of his. The dress had achieved its goal. The rest was up to her.

"Shall we stroll around the deck?"

He crooked his arm. She nodded and placed her hand on his sleeve. He shortened his long-legged gait to match hers. She smiled, glad to be the woman by his side.

Tomorrow morning they would dock in Galveston. Tonight would be their last night together. But perhaps, somehow, something wonderful would happen.

"The seas have calmed," he commented.

"Mmm. My stomach noticed."

"Are you hungry?"

"A little."

"Captain Bligh would starve on what you've eaten since we left New Orleans."

Laura Lee chuckled. "I hope you're not going to offer me a late-night snack of birdseed."

They rounded the corner. Piano music and laughter could be heard coming from the main saloon. Until now, the only activity in the evening had been a poker game that went on into the wee hours of the morning.

"The saloon appears to be busy," Jack observed, motioning to the people coming and going through the swinging doors. "Come to think of it, I did overhear someone mention that there would be entertainment tonight."

"A farewell party."

Her smile began to wilt. Farewells denoted final endings. Was this the last time Jack would be her escort? Don't think, she silently told herself. You'll only spoil the precious time that remains!

"Let's see what's going on. Maybe I can scrounge up something for you to eat."

All melancholy thoughts vanished the moment they stepped into the saloon. A squat black man with a fat cigar clenched between his grinning lips pounded his fingers on the yellowed keys of an upright piano; his feet pounded on the floor in perfect rhythm to the bass notes he struck. Another musician with a banjo on his knee sat cross-legged in a straight-backed chair, strumming and singing in a falsetto voice. The last member of the trio puffed on a harmonica, his shaggy eyebrows bouncing in time to the notes he played.

"There's an empty table. Follow me."

Her hand automatically slipped into his. Her eyes went round with surprise when she noticed that the waiters weaving their way between the small tables were carrying trays filled with beer mugs and whiskey glasses. Ladies seldom drank alcoholic beverages—and never in public. Just once, at Christmas, her mother had given her a sip of white wine. But here no one seemed to notice or to care who was drinking what.

"Here we are," Jack said, whipping his handkerchief from his pocket and dusting the chair before he held it out for Laura Lee. He motioned to a waiter before seating himself across the small table. "It's kinda loud!"

The footloose-and-fancy-free gaiety reminded her of the grown-up parties she'd watched from the balcony at

Blythewood when she'd been too young to participate. It was as though the war had never taken place. Within seconds her foot was tapping and laughter was bubbling from her lips.

"What's it gonna be, mister?" came from over her shoulder.

"Whiskey. Neat. Any chance of getting something to eat?"

"This ain't no restaurant, mister. Does the lady want something?"

Jack frowned.

"Beer," Laura Lee answered. "Neat."

The waiter tossed his head back and roared with laughter. "Okay, lady. Beer with no ice."

"On second thought..." Ice was an unaffordable luxury back home. The frothy golden-yellow beverage had to taste better ice-cold.

"No...uh, never mind." Jack winked at the waiter. "She'll take hers straight up."

"What's so funny?" she demanded when she saw his devilish eyes laughing at her. He'd covered his mouth with his hand.

"Nothing. You. Everything." He settled back in his chair and lowered his hand.

As infectious as the lighthearted music, his grin brightened the dimly lit room. She couldn't be angry with him; a sappy smile of pure contentment parted her lips.

"Hey, mister! Ready to pay for your cigar with a poker hand?" said a voice from the large table tucked away in the corner of the room.

"Later."

"You play poker?" Laura Lee asked with mild interest. Her father had loved "ruffling the pasteboards." She'd learned the rudiments of the game from Beau at an early age. Within hours she'd been able to beat the socks off him.

"What cowpoke doesn't? Cards are a pleasant way to while away the lonely evenings out on the range."

He scooted his chair close to hers so that she could hear him without his having to shout. The waiter returned, setting a mug in front of Laura Lee with a bang that was loud enough to rival the foot-stomping musicians. White foam sloshed over the rim of the mug.

While Jack paid the man, she gingerly raised the mug to her lips. She thought he wasn't looking when she darted her tongue into the miniscule bubbles. She'd expected her drink to be sweet, with its light color and foam. Her nose wrinkled at its bitterness. Beer looked like strong lemonade, but it sure didn't taste like lemonade.

He must have been keeping one eye on me, she thought. His insufferable bemused smile had his mustache tilting sideways again.

"Now what am I doing that amuses you?"

"I don't think I've ever seen anyone hold a beer mug like a china teacup." He waggled his little finger at her. "You don't have to drink it if you don't like it."

"Sugar and ice might improve the flavor," she said, after taking a sip and getting past the foam. The yellow liquid had a stronger flavor than the white foam.

Her comment brought a deep rumbling laugh from Jack. He yanked his handkerchief from his breast pocket, reached over and dabbed at the foam on the tip of her nose.

"There must be a real knack to drinking this stuff without a handkerchief. Want to swap drinks?"

Jack shook his head, raised his arm and motioned to the harried waiter. "Mixing beer and whiskey is the best recipe I know to make you deathly ill."

"Ready for another?" the waiter called.

"A sarsaparilla for the lady. And a bag of peanuts."

Laura Lee took another glance at the card table. A woman had joined the three men, much to Laura Lee's surprise. Beau had told her that women weren't allowed to gamble. Her fingers were fairly itching for a chance to play for real.

"Jack." She nodded toward the poker table. "Do you think they'd let me play a few hands?"

"Probably."

"Would you mind?"

Jack smiled broadly. Despite the feminine finery, the irascible little hoyden he'd come to love lurked just beneath the skin of the lady next to him. "Go ahead. Be my guest."

She was on her feet and heading for the table before Jack could pull her chair back for her. He had a hell of a time signaling the waiter and catching up with her. Reaching into his pocket, he pulled out a few silver dollars and handed them to her.

"Here. You'll need these. Don't be disappointed when you see them raked into one of those men's piles."

Only the gambler Jack had previously met got to his feet. "Welcome. Seth Jones is my name. Poker's my game. There's always room at my table for a gambling man who brings along a charming young lady for good luck. Care to join us?"

"I'm afraid my wife brought me along."

Dazed by his glib statement, Laura Lee barely heard the introductions. She did catch the other woman's name: Charity Lane. Strange name, she thought, noting the subdued dove-gray dress with its frayed white cuffs and the meager stack of silver dollars Miss Lane guarded with both hands. She recognized fear on the woman's face; she'd seen it in her own mirror many a morning.

"No problem," the gambler replied, returning to his seat. "With this ruckus going on tonight it's too noisy for a serious game."

"Five-card stud? Four up and one in the hole?" Laura Lee asked as she looked at the position of the cards.

Automatically she began figuring the chances the other woman had of winning. With four hearts showing, the odds were in her favor of her filling in another heart. Since the last card to be dealt would be down and dirty, Miss Lane could always bluff.

Laura Lee smiled encouragingly across the table at her and was slightly appalled when Jones dealt the last card and the woman's lips drooped.

No! Laura Lee implored her with her eyes. You're giving your hand away. She almost groaned aloud when she watched her gather her cards and turn them facedown.

Within seconds the professional gambler had won the hand, but not before Laura Lee had studied the faces of the other two men. The round-faced man on her left had fidgeted with the corners of the cards—a dead giveaway that he had a losing hand.

Surreptitiously she watched the whiskered face of the man on her right. She'd bumped into him earlier. If Jack hadn't been standing right behind her she'd have felt uneasy. There was something about him that made her skin crawl.

She silently scolded herself. Don't be silly. You can't judge him just because a scar has disfigured his face. You've seen plenty worse than this one. For all you know he could be a war hero like Bill Carpenter. But the red scar parting his eyebrow and puckering his nostril still gave her the creeps, as if it were something evil.

"You'll have to excuse me," Miss Lane said, counting her coins and picking them up with a shaky hand. "Mr. Wynthrop, you're welcome to take my place."

Just as she had taken an instant dislike to the man on her right, she felt she had found a kindred spirit in this woman with the soft Southern drawl who was leaving with little more than her dignity to show for her efforts.

Jack winked at her as he seated himself between the gambler and the nervous gentleman next to her.

"Ante up a dollar, folks," Jones said. "Here comes Lady Luck, smilin' at me again. Mr. Alden, you aren't thinkin' of droppin' out, are you?"

"Just deal the cards, mister. Lady Luck is fickle. I can feel her moving around in my direction."

The rollicking music and jovial laughter in the room faded into the background as Laura Lee concentrated on the first round of cards dealt. She looked at the queen of hearts in front of her and took it as a good omen. Jack, Alden and Scarface had low cards.

"Thank you, Lady Luck," the gambler crowed.

Lo and behold, Jones had dealt himself the ace of clubs with hands quicker than the average eye. But Laura Lee had more than an average eye. Beau had not only taught her how to fan the cards to check for a marked deck, he'd also taught her how to deal from the bottom of the deck, along with a few other choice card tricks. The gambler would bear careful scrutiny, she quickly decided.

She leaned forward and placed one finger on her card. "My, oh, my," she said, fanning her eyelashes, "I do believe my queen is the only face card. I just bet—"

"Whoa there, little lady..."

Jack pointed at the dealer with his thumb. "His ace beats your queen."

"Oh." Her voice dripped with feigned disappointment. "That means he gets to wager first, doesn't it?"

"I'll make it easy on you. How 'bout two dollars?" He flicked his wrist, and two silver dollars landed in the center of the table.

Two dollars from the man to her right matched the gambler's bet.

She'd have tossed two off her pile, but Gambler Jones's condescension as he said, "Your bet, little lady," raised the number of coins she slid to the growing pile, as well as her hackles.

"You're raising? On the first card?" Jack asked, surprised by her boldness, though he knew he shouldn't be.

Jones made a *tsking* sound. "Poker isn't a game for partners. Let the little lady play her own cards. You can win your money back when she drops out."

Like hell, Jack thought, catching on to her ploy when he looked at her simpering grin. She might look dumb enough that a man could blow in one ear and feel a breeze coming out the other ear, but he knew better.

Alden plunked three coins in the center of the table.

"I'll fold," Jack said, leaning back on two legs of his chair to watch the action. Go get 'em, hoyden!

By the time the last round of cards had been dealt Laura Lee felt confident that she'd convinced everyone but Jack that she had a head full of feathers and a purse lined with silver. She had a queen and a pair of sixes and a nine showing. She lifted the corner of the last card. Beaming inwardly, pouting outwardly, she waited for her turn.

In her estimation, the only competing hand was held by Jones. She had a gut feeling he had another ace to match the one he had showing. Maybe not from the deck, she mused. Maybe from behind the silky hankie that spilled from his coat pocket.

The whiskered man with the scar folded.

"Can I raise . . . say five dollars?" she cooed, deliberately putting both her hands on the last card.

"Sure can," Alden said, matching her wager and thumping his cards with his forefinger. "You're awfully proud of those sixes, aren't you?"

"I'll call. What've you got?"

"A pair of sixes—"

Alden flipped over his last card. "My nines beat those."

"And my pair of aces beats your nines," Jones said.

Jack raised an eyebrow as the gambler's hands circled the pile of silver.

Surprise, surprise, Laura Lee mused, grinning. "But, gentlemen," she protested, "don't my queens count?"

All eyes were on her fumbling fingers.

"I'd say my wife won that hand, gentlemen."

"Nothing unusual about beginner's luck, folks," Jones said, shoving the pot toward Laura Lee, who was clapping her hands enthusiastically.

"I told you the luck was heading my way."

For the next few hands Laura Lee led them to believe that she was depending on luck. She deliberately played badly, letting Alden peek slyly at her hole card, counting aloud when it was her turn to deal, and not declaring a straight that was there for the entire table to see.

What a conniving little cardsharp, Jack thought, at once amused and worried. Her timing had to be perfect, or he'd be forced to use the pistol strapped to his thigh to keep these men from pitching her overboard.

Twice he'd tried to extricate her from the table, but his "wife" had begged prettily to stay for "just a couple more hands." When her pile began growing, he excused himself, shooting her a nasty look.

She puckered her mouth in a charming moue. "I just can't understand why he wants to go back to that stuffy old cabin. I can't possibly leave when I'm winning, now can I, gentlemen?"

The men nodded in agreement.

"Why don't you have the waiter come over here with a round of drinks?" she suggested to Jack. "That'll get rid of some of this dirty old money."

Jack circled the table. Her graciousness would make him appear churlish if he refused. "What can I get you, m'dear?"

"Water, please." Impatient to start playing again, she fluttered her eyelashes and asked, "Should we wait until you get back to deal?"

A card slid under her hands in silent reply.

Jack bent over her shoulder and whispered, "Hoyden!"

Her ready blush served to further distract the male poker players from their game. From the expression on their faces Laura Lee felt certain that they were itching to do things that had nothing to do with cards.

Jack took his time getting the drinks. He returned to the table just as Alden tossed a folded document on the table and called Laura Lee's healthy bet. The place in front of her was empty of silver; her winnings were neatly stacked in the center of the table. The professional gambler was still in his place, but the whiskered man who'd been seated to her right had vanished. Her small hands were tensely holding the cards that she had yet to deal.

A small frown knitted twin lines on her forehead. She'd thought she could buy the pot and narrow the game down to the gambler and herself. Why didn't you drop out of this hand? her eyes silently asked Alden. The odds against his filling a royal flush were phenomenal. She had a pat hand: three of a kind, with a king for a kicker.

"It's the title to the Golden Spur Saloon in Galveston. A gold mine, actually." Alden laughed; his boot heel nervously tapped the floorboards, rustling the taffeta of her skirt. "Worth twice what's in the pile."

"What would I do with a saloon?"

"Run it. Sell it. Tear it down and build a hat shop, for all I care."

"Last time I strolled by the Golden Spur it was boarded up tighter than a whiskey keg," Jack said, depositing a shot glass in front of each man.

"I shut it down for the winter while I was back in St. Louis looking for a business partner who had some money. The saloon needs some fixin' up, but . . . hell, I don't plan on losin' this hand. Beginners luck should have run out by now."

"Mr. Alden, my winning is more than luck," Laura Lee told him. What had started out as good fun had suddenly taken a serious turn. She didn't want to deprive the man of his property, she didn't want the responsibility of disposing of it. "I've been playing card games since I was old enough to deal. Why don't I just take back—"

"Oh, no, you don't." Alden blocked her hands with his beefy arm. "Just deal and weep."

She glanced at Jack; he shrugged.

"Down and dirty," she murmured as she dealt each of them a card. She turned hers faceup. "A king, Mr. Alden. I'd say that makes a full house."

"That leaves me suckin' the boar's hind—" a threatening look and the sound of a hand slapping leather was enough to choke back the crude remark "—end. You win, lady."

"That's it for me, too," the gambler said, edging his chair backward.

Laura Lee raked in the pile of silver—more money than she'd had in her possession in several years. And a title to boot! Generously she flipped a silver dollar high in the air toward the gambler.

"For my husband's cigar," she said grandly.

Laughing, Jones snagged it in midair. "Thanks for the cigar, and for the poker lesson." He doffed his hat, then turned to Jack. "A smart man would let her open the Golden Spur. She'll make you rich in no time."

"I don't suppose you'd hire me as a bartender, would you?" Alden asked, his voice shaking. He gulped down the whiskey Jack had placed in front of him. "I'd work for a percentage of the profits, and I wouldn't cheat you."

Smiling, not sure what she'd do, she answered, "I'll think about it and let you know before we dock."

Later, sprawled on her stomach across the narrow bunk in her cabin, she did think about it. She could almost hear the silver and gold coins being raked into the cash drawer as she heard the gambler's words, "She'll make you rich in no time."

Hadn't that been her goal before Jack had arrived at Blythewood and complicated her life? She traced the folds of the deed with her fingers. Now she had the means to reach her goal. She could earn the money to support Blythewood.

"I don't need the Wynthrop money," she muttered, tapping her lower lip with her forefinger. "I need to be with Jack, but not as his brother's wife—especially since he's considering leaving the Rocking W Ranch because I'll be there. We'll all be better off with me in Galveston and both Wynthrop men at their ranch."

"Awwwk! I love you!" came from the cabin next door.

Chapter Eleven

"The Golden Spur? That's no place for a lady!" Jack put his arms around the tiny waist of the bullheaded woman glaring at him. "I'm taking you to the Rocking W Ranch. Period!"

Squirming, Laura Lee stomped on his big toe with the sharp heel of her shoe. She might as well have kicked a boulder; his arms remained around her waist.

"I won't allow—"

"*You* won't allow! My fiancé is the only man who has any rights over me." She glanced around the small cabin as though she were looking for someone. "He isn't here, so I'll do as I damn well please!"

"Be sensible, Laura Lee."

"It's because I am being sensible that I'm starting a business in Galveston." She stiffened every muscle in her body to keep from melting against him. Her tenacity and fortitude weakened considerably when he held her in his arms. Her eyes pleaded with him for patience and understanding. "The same mathematical skills that earned me pennies a day at Luke Reynolds' bank can be used to earn dollars. I'll be able to pay you back and keep Blythewood afloat financially."

"What about the written agreement between our fathers?"

"My father wanted me to be financially secure."

"And safe. You sure as hell won't be safe in a saloon."

"Mr. Alden offered to tend the bar. This morning I talked to Charity Lane."

"This morning! You've been on deck? Alone?"

"I have a gun in my purse."

"You'll need it if Luke Reynolds or one of his hired guns finds you alone."

"Luke Reynolds is in Louisiana. I'm out of sight—and out of mind, I hope."

"You are out of your ever-loving mind if you think he doesn't want revenge." Jack couldn't help remembering the shot that had nearly killed Laura Lee aboard the Mississippi paddle wheeler. But from the stubborn set of her chin he could tell that she considered the Reynolds episode finished. Geography wouldn't dissuade Reynolds, though. A man with money had long arms. "Is that gun you're so proud of the same gun I took away from you?"

Laura Lee nodded. "And I do know how to use it. Beau taught me."

"You're in Texas. Waving a gun in a drunken sidewinder's face will get you shot out here." He wanted to shake some sense into her head; he wanted to hold her and never let go. "That's if you don't shoot yourself in the foot before he fires a round."

She turned up her nose. "Nevertheless, I've hired Alden and his double-barreled shotgun to tend bar, and Charity to supervise the serving of refreshments."

"Serving refreshments?" He waggled his finger in her face. "Beer and rotgut whiskey isn't tea and crumpets! I can't picture Miss Lane serving warm milk to a man, much less a shot of whiskey."

While she'd been reasoning with him, she'd relaxed. He released her as if she were a fiery coal. If he wasn't careful, he'd be nestling her against his chest and trying to use friendly persuasion. He wondered how many sleepless nights a man could endure without exhaustion having the same effect on him that locoweed had on cattle. He was half crazy with desire, and he knew he needed a respite from her companionship.

"Calm down and lower your voice. That vein throbbing on your forehead is going to burst." Laura Lee whisked the skirt of her dark gray traveling dress sideways so that she could get by Jack without so much as her hem touching him. "The war orphaned Charity, too. She's heading west to start over."

Jack snorted. "Charity is the marrying kind. She wants a husband and kids."

"So? What's she supposed to do while she's waiting for Mr. Right to ride in on a white horse? Starve? She can't thread a needle and she can't read a book. Working for me won't pay much at first, but she'll have a roof over her head and food on her plate."

"Women! If you're so all-fired worried about her, bring her along to the ranch."

"Can't you get it through that thick head of yours that I'm staying right here?" She'd raised her voice; it was something she'd vowed to refrain from doing. Purse in hand, she marched to the door. "You have a job, too. Someone has to go to the ranch and inform John of the change in plans."

"Great! Just great!" he commented sarcastically. "You've got everyone assigned to their respective duties. What about you, Laura Lee? What are you going to do? Sit in the back room behind the bar and count piles of gold?"

She'd purposely avoided revealing how she fit into the scheme of things. Her hand on the door latch, she answered, "I'm going to do what I do best—play poker."

And with that pronouncement she made a quick exit. Jack pursued her up the flight of steps to the deck. He silently swore at her pigheadedness, at her winning the Golden Spur and at the way that damn bustle waved in his face like a red flag. Some clever woman must have devised that contraption; a bustle tempted a man far more than a luscious red apple!

"You'd better wait and see what you're getting into before you decide to stay here. John won't want a saloon owner for a wife."

Delighted with the idea, Laura Lee stopped.

Jack was three steps behind her and unprepared for a quick stop, and before he realized what was happening, his face buried in the soft folds of her pert bustle.

She grinned. "What about you? Do you have an aversion to businesswomen?"

She climbed the last few steps, then turned around and lazily imitated his sexy wink.

"You'll change your mind pronto once you've seen the place."

"It'll have to be a filthy hole-in-the-wall to change my mind."

It was. She couldn't have described the Golden Spur better if she'd seen it first.

An hour later, after they disembarked and loaded a buckboard with their belongings, they rode through downtown Galveston and arrived at the Golden Spur.

Alden jumped down from the wagon and ripped the boards off the two windows and the double-width swinging door. The moment Laura Lee stepped inside she dug in her purse for her rose-scented hankie. The smell of stale perfume and whiskey permeated the air. Dust motes and spiderwebs vied for space in the beams of sunlight. Broken chairs and overturned tables littered the floor. The upright piano leaned back against a raised platform. Only the long bar and the mirror behind it were intact.

Charity coughed; Jack chuckled; Captain Bligh squawked.

"I told you the place needed a few repairs," Alden said, looking embarrassed. "The night I left, a few ranch hands got a little rowdy."

Overwhelmed by what appeared to be an impossible task, Laura Lee squeezed her eyes shut in dismay.

"Just needs a woman's touch and it'll be as good as new," Alden added. "Drinkin' men don't notice a little dirt."

"Ready to go?" Jack prompted. "I guarantee the big house at the Rocking W doesn't stink like this place."

Laura Lee lowered her hankie and took another look. What had she expected? Fancy chandeliers? Brocade drapes? Carpeted steps leading to the second-floor balcony?

"What's upstairs?" she asked.

Alden blushed; Jack grinned; Charity gasped.

"Uh . . . well, uh . . ." Alden muttered.

"Bedrooms?" Jack asked with feigned innocence. He knew damn well that the saloon girls served one hell of a lot more than cheap booze. Sweet little Laura Lee would take one look at them and come screaming down those rickety steps, begging to go with him. "Why don't you take a look at them?"

Laura Lee drilled him with a glare. Innocent she was, but not that innocent. Dr. Wainwright's "bad" women must have occupied those rooms, she deduced from the lopsided smile on Jack's face.

She counted the upstairs doors. Six rooms. She removed her spotless white gloves, one finger at a time. The upstairs rooms would provide living quarters for Alden at one end and Charity and herself at the opposite end. She'd use the other rooms as private gambling rooms for the elite.

Without realizing it, Laura Lee had made her decision.

"First we'll give the place a thorough spring cleaning. Then we'll redecorate—using the money I won at the poker table—and then we'll rename it something catchy."

"Bordello?" Jack said through clenched teeth. "That's a fancy name for a—"

Laura Lee interrupted him before he could finish. "Mr. Alden!" Her smile was as empty as the bottles behind the bar. "Would you be so kind as to escort Mr. Wynthrop to the door? He's in the wrong establishment."

"Awwwk! Keelhaul the swine! Awwwk!"

"You heard the bird," Alden said, lifting the shotgun he was carrying. "Git!"

Through narrowed eyelids, Jack's black eyes blazed with ill-concealed anger. "You're ordering me out of here?" he asked the new proprietress.

"Come back when you've done your . . . your family duty." Her chin was threatening to wobble. Her eyes pleaded with him, silently, eloquently. Please, Jack, this is the only honorable solution. We'll disgrace both our families if I go with you.

From the hard line of Jack's jaw and the hand resting on his six-shooter she could tell that his ears were deaf to her plea. But something must have clicked in his head, for he turned on his heel and strode toward the swinging doors.

Her gaze lowered to the bird cage on the floor next to where Jack had been standing.

"Don't be a stranger. Come back and I'll buy you a free round of drinks at—at the Golden Parrot."

The doors swung violently behind him; one fell off its rusty hinge and crashed to the floor.

He'll be back. He's got to come back!

Laura Lee wiped away the lone tear trekking down her cheek with her hankie. She had work to do. She'd shed buckets of tears on the ship—for Tad, for Blythewood, for Jack and for herself. The time for tears was long past.

She lifted her shoulders and squared them. Charity and Alden seemed to be holding their breath, waiting for her to indicate where to begin. "Let's get busy." She marched to the dust-covered bar. In a stronger voice, one filled with determination, she added, "We've got to run out of work before I run out of money. With what we'll have to buy, I figure we can't last more than two weeks." As though saying it aloud would make it come true, she added firmly, "A week from Saturday we'll open the doors of the Golden Parrot for business."

Outside Galveston, on the trail that would eventually take him home to the Rocking W, Jack raised his bandanna over the bottom half of his face to keep the windblown sand from getting into his nostrils and mouth. Hellion, the horse he'd stabled in Galveston before he'd set sail for New Orleans, whined in protest at the delay. Jack calmed the prancing stallion by stroking his solid back haunch. Then he squeezed his heels together. Fresh from lack of exercise, Hellion rolled his tongue until the bit was between his teeth and lunged forward.

Jack needed the burst of speed; he shifted the reins to his right hand and pulled his Stetson low on his brow. With the horse in control, his mind raced at the same pace as the thundering hooves carrying him to his destination.

Short of disarming Alden, kidnapping Laura Lee and throwing her over Hellion's rump, Jack knew, there was little he could have done. Hell, he silently swore, she'd limited his choices long before those wild bluebonnet eyes of hers had begged him to leave peacefully.

She was one hell of a woman. He couldn't deny that. And he couldn't deny that she had a reasonable chance of converting that broken-down saloon into a thriving business. She didn't need him or his brother to help her save Blythewood.

He rubbed his chest. It felt as though a strand of that newfangled barbed wire were wrapped around his heart. Yeah, he admitted, it hurt his pride to think that a little bitty woman could tie his stomach up in knots and then order him off the premises, calm as you please. He hadn't realized that he was the kind of sucker who would fall in love this hard.

Wasn't he the one who'd ridiculed John's choice by saying that a Southern magnolia couldn't survive under the hot Texas sun? Fate must have been chuckling up its sleeve when he'd spoken that blasphemy. Laura Lee had been born with strength and determination.

She'd survived having her homeland invaded. She'd robbed Luke Reynolds and made a laughingstock out of him to boot. She'd fought him physically, tooth, nail and elbow. And she'd won herself a stake in the future with the flick of a card.

"A whole lot of woman in a pint-size package," he said to Hellion, seesawing on the reins when the horse began to sweat. Hellion reared up on his hind legs, dropped his forelegs and slowed to the pace his master wanted.

"So what do you think I oughta do, Hellion?"

Like most cowpokes, Jack talked to his trusty steed. Unlike Captain Bligh, Hellion didn't have a smart mouth. At most he would toss his head or whicker a reply. Most often he just kept silent.

Jack had his answer long before he reached the Rocking W. He'd tell John the truth—the unvarnished truth. He loved Laura Lee Shannon. Be she the naive, innocent mistress of Blythewood or the proprietress of a bawdy house, he loved her.

Three days later, in the middle of the night, he rode into the stable behind the ranch house.

"Steady, boy," he murmured to Hellion. Hellion whinnied, perhaps in reply, perhaps to communicate with the other horses in the barn. "Yeah. It's good to be home, huh, big fella?"

He'd ridden Hellion long and hard. A man saw to his horse's comfort before seeking comfort for himself. He lit an oil lantern, unsaddled Hellion, led him back to his stall and unbridled him.

As he fed and curried his horse, his thoughts were on John. He had repeatedly rehearsed what he planned on telling his brother, but the closer he came to actually confronting him the higher his anxiety level rose. Deep in thought, he didn't hear anyone approaching until the sound of a shotgun being cocked caught his attention.

"Mist' Jack? Is that you in there?" a cautious voice called from outside.

"Yeah, Seth." He grinned as the tall, burly black man who was John's companion and friend strode along the row of stalls. "That's some welcome party you're holding in your hands."

"What'd you expect when you come riding in here unexpected? Why didn't you telegraph and let us know you were coming?" While he spoke, his head swiveled around. "Where's Miz Shannon?"

"Whoa! One question at a time. Miss Shannon is still in Galveston. I rode on ahead because I needed to talk to John."

"He's gonna be right disappointed that she isn't with you."

Jack gave Hellion one last swipe with the curry brush. "That'll have to do for tonight, big fella." He strode through the gate, latched it, then turned to Seth. "I don't suppose you could rustle something up in the kitchen for me, could you?"

"S'long as you don't wake Mist' John up eating it, I reckon there might be some beefsteak left over from dinner." Seth shifted the shotgun to his left hand and clapped Jack on the back. "Good to have you home, Mist' Jack, even if you didn't bring the little lady with you."

"The little lady pretty much goes where she wants to go," Jack responded dryly. And stays where she wants to stay, he tacked on silently as he turned the knob on the lantern to extinguish the flame.

"Mist' John surely is looking forward to her arrival. 'Course, he'll be glad to see you, too."

"How is he doing?"

"Better. Fewer black spells." Seth's brows knit together. "He's stronger. Wants to do more for himself. The other day he said he felt a prickling in his big toe."

"Do you think I ought to send for a specialist in Dallas again?"

"You can." Seth pondered the consequences of building his friend's hopes up again. "You know how disappointed and frustrated Mist' John was after the doctor left the last time. I spent two weeks cleaning up the broken pottery he threw against the wall."

Jack pushed against the barn door and stepped out into the barnyard. The full moon and the stars that studded the sky lit the path leading to the rear of the ranch house. An uncomfortable silence settled between the two men as both thought about the invalid sleeping in the house.

Up until the accident, John Wynthrop had been even-tempered, slow to anger and quick to forgive. John had often teased him about his having inherited Jack's share of the "genteel Southern blood." Back then John had chuckled quietly and attributed his brother's hot temper to the jalapeño peppers in his food.

But the past few months John had vacillated between self-pity and open hostility. His moods shifted quicker than the winds blowing across the hillside, from hot and sultry south winds to chilly north ones. Physically a powerful man, John resented having to depend on Seth to dress him, bathe him and wheel him from room to room. His black scowls had everyone in the household, Jack included, catering to his slightest whim.

Jack suffered the most. Guilt had sharp claws. As he opened the wrought-iron gate to the courtyard he could feel them scoring his back. Only when John spoke of Laura Lee did his eyes light up, Jack mused. The progress his brother had been making would disappear when he heard of Jack's latest perfidy. How the hell was he going to tell John that he'd fallen in love with his fiancée?

"Don't contact that quack," Seth said quietly. "Mist' John having Miz Shannon here with him will be better medicine than what's in the bottles of that sawbones' black bag."

"I checked up on him." The mutual disdain Seth and the specialist had for each other had become a joke in the bunkhouse. The men were placing bets on how long it would take Seth to run him off the Rocking W Ranch. Jack wasn't partial to the man, either, but he'd have put up the devil himself if he could have helped his brother. "He is the best medical man in Texas. And he did say he might be able to get John walking again."

"Medical man?" Seth snorted. "I'd trust the horse doctor more than that snooty little bastard. I can still hear the nasal twang in his voice when he told me to quit interfering, that *he* was the practicing physician. Me! Interfering! He strutted his skinny butt around here like he was the master and I was his slave."

Jack grinned at Seth's indignation. Taking care of John was more than just his job; it was a labor of love. As boys, he and John had played together; as young men, they'd hunted the swamps and bayous for black bears; as grown men, they'd worked side by side. Jack knew that his brother had secretly taught Seth to read and write when state law had strictly prohibited educating slaves. When Jacob Wynthrop had given Seth his freedom papers, Seth had left his relatives in Louisiana and trekked to Texas, riding beside John as his equal. And when John had been at death's door from the injuries he'd sustained, Seth had nursed him back to health. He'd become John's legs. No snooty doctor was going to give him orders!

"I remember what you said that had him packing his bottles into his bag and hightailing it out of here, too."

"I just told him I wasn't going to let him practice on Mist' John until he figured out what the hell he was doing." Seth opened the kitchen door, turned up the lamp and crossed to the cupboard where Mama Garcia, the cook, stored the leftovers. He pulled a platter off a shelf and banged it on the wooden table. "I couldn't catch him, but I suspected he was out at night gigging horny toads to brew into that foul-smelling medicine he gave Mist' John. Damn witch doctor," he muttered under his breath. "But did I tell you Mist' John seems to be doing better? Just knowing Miz Shannon was coming must have been good tonic for him. He won't let me help him in and out of bed or push his wheelchair. Except for his legs, he's doing more every day. But I keep an eye on him. He's still restless at night."

While Seth got the food, Jack got a knife and fork and sat down at the kitchen table. "You're going to be the one who wakes up John," he said teasingly, carving a hunk of meat off the thick slab.

"I'd better check on him." Seth's eyes raked over Jack's stubbled whiskers, tired eyes and dusty clothes. "You look like you could use a good night's sleep, too. Nita and her mother have been fussing at each other while they polished and aired the rooms, preparing for Miz Shannon's arrival. I reckon your room stinks like beeswax and your sheets are starched stiffer than a board, but it'll be better than sleeping on the trail. I'll see you in the morning."

His mouth full, Jack nodded, knowing he wouldn't sleep a wink. It would be his butt that Seth kicked off the ranch after he told John that he'd fallen in love with Laura Lee. His gut twisted. He dropped his fork on the table and pushed the plate aside, then folded his arms and rested his head on them.

His mind was still racing, but exhaustion claimed him nonetheless. Within minutes he was asleep.

Before dawn's light entered the kitchen windows, John shook his brother's shoulder. He'd wanted to get up hours before, when Seth had unintentionally awakened him by tucking his blanket under his chin and had told him of Jack's return. He'd waited impatiently, letting him get a few hours' sleep before levering himself into the wheelchair and seeking him out. He had to find out why Laura Lee was still in Galveston. The longer he'd waited, the shorter the fuse on his temper had become.

Jack jerked upright, his hand sliding automatically to his holster. A sheepish grin curved his mouth when he recognized his brother's voice. For a moment he'd thought he'd been caught catnapping out on the trail.

"You look like hell, little brother," John said, his usual politeness entirely absent. "Where is she?"

"In Galveston." Feeling as though a pack of demons had spent the night tying knots in his back, Jack stood and stretched, then massaged the small of his back with his fingers. "How are you, John?"

Ignoring his brother's question, John gritted his teeth and said, "You promised to bring her back here. I thought you were the one man I could trust to wade through fire and brimstone to keep his word."

"John—"

"Sit down! I hate straining my neck while I'm talking to you!"

"Why don't I just turn around? Then we'll both be at the right height for a proper ass-chewing," said Jack, relying on his brother's sense of humor to cool his hot temper before it reached the boiling point. The corner of John's mouth twitched. Then Jack presented his backside, and he chuckled.

"I ought to make you grab your ankles, the way Father did. He always said you needed a sound beating to curb your tongue." John administered a brotherly swat. "Fix us some coffee while you tell me about Laura Lee."

Glad he'd been able to postpone telling John why he'd arrived without her, Jack crossed to the stove and stoked the banked embers with kindling until it was burning brightly.

"She looks the way you remembered her. Petite and pretty." He removed the lid from the coffeepot and strode to the water pump. He worked the handle vigorously. "But I have to disagree with you about her being a sweet Southern magnolia. Your magnolia grew thorns."

John scowled. "Self-defense, I imagine. With her father and mother dead and Beau missing, I knew she had a rough time. I wanted to go back sooner, but . . ."

"You weren't ready to tie yourself down to one woman?" Jack glanced over his shoulder and winked at his brother. It wasn't until John was flat on his back that his obsession with returning to Louisiana had changed to a determination to bring Laura Lee to Texas.

". . . but you were boneheaded about my leaving the ranch," John said. His mouth tugged upward into a wry smile. "And I'll admit that I wasn't going back for the sole purpose of marrying Laura Lee. When we left for Texas she was still a schoolkid tagging along after Beau and me. Knobby knees, dirty face and grubby hands—a genuine pest."

Water splashed on Jack's hand; he wiped it away on his pant leg. John's description reminded him of how Laura Lee had looked when he'd dumped her on the davenport in the parlor at Blythewood. His heart slammed against his chest as he compared John's memories of her with how adorable she'd looked sprawled across their bed at the St. Charles Hotel. His hands shook as he measured ground coffee from the canister, put it in the pot and set it on the stove to boil.

"Be honest with me, John." Jack swiveled around and leaned against the sink. "Would you have honored the Wynthrop-Shannon agreement and married Laura Lee if you hadn't been hurt?"

"Yeah. I would have. Father's idea of joining Heavenly Acres with Blythewood is still practical."

"Practical," Jack muttered under his breath. What he felt for Laura Lee had nothing to do with practicality. "What about love?"

John shrugged his massive shoulders; his eyes dropped to his useless legs. "That's something I don't have to worry about, isn't it?"

Familiar pangs of guilt raced through Jack. Heartsick, he stared at the pot and willed it to start boiling. He needed a strong cup of coffee. How could he find the courage to tell John he'd fallen in love with Laura Lee?

"Why'd she stay in Galveston?"

"She won the Golden Spur in a poker game aboard the *Matadora*." Jack's black eyes darted to the wheelchair when he heard John laugh unexpectedly. "What's so funny?"

"I just remembered how she used to beat the pants off Beau playing cards. At ten she could keep track of every card played and pretty well guess what cards he was holding in his hand." John chuckled again and slapped the arm of his chair with his hand. "Once, in a fit of temper, Beau threatened to bar her from sitting in on his arithmetic class. The little minx fluttered her eyelashes, rolled her tongue in her cheek and let him win the next few hands." Long-forgotten memories of the fun he'd had with her brother buoyed his spirits. "God, I miss Beau. It'll be good to have his sister here."

"She says she isn't coming to the ranch," Jack said bluntly.

"You'll have to ride back to Galveston and change her mind."

"John—" Tell him! Tell him you're in love with her! his conscience demanded.

"Don't argue with me. I can't believe Laura Lee will refuse to marry me, either. She may have been a ragamuffin cardsharp, but I remember her pride and her sense of family honor. Her father promised she'd marry me, and she did, too. She won't break that promise."

"I'm in love with her, John," Jack whispered, "and I think she's in love with me. That's why she stayed in Galveston. She doesn't want to have anything more to do with either of us. But I want to marry her, if you'll just give me your blessing."

Only the bubbling of the coffeepot penetrated the silence in the kitchen.

"Like bloody hell you will." John wheeled himself to the kitchen door, then twisted at the waist until he could see his brother's back. "You gave me your word that you'd bring me my bride. By damn, I expect you to keep it. We'll just see who she's going to marry!"

"Belly up to the bar, gentlemen. Welcome to the shiniest star in the Lone Star State!"

Alden bellowed his invitation with jovial glee above the rinky-dink clattering of the piano. An odd mixture of cowhands and businessmen crowded the Golden Parrot Saloon.

Two weeks of elbow grease had worked wonders on the dilapidated rooms. A hard taskmistress, Miz Shannon had hired a crew for the heavy work and added the finishing touches herself, while Miz Charity had rounded up other Southern women with limited resources and trained them in ladylike ways of keeping men at a distance. Most of the newly renamed ladies had pitched in and helped, and the saloon fairly sparkled—from the crystal lamps on the walls to the brass spittoons strategically placed near the bar rail.

"Miz Charity and the prettiest little wildflowers in Texas—Daisy, Clover and Cactus Flower—will fill your beer mugs and your eyeballs! You can look, but don't touch. Them's the rules. Oh, yeah, I almost fergot. Keep your damn fingers outa the bird cage unless you don't need your trigger finger. An' one more warning." He glanced toward the shotgun mounted on the wall. "*My* trigger finger is itchin' to pull on anybody cheatin' at Miz Shannon's poker table. She isn't gonna cheat you, and you sure as hellfire aren't gonna cheat her. Five-dollar ante and hundred-dollar limit—no point in goin' over there with empty pockets, fellas. You pass the word, and I'll pass the beer!"

Loud guffaws, nodding heads and the Captain's squawking accompanied the gurgling sound of the first beer being drawn from the tap. Free beer, good-looking women and an honest gaming table had been the news circulated by word of mouth throughout Galveston about the grand opening of the Golden Parrot.

Laura Lee sat at a round green-felt-covered table. She wore a perfect poker face, but her prudish heart was pounding, and her skin was peppered with goose bumps underneath the blush-pink silk gown Jack had given her in New Orleans. Her hands swiftly dealt the cards; only someone who knew her well could have detected her nervousness.

And someone who knew her very well was standing directly across from her, grinning a lopsided grin and watching her closely with devilish black eyes.

Jack Wynthrop had the relaxed stance of a man enjoying a Saturday night out on the town. His crisp fawn suit molded his broad shoulders and muscular thighs to perfection. He looked more like the owner of the establishment than did Laura Lee, who was losing hand after hand, silver piece after silver piece.

She noticed that none of the men circling the table, watching, jostled him. A few of the toughest customers might risk the wrath of the bartender's shotgun, but no one wanted to slap leather against Jack Wynthrop.

"Pot's right, gentlemen," Laura Lee drawled softly. "The name of the game is five-card draw."

Concentrate on the card game, she told herself silently. Keep your eyes on the cards. Figure the odds. Don't count on lucky draws. Skill is the real name of this card game.

She spread the five cards she'd dealt. Ah, at long last, my losing streak is over—four small spades. Good chance of getting the fifth spade for a flush. Watch their discards.

"How many?" she asked the man to her left.

"Gimme three good ones."

A pair, she guessed—or, from the dismal look on his face, nothing.

"And you, sir?"

"One."

Her heart sank, but she smiled. Two pair? Or is he hoping to fill a flush?

"He's bluffing. I'll take two, just to show you I'm an honest man."

"Dealer takes one."

She placed the new card on her hand, picked it up, held it close to the bodice of her pink dress and slowly spread the cards apart. Five of spades. So much for Jack being able to jinx my luck—no, skill. Steady. Keep your eyes at half-mast. Watch their faces.

To her delight, the man accused of bluffing doubled the pot and the other two men dropped out of the hand.

Her remaining opponent grinned broadly. "You calling or folding?"

Laura Lee returned his smile. "I'll call. Let's see what you're so proud of, mister."

"Two pair. Tens and eights, with a jack for a kicker."

"A spade flush."

"It's a one-eyed jack. A wild card."

"You lose, friend" came from over the shoulder of the man with the losing hand. "Time to vacate your chair and let someone else try his luck."

"Who are you to tell me what to do?" The man swiveled at the waist, saw the man behind him and paled visibly. Jack Wynthrop had a reputation for being short-tempered and damn fast clearing his holster. He pushed the pile of silver toward the dealer. "Yup. Guess I'd better drink a keg of that free beer to make up for my losses, huh?"

"Be my guest." Laura Lee got to her feet gracefully and motioned for Cactus Flower to take her place. "If you gentlemen will excuse me, I'll see that my other customers are enjoying themselves, too."

Jack shadowed her. His spurs jingled, but he didn't speak. The men she greeted took one look at the powerful man towering behind the diminutive lady and seemed to choke on their drinks.

Finally Laura Lee spun around and said, "What the devil do you think you're doing?"

"Observing."

"Intimidating!" She smiled for appearance' sake, but inside she was burning with indignation. "I don't need to have you following me around, scaring the bejasus out of my customers."

"On the open range a man takes measures to protect his property. I'm just letting the men here know that I won't appreciate trespassers or cattle thieves."

"Do you see a Rocking W brand on my backside?"

Jack's wicked eyes paid homage to Laura Lee's dress by straying down the deep vee in front. "I do prefer the hat with the magnolias to those pink ostrich feathers in your hair, though."

Laura Lee's cheeks flamed. "Excuse me." Sweeping her skirt up in one hand, she moved toward the steps. Scoundrel! she silently blasted.

She heard a jingling behind her on the steps.

"Customers are barred from the private quarters upstairs," she said emphatically. "Before you take another step, I strongly recommend that you take a look at the bar. Unless you want your trousers filled with buckshot, you'd best change your direction." Feeling like a recalcitrant heifer that had been prodded with a sharp stick, she moved forward, up another step and out of his reach. "You don't order me around, Mr. Wynthrop."

Frustrated but aware that she had the upper hand, he doffed his hat respectfully. "You never take the easy path, do you?"

"Good evening, Mr. Wynthrop." Her knees were weak; she clutched the banister to maintain her balance. "I'll see that this gown is returned to you."

Her head held at an imperious angle, she regally climbed the remaining steps. She didn't have the heart to turn around once she reached the balcony. She longed to signal to Alden to drop the barrel of his gun, to motion for Jack to follow her. She hesitated, inexplicably winded.

You can't let him waltz back into your life and disrupt it, her mind told her. You're a woman of independent means. With part of tonight's receipts you'll be able to make the first payment on what you owe him. Cash on the barrelhead—that's how you settle old family debts.

Resolutely she marched toward her room.

Jack admired her fortitude, and he respected her grit, but he sure as hell wasn't going to let a woman dictate terms to him—even if there was a gun pointed at his head. He had a few aces up his sleeve that she hadn't planned on.

Chapter Twelve

From behind the privacy screen in her bedroom, Laura Lee answered the sharp knock on her door by calling, "Who's there?" as she streaked across to the nightstand where she kept her gun.

The brass doorknob turned. "Unlock the door."

"How'd you get up those stairs without getting blown to bits?" she asked, feigning irritability, as she slipped her arms into her silk robe and cinched the knot at her waist. She'd spent the last ten minutes curbing the urge to go back downstairs to find Jack.

"I disarmed the bartender."

She turned the key, fuming at his audacity. "What did you do to him?"

"Taught him a lesson in Texas law. It's not who has the biggest gun that counts, it's who has the most guns. A couple of my men persuaded Alden to be a real law-abiding citizen."

"So help me, Jack Wynthrop, there had better not be so much as a hair on his head out of place!"

"Or you'll do what? Shoot me yourself?" He chuckled. "Not likely."

Jack stepped inside, closed the door and secured their privacy by twisting the key until he heard it lock. Laura

Lee's hands were on her hips, her hair was mussed, and her eyes were shooting sparks in his direction. Jack felt certain he'd never seen a more beautiful woman.

"I'm not going to listen to your cow clap!"

"Cow clap? You've picked up some Texas slang since you've been here. Much better than using the swear words your brother taught you." He crossed to the whiskey decanter on the dresser and helped himself.

Casually he removed his jacket. He tossed it over a chair, then made himself further at home by removing his tie and kicking off his boots. The gun strapped to his hip met a similar fate.

"You can stop making yourself at home. You're leaving!" She strode toward the door. "I'm going to bang on the door until the sheriff comes up here to investigate."

"Sheriff Preston? He's an old friend of mine. Before he pinned a badge on his chest he used to ride for us."

Smiling, he watched her raised fist drop to her side. He reclined against the brass headboard on her bed, sipped his whiskey and unbuttoned his shirt to the waist.

"Out!" Outraged, she dived at him, spilling the contents of the shot glass as she hammered on his chest. "You can't just come in here acting like you own the place. Damn your stinking hide! Stop laughing!"

Jack dropped the shot glass on the floor, clasped his arm around her waist and rolled on top of her. "Have I told you that you're a very, very sexy lady?"

"Get off me. You weigh a ton," she gasped. Flattery wasn't going to earn him a night in her bed! But those peculiar feminine feelings he caused attacked in full force when she tried to buck him off her. She was fighting her own inclinations far harder than she was fighting Jack.

"And you're a featherweight." He nuzzled the swell of her breast, which threatened to burst from beneath the edge of her gown. "Oh, God, Laura Lee, have I told you I've missed you?"

"No." Her back arched upward in response to the delicious feel of his lips on her skin. She couldn't just let him waltz into her saloon, play her with sweet, loving lies and let him make love to her. She stuck a work-reddened hand in his face. "I've been too busy to miss you."

Her stubborn determination to remain aloof disappeared under the sweet ministrations of his kisses on the back of her hand. The tip of her tongue darted between her dry lips. Memories of his kissing more intimate spots made her heart race.

On the verge of surrendering, she snapped, "I've talked to a lawyer about my father's agreement."

He tongued her fingers, kissing each knuckle, then circling the tip of her longest finger. A shudder ran the length of her small body, communicating louder than her protests. For all that she was a sweet innocent, he thought, she had the soft, womanly curves of a temptress.

"And I talked to my brother. I told him we loved each other. I asked him to let us marry."

She was helpless in his arms. Her cheeks burned as she realized how easily he could coax her into surrendering to him.

He lifted his head to the side of her neck and nibbled on her shell-shaped ear, the tip of his tongue swirling around the outer rim.

"I've come for you," he whispered reverently. "I love you. I'm going to take you back to the ranch with me, come hell or high water." His lips nuzzled her throat. "But John's my brother. I love him, too. I'm hoping you'll love me enough to let me do what's right. In all fairness, I have to give John the chance he's asked for. I owe him that, at least."

Laura Lee started to protest.

He brushed a kiss across her lips to silence her. "After tonight I have to back away from you." He wondered if that was humanly possible. He ached from loving her, from wanting her to be his wife.

"No."

"Yes, sweetheart. I couldn't look at myself in the mirror in the morning if I didn't give John a chance. He'd hate me, and I wouldn't blame him. We'd both feel guilty, miserable."

Laura Lee watched, helpless, as Jack's head followed the trail his fingers were blazing. She couldn't ask him to give up his brother and his home for her love, but she couldn't marry John, either. No, it was best that she stay here in Galveston. Maybe she could make enough money to return to Blythewood. Her heart ached at the thought of never seeing Jack again, but she knew it was for the best.

Jack's mouth opened. His hot breath and the sight of his tongue teasing her heated flesh sent shivers straight to her curled toes. His fingers untied the knot at her waist; her silk robe slithered to her sides.

She moaned, melting into his touch. Soul-stirring sensations seared through her. Ecstasy rippled beneath his clever fingers.

"I love you, Laura Lee," he whispered.

She knew she shouldn't listen, but her heart could no more refuse his love than her body could refuse his caresses.

"I love you, too," she whispered, opening her arms to him.

He covered her, kissing her with all the pent- up love and tenderness he felt for her. Her tongue twined against his. Silently, with the thrust of her tongue, with the arch of her hips, with her fingers weaving into the mat of hair on his chest, she showed him how much she loved him.

"I did miss you, Jack." She showered tiny kisses over his face. "Working my fingers to the bone was the only thing that kept me from going crazy and chasing after you."

He nudged her knees apart and sank into her sleek softness. She was ready for him; he couldn't wait any longer. Later, perhaps he could tell her what happened at the ranch. Right now, they were both going straight to heaven's gates.

Much, much later, when he heard her name being shouted from downstairs, he shifted drowsily and pointed to the door. "What's going on down there?"

Laura Lee giggled. "I think they want me to come back down."

"Hell, no. You're not leaving my side. I don't care if Sherman's army comes and burns the place to the ground. You're staying here with me."

"You wouldn't rather be down there than in here?" she asked him teasingly.

"In here." He let his hand roam between them until he was touching her. "Definitely in here."

For long, luscious hours, neither of them heard the boisterous shouts or the tinny piano or the groans of the men when Alden shut off the free beer and closed the bar for the night. Nor did they hear the whispers and giggles as the women climbed the steps and went to their rooms.

Drowsily Laura Lee shifted onto her side, curling against Jack. Captain Bligh's zealous squawking from downstairs brought a sleepy yawn from her.

Someone must have forgotten to put the cover over him, she thought. Her long fringe of eyelashes slowly parted.

"What's that smell?" she mumbled. She wiped the back of her hand beneath her nose. "Smells awful."

Jack awakened abruptly. Instantly alert, he recognized the odor: coal oil. Down below he heard someone stumble and curse.

A second later he heard running feet and heard Alden bellow, "Hey! What the hell do you think you're doing?"

He shook her shoulder and flung back the bedclothes.

"Get up, Laura Lee!"

She started to rise, then flopped back on her pillow. A lazy grin curved her mouth. "Can't. What's that smell?"

"This is no time for more questions. Something is going on downstairs!"

He'd barely issued his command when he heard a crackling. Grabbing his trousers, he yanked them into place, then felt around on the floor for her robe. An eerie red glow gradually lit the room.

"Dammit! Get up! Somebody's set fire to the saloon!" He located her robe and tossed it to her. Familiar with the upstairs quarters of other saloons, he asked, "Are there steps from up here to the alley?"

"Cactus Flower's room! Second door down on your right!" She pushed her arm through the sleeve of her robe as she scurried from the bed. "Oh, my God, wake her up! The other girls are in the adjoining rooms!"

"You wake them! I'm going downstairs!"

He was through the door before she cried, "Nooooo!"

Scared witless, she ran barefoot down the length of the corridor, banging on doors, flinging them open, screaming, "Fire! Get out through the window in Cactus Flower's room! Everybody! Get up! Get out!"

She darted for the steps. The stairs were like a chimney, with thick black smoke billowing upward. Laura Lee covered her nostrils and mouth with the sleeve of her robe. Dry timbers crackled. She could feel the heat penetrating to the soles of her feet.

"Jack! Jack!"

She couldn't see anything. Smoke crept between the cracks in the floor, filling her lungs with each breath she took. From behind her she heard a high-pitched scream.

"Stop it!" she heard Cactus Flower bellow over the shrill cries of the other women. "Charity! You're blocking the window! Git, girl, or we'll all be roasted! Put this wool blanket over your head and run! Laura Lee! Where the hell are you?"

"I'll be there. Don't wait for me!"

Her hand gripped the banister. She swayed indecisively, poised for action, but her mind twisted back to another fire, bigger, hotter, more fierce. Heavenly Acres burned in her memories.

In the few fleeting moments that had passed the fire had begun to blaze ferociously, like a hungry monster consuming everything in its path. Piano wires snapped, making a weird pinging noise, and Laura Lee could hear other sounds: fists pounding flesh, grunts of pain. Glass shattered.

The Captain whistled. "Awwwk! Hang him from the mast! Awwwk!"

Water! she thought desperately. Put the fire out! Move! Don't just stand there like a nincompoop!

"Get the hell out of here!" boomed a voice from below. "We're too late to stop the fire from spreading!"

She could hear Jack dragging something or someone heavy toward the back storage room.

"Awwwk! Tarnation!"

"I've got the Captain. Dammit, woman, I can't get back up the steps. Get out of here!"

Mesmerized by the sight of the yellowish flames licking at the draperies she'd hung below the balcony, she froze, unable to move. Smoke-induced tears streamed down her face. Her legs crumpled, and she fell to the floor.

Get out! she ordered herself, but she couldn't budge. You're going to die if you don't move!

She coughed, again and again. Here, on the floor, the smoke was thinner. Her instinct for self-preservation motivated her. With painful slowness, she crawled toward Cactus Flower's room.

Faster!

"I can't," she mumbled. Her knees slipping on her robe, and the collar jerked until it bit into her neck.

You can! You must! Dammit, you can't die in a saloon fire!

She was wheezing and choking from the smoke, and she could hear the fire crackling, snapping, spreading behind her. From outside the window she could hear someone shouting her name.

"Where's Laura Lee?"

"Laura Lee!"

Jack! her mind screamed.

She made it to the window and heaved herself to her feet. Fresh night air filled her lungs when she inhaled deeply.

"I'm going to make it," she croaked hoarsely. "I'm coming, Jack!"

An explosion from directly below her broke the downstairs windows, and flames shot up the front of the frame building. Laura Lee rocked painfully back against the windowframe. Her head struck wood solidly. She collapsed, half in and half out of the window, and sank into oblivion.

"Oh, my God!" Charity shrieked. "The steps caught on fire! Somebody do something!"

Jack summed up the situation the instant he rounded the corner from the alley. He dropped his heavy burden and the bird cage. He whipped the blanket off Charity and raced to the steps.

Flames danced around his trouser legs as he flew up the steps. Weakened by fire, the third step crashed beneath his foot. Lightly he sprang over the charred tread. He had to get to her. He raced the flames climbing the timber that partially supported the landing.

"Laura Lee!" he called when he reached the window. He grabbed her under the arms and hoisted her limp body over his shoulder. She can't be dead, dammit! She can't! He threw the blanket over her.

He turned. The steps near the ground were enveloped in fire. He mentally measured the distance to the ground. He could jump. What if he landed on Laura Lee? He'd crush her! He couldn't take the risk.

"Douse those steps!" Alden shouted to the men carrying pails of water. "Come on, Jack!"

Jack took the steps two at a time. Water sizzled as it splashed the flames. He leaped over the charred structure, hitting the ground and rolling over and over in the sand.

"Awwwk! Prrretttty girl!"

Scared to death, Jack untangled himself from Laura Lee and pushed the blanket aside. Streaks of soot marred her face. There was a lump the size of a hen's egg on her forehead. He placed his hand on her neck.

"Get back, everyone," Cactus Flower shouted, pushing her way through the circle.

"Don't die." Jack chafed her wrists helplessly.

"Let me see her."

"No," Jack barked. His stomach clenched into knots; he felt physically ill. "Nobody's gonna touch her but me."

"Breathe into her mouth," Cactus Flower ordered. "Pinch her nose and breathe hard into her mouth! She needs air, dammit!"

Laura Lee stirred just as Jack's lips covered hers. She had no idea where she was or what had happened, but she felt Jack's breath press forcefully into her lungs.

Her eyes sprang open. She twisted her head aside and coughed deeply.

"She's all right," Jack gasped. "She's gonna be okay."

Laura Lee felt certain her lungs had caught fire. Each coughing spasm brought foul-tasting blackness into her mouth. She rolled to her knees with Jack's help and spit it out on the ground. Tears blurred her vision, washing away the burning sensation caused by the smoke.

"Who?" she asked in a strangled voice. "Fire. Who started it?"

Jack lifted his head. Alden was fighting the fire, along with the other townsmen, who had formed a bucket brigade and were dousing the exterior of the adjoining buildings. It looked as though they'd contained the spreading flames, so Jack didn't join them.

The fire had devastated the Golden Parrot, but they'd stopped the fire from burning down the entire block.

"I thought it was Alden." Jack paused, reconsidering what he'd thought he'd seen. "It had to be Alden." But Alden had worked as valiantly as any to put it out.

"I don't believe it," Laura Lee said.

"He swears he heard someone downstairs, but when I got there he had the cashbox under his arm and was headed out the back door."

She clutched her waist, shaking her head. "No. I'm certain Alden didn't start it." She blinked until her vision cleared. Jack's face was smoke-streaked, but there were no cuts or bruises. "Did you two fight?"

"I did. He didn't. He blocked my fists, but . . . he never landed a punch. I knocked him out and dragged him out back in the alley." Jack scratched his head in bewilderment. "Here he comes now. I've got a few more questions for him."

"Jack, let me talk to him . . . please."

Alden circled them warily until Laura Lee was between him and the man who had given him a sound thrashing. He wiped his sweaty brow nervously on his sleeve. "I'm no barn burner, Miz Shannon . . . and I don't set fire to saloons, either!"

"Do you know who did start it?" Laura Lee asked, her voice still husky.

"No, ma'am." He nodded toward Jack. "He tried to beat my head in while I was trying to save the cashbox. For all I know, he could have started it."

"That's impossible," Laura Lee replied. Jack had been beside her in bed. He couldn't be two places at once. "Neither of you would light a match to the Golden Parrot."

But someone had. Who?

Chapter Thirteen

"I saved Miz Shannon's money. Or I tried to save it. I don't know what happened after you hit me over the head with the whiskey bottle." Alden shook his finger at Jack. "What'd you do with it?"

Bruised, battered and feeling slightly charred around the edges, Laura Lee had to concentrate on each man as he spoke to absorb the meaning of what had been said.

"It's still in there," Jack replied quietly. Laura Lee was too quiet. Shock? he wondered. Or had Alden's suggestions that he might have started the fire caused her to doubt him? "Sweetheart, I didn't rig anything to start the fire while we were upstairs. I'll admit I came to Galveston determined to take you back to the ranch with me, but I wouldn't start a fire to force your hand."

"I know you didn't. I'm just trying to think of who did." She bit her lip nervously. This fire hadn't started accidentally. There had been too many coincidences. Her voice shook as she asked, "Do you think it was the same man who winged you on the boat? Maybe I didn't imagine someone following us in New Orleans."

"I don't know, Laura Lee. It could've been the same man. I won't feel safe until you're out at the ranch. I shudder to think of what would have happened if you'd been asleep."

She reached up to touch the back of Jack's hand. Only what remained of the fire provided light, but she could tell that the hairs there had been singed. "You saved my life, Jack. 'Thank you' seems pitifully inadequate..." she raised her shoulders "... but thank you."

"He could have helped me try to put out the fire." Alden puffed himself up to his full height. He was several inches shorter than Jack. "We might have been able to save something!"

"It doesn't matter. Don't worry about the cashbox. It's metal. Maybe the fire's heat won't melt it... and even if it does it won't be the first time I've been penniless. I'll think of something." She pushed a mass of sooty hair back from her face.

"You've been a genuine lady... treatin' me like I still owned the place... askin' my advice. I wouldn't do anything to hurt you or the other ladies." Alden threw a suspicious look at Jack. "I know you think he's innocent, but it's damn peculiar that we didn't have any trouble until he arrived."

"Hush, Alden. Mr. Wynthrop was with me." Beneath the dirty streaks, Laura Lee's face turned pink. "He couldn't have started the fire."

"Then who did? For such a pretty little thing, you have a powerful lot of enemies, Miz Shannon. Somebody hates you real bad."

Laura Lee shivered as though someone had walked on her grave. There was only one man who hated her enough to try to kill her. She whispered, "Luke Reynolds."

Jack could barely contain his frustration. The thought of a killer stalking Laura Lee made his trigger finger itch. If he weren't afraid of leaving her alone he'd sail back across the Gulf and up the Mississippi to personally settle the problem of Luke Reynolds—with a six-shooter!

Laura Lee started to rise. He caught her elbow and pulled her up against him. She leaned forward and patted Alden's sleeve with real affection. He looked miserable. He wasn't the arsonist, he was just another person who had hit hard times and had done what he had to in order to survive. "Would you do something for me?"

"Anything, Miz Shannon. You name it."

"Stick around here until dawn. Sift through the ashes and search for the cashbox. If you find it, I want you to split the money with the ladies. They're going to need something now that we've been burned out of business."

Jack could tell from the way she was leaning heavily against him that she was at the end of her tether. "C'mon. I'm taking you to the nearest hotel. You'll feel better after you're cleaned up."

It felt good to be under his protective arm. Her streak of independence had narrowed to the point of being invisible. Willingly she allowed him to take care of her.

"Alden, I still don't trust you any farther than I'd trust a skunk with his tail raised, but if Laura Lee says she trusts you, then I guess I have to, also."

"Jack?" Her muscles protested as she stepped forward. "Where's the Captain? We can't leave him."

"I'll get him," Alden volunteered, anxious to get away from the big Texan as quickly as possible.

Jack pointed toward the alley and chuckled. "That won't be necessary. Miss Lane is bringing him."

Charity advanced toward them. She was holding the cage as far in front of her as her arm would reach. Captain banged against the bars with his wings. "He's been cussing something awful."

"From the look of him, I'd say he earned that privilege tonight." Alden stuck his finger into the cage and remove the soot from the golden feathers on the Captain's head.

"Awwwk!"

"Don't!" Laura Lee said, but it was too late.

Alden jerked his wounded finger back and stuck it in his mouth. "Damn bird," he muttered in disgust.

"Awwwk! Damn landlubber!"

The following morning Jack sat in a carriage flanked by two trail hands on horseback, waiting outside the boarding house where Laura Lee had spent the night. He'd tied Hellion's reins to the back of the buggy, where Captain Bligh's cage hung.

For the sake of propriety he'd spent the night with his men. Before the dry goods store had opened for business he'd been pounding on their door, anxious to buy clothes for Laura Lee. Nothing was going to delay his getting her out of Galveston to the ranch, where she'd be safe.

His brow puckered when she came down the steps. Her eyes swept up and down the street, as though she were making certain they weren't vulnerable to attack.

Jack hopped out of the carriage. "Everything fit?"

"You've got a good eye for size. Thank you for the clothes."

"You should have seen the store clerk measuring the circle I made with my fingers to get your waist size."

Laura Lee smiled, but it was a strain. During the night she'd slept only fitfully. Images of orange-and-red flames had leaped at her. The dark, threatening shadow of a faceless man had been silhouetted against the flame. An eerie laugh had floated along the edges of her subconscious. She'd been too afraid to sleep.

Jack lifted her into the buggy and climbed in beside her. He clucked his tongue to get the horse moving. "Don't worry, sweetheart. You're too precious for me to let anything happen to you."

"Awwwk!"

She turned in the seat and lifted the cloth covering the cage. Captain Bligh blinked and preened. The movement of the carriage made him sway on his perch as though he were aboard a ship at sea. She blew him a small kiss, glad that at least one of them wouldn't mind this journey.

Laura Lee made it through the next few days with false cheerfulness. While she jostled against Jack in the two-seater buggy along the road that led to Austin with the two ranch hands trailing close behind them, she contemplated her life.

From the moment she'd lit the candles on Luke Reynolds's birthday cake until the night she'd watched the Golden Parrot burn she'd been trying courageously to alter the inevitable. She'd repeatedly struggled against fate, and she'd been defeated at every turn. With each defeat she'd walked away poorer than she'd been before.

The destruction of the Golden Parrot had left her penniless. Not even the clothes on her back were her own. Wynthrop generosity had provided her with store-bought dresses and sunbonnets. More clearly than ever she understood how Brandy had felt when she'd arrived at Blythewood.

As the miles stretched between Blythewood and herself she began to wrestle with the possibility that while her clever innovations and her grim determination might have postponed the final outcome she would still meet the same fate: destitution and heartache.

She could smile and accept her fate, or she could be like Captain Bligh. He batted his wings against his gilded cage—and got nowhere. His smart mouth earned him a scolding or amused his listeners, but he wasn't taken seriously by anyone. We're both birdbrains, she mused glumly, staring at the sprawling Spanish-style hacienda in the valley below where Jack had stopped the buggy.

"You men go ahead," Jack called over his shoulder. "Tell John we'll be there directly."

With a boisterous, "Yip, yip, yippee," the men galloped toward a rail fence that ran as far as the eye could see. The road led to an arched gate with the Rocking W brand like a family crest in the center.

"What do you think of the ranch?"

Laura Lee heard the pride in Jack's voice. This was his home, the place that had been the Wynthrops' sanctuary during the war that had devastated their Louisiana home. For a moment she honestly didn't know how to answer him. She relied on the good manners that had been drummed into her head as a child and replied, "It's lovely."

"But different? Did you expect a replica of Heavenly Acres?"

"No, I don't think I did." Her eyes swept to the far corners of the valley. Small cabins dotted the landscape. There was a long, narrow dwelling set apart, close to the biggest barn she'd ever seen in her life. "It looks different, and yet...it's like a small town...just like Heavenly Acres, isn't it?"

Jack grinned. "Yeah. We're fairly self-sufficient. Cattle provide meat. You can't see it, but there are several acres of gardens and fruit trees on the other side of the next hill. See those corrals?" He pointed to the right of the main house. Horses, their heads bent to the lush green grass, grazed lazily in the late-afternoon sun. "We started raising them during the war, when a good mount was damn near impossible for the cavalry to locate. Lately a few of our wranglers have been training them for the trail drives."

Jack searched her face. He'd stopped the buggy to have a few moments alone with her, to tell her . . . what? Neither of them had mentioned what had taken place between them the night of the fire. During the trip to the ranch the two ranch hands had been diligent chaperons, seldom giving them a moment's privacy. Each night when they'd set up camp his bedroll had been placed on the opposite side of the campfire from hers. He'd lain awake, counting the stars, thinking of a multitude of things he wanted to say and couldn't.

"John and I divided the work after . . . after the accident. He handles the business end of ranching—ordering the supplies we don't make or grow, keeping track of cattle production, making arrangements for the cattle drives. I'm responsible for the outdoor work."

"I won't be seeing much of you, will I?" She smiled up at him, trying to maintain a cheerful attitude. "You're going to stick by your decision to give John a chance, aren't you?"

"I have to be fair to John."

"All's fair in love and war," she muttered. It was an old cliché she'd heard somewhere. "Aren't you being unfair to us? We love each other."

"Fairness isn't the only reason I moved my belongings into one of the cabins before I returned to Galveston. Perhaps you'll find you want to marry John. Women have always preferred him over me. I'd hate to look up from my plate one day and see you mooning over John."

"That's ridiculous."

"Women have been known to be fickle."

"There isn't a fickle bone in my body. You, of all people, know that I don't readily change my mind once I've made a decision.'' She studied his face, searching for the real reason. His features might have been carved out of stone; they revealed nothing. Only when she noticed that Jack was rubbing his thigh did she gain insight. ''It's John's injury, isn't it? You still think you should give him a chance to make up for his getting hurt while he saved your life.''

''I owe him a chance at happiness, don't I?'' His fingers balled into a fist. ''I've been a selfish swine all my life. Just this once I'm going to put John's needs in front of mine.''

Her heart was in her eyes. She loved him; she couldn't hide it. She wanted to cling to him, to have him embrace her one last time.

''Laura Lee, you'll be safe here. John will be good to you.'' Those weren't the words he wanted to say, but they would have to do. ''I'm hoping you'll be good for him, too.''

''I'll do my best,'' she said. The hand Jack had dealt her was second-best. There would be no more bluffing or relying on luck. She would quietly fold her cards, get up from the table and walk away. She'd use her God-given mathematic skills to help John run the ranch.

''We'd better go.'' He made a clicking noise to the horses and dropped the reins across their backs. ''John will be anxious to see you. He's waited a long time.''

John rolled his cumbersome wheelchair to the carved oak door. Full of anticipation and nervous as a calf with a branding iron hovering over its rump, he raked his hand through his thick, dark hair for the tenth time in sixty seconds.

''Can you see them yet?''

''Yes, sir. They've just come through the gate. Quit fussing with your hair,'' Seth told him. Turning to Nita, he said, ''Comb it, again.''

Nita removed a comb from the pocket of her skirt. Her fingers moved more slowly than necessary through John's hair. Her dark eyes dared Seth to make a comment.

Seth's eyes narrowed. Nita was a handsome woman—tall, slender, with waist-long black hair caught up on one side with a silver comb—but, like the doctor he'd booted off the ranch, she was a mite uppity. She refused to wear the all-white homespun clothing the other servants wore. When he'd tried to insist on it, she'd lifted her thin, aristocratic nose and calmly told him that she'd make do with the clothing she'd worn before the Garcia family had lost their hacienda. She was a lady, not a servant.

Nita's devotion to John stuck in Seth's craw. He wanted to tell her to put the comb back in her pocket, but he knew John would give him a reproachful look. John was totally unaware that he was on the receiving end of those adoring eyes of hers. Seth guessed that Nita loved him, but he knew she was the wrong woman for him. John wanted Laura Lee Shannon, and, by God, Seth was going to do everything he could to thwart Nita's affections.

Intent on what was happening outside, John absent-mindedly thanked her, then used the powerful muscles in his arms and shoulders to lift himself a few inches higher in his chair.

"Does she look the way I described her?"

"She'll do," Seth said teasingly. He gestured to Nita to stand aside, then pushed John to the long window so that he could see for himself. "What do you think?"

"She looks like she hasn't grown an inch. She's a tiny little thing, isn't she?"

"You're the one who always complains about getting a crick in your neck from looking up at people." He glanced at the tall young woman who was standing behind John's chair. Misery was clearly written on her face. Seth's straight white teeth snapped together when he grinned. "I'd say Miz Laura Lee is the perfect size for you."

"I wish she wasn't wearing a sunbonnet," John said. "It's the only thing I remember most about her. Waist-long, silver blond and curly as a piglet's tail."

"A piglet's tail?" Seth's belly jiggled as he laughed. "I'd save that compliment. She might not take it kindly."

"Guess my silver tongue is a little tarnished from lack of use, huh?"

"A mite." Seth cuffed his friend on the shoulder. "And I reckon Mist' Beau would have knocked your block off if he'd known you were watching his little sister."

The lines bracketing John's mouth, lines caused by constant pain, deepened. "It was Beau's idea for his father to add that paragraph about taking care of the Shannon women to the agreement."

"My, oh, my," Seth said as the buggy stopped in front of the house. "Look at that smile of hers. Makes you feel good all over, doesn't it?"

John nodded, excited. "Open the door, Seth. Let's get a better look!"

Jack circled Laura Lee's waist and lifted her down from the buggy. It took all his self-control not to let his arms slide around her and pull her close. The place on his forearms where she'd put her hands felt blistered.

"I'll be within shouting distance," he whispered huskily. Stepping back, he pointed to a log cabin down the road a short piece. Backing away from her to unhook the parrot's cage from the buggy, he said, "Call if you need me."

She pretended concern for her appearance by shaking the wrinkles from her skirt and shoving a stray tendril of hair up under her bonnet. All the while she was wondering what reaction she'd get if she said, "Jack, be selfish. I need you. Now. Don't leave me here. Take me with you."

Her vow not to push her luck curbed her impulsiveness.

"Thanks." She held out two fingers so that he could hook the cage on her hand and tilted her head back to look into his eyes. "I seem to perpetually be thanking you, don't I?"

"It is I who should be thanking you." Sweat trickled unnoticed along his jaw. "I'll be eternally grateful to you for settling a debt of honor that I owe my brother."

She sensed his eagerness to depart, and she summoned up a weak smile. "You go ahead. I'll reacquaint myself with John. He and Beau were good friends."

Her kindness sapped his remaining reserves of self-discipline. Such a brave little hoyden, he thought, brushing his lips against her forehead. A small bruise remained there. It served to remind him of that last night when she'd belonged solely to him. John couldn't deny him this innocent kiss. By walking away from her he'd be paying the ultimate price for this brief moment of pure selfishness.

While he tightly held her, she inhaled his masculine odor and imprinted the feel of his muscular body in her mind. She'd suffered many material losses, but none had been as devastating as losing Jack.

"Laura Lee! Welcome to the Rocking W Ranch!" John shouted from inside the doorway. "Come in here!"

She jumped guiltily away from Jack.

He tipped his Stetson in his older brother's direction. "I'm going to the corrals."

"Hey! Wait a minute, Jack! Seth fixed mint juleps. You don't have to rush off."

Jack did. His knees buckled. Lifting his head toward the cloudless blue sky, he muttered, "God, give me the strength to walk away from her."

"Say a prayer for me, too." She blinked to stop the tears brimming in her eyes from betraying her inner turmoil by sliding down her cheeks. "See you."

Half running and half skipping, she hurried up the path.

John beamed, his arms wide. "The Shannons don't know how to walk. Beau could always run circles around everybody. C'mere, Laura Lee. Let me take a look at you."

She spun around slowly, then took his hands in hers. To compare John and Jack was like comparing the plantation to the ranch. They were incredibly different in coloring and build, but she sensed they were essentially similar—kind and generous, with a keen sense of fairness.

When she touched his hands, she noticed that they were soft. His pallor was that of a man seldom in the sun. The dimples in his clean-shaven cheeks had been transformed into long slashes. His dark, soulful eyes were his most prominent feature. A handwoven rug was draped over his useless legs; it contrasted sharply with the loose-fitting snow-white shirt that covered the powerful muscles of his arms and chest. What he lacked in physical strength below the waist he'd compensated for by developing his torso.

"Isn't she beautiful, Seth?" John gallantly kissed the back of one of her hands. "Oh, I beg your pardon, Laura Lee. You don't remember Seth, do you? And you haven't met Nita, either."

"Of course I remember Seth. Beau often told the story of the monstrous catfish you caught down by the boat landing. Eight feet long, wasn't it?"

Seth chuckled; his belly danced beneath his wide leather belt. "Well, missy, I reckon that fish growed a foot each time Beau told the story."

"Awwwk!"

"Meet Captain Bligh, terror of the high seas." She lifted the green velvet cover on the cage. "Captain, meet John and Seth. Don't stick your finger in his cage. He bites."

"Ah, yes." John chuckled. "A golden bird and a golden lady. I'm twice blessed."

"Where are your manners, Captain? Aren't you going to say hello?"

Captain stared round-eyed at John. He blinked once, then put his head under his wing.

"It's been a long, dusty journey," Laura Lee explained. "You'll have to pardon him for being shy."

"Nita, why don't you take Captain Bligh out to the courtyard?" Seth said. He relieved Laura Lee of the cage and handed it to the other woman. "It looks as though he needs water."

"It's been a long trip for you, too." John was grinning from ear to ear. "Why don't we join Nita in the courtyard? It's cooler out there, and she has refreshments waiting." He clamped his hands on the wheel of his chair and rolled it across the clay-tiled floor toward the arched doorway.

"Why don't you take off your bonnet? I was just telling Seth that you weren't just the prettiest girl in the parish, you had hair like an angel."

"My hair is a fright," she protested, blushing at the effusive praise.

She'd forgotten that such lavish compliments were an innate part of a Southern gentleman's nature. John Wynthrop was confined to a wheelchair, but he could still charm the birds from the trees.

"Nonsense. I hope Jack made your journey to Texas pleasant. He told me about you winning a saloon in a poker game."

Untying the droopy bow, Laura Lee felt her blush fade to a dull pallor. Automatically her hand lifted to the bump on her head. "I did, but it was destroyed by fire the last night we were in Galveston."

"You belong here, Laura Lee."

Laura Lee could hear the ring of authority in his voice. Her chin raised a fraction of an inch. Beneath his mild manners, she felt certain, there was a core of steel.

"Your father would roll over in his grave if he thought I'd let you become a saloonkeeper." He smiled to take the sting out of the remark. "We'll appreciate having the scent of magnolias in the air. The Shannons are sturdy stock. You'll sink roots in the Texas soil in no time."

Homesickness swamped her.

She missed Tad and Brandy. And Blythewood. Her roots in Louisiana ran deep. She wouldn't disagree with John, but she doubted that adjusting would be as easy as he thought. It wasn't as if she would have Jack at her side.

"Most people think Texas is one big arid desert. Sagebrush and cactus. Cockroaches and scorpions . . ."

John continued the one-sided conversation, and Laura Lee nodded in agreement or shook her head at the appropriate moment. Her inquisitive eyes panned the courtyard.

The house was U-shaped, with stucco arches leading to a center courtyard. Vast growths of unfamiliar plants with vivid pink, yellow and red blooms hung from iron hooks in every nook and cranny. Vines with viridescent foliage clung to the rough walls. Wicker chairs holding plump cushions circled a wooden table.

She watched Nita fill a shallow pottery dish with water and cautiously open the cage door. The lithe, graceful Nita performed the task with the flair of a woman whose hands could flutter a lacy fan with the greatest of ease. To think of her as simply gorgeous would have been to underestimate her. When she compared herself to her, Laura Lee felt short and dowdy.

Nita placed the dish in the bottom of the cage. The Captain squawked and swiveled his head, taking in his new environment. "Prrretttty girl! Cap'n wants a cracker!"

Nita smiled, and her entire face lit up.

John followed the path of Laura Lee's gaze. "Nita and her mother are the only other females here. Women are scarce as hen's teeth and precious as gold to a Texan."

Nita's adoring black eyes lingered on John before they lifted to blankly stare at Laura Lee as though she were a bug trapped in a box—a rather unimpressive bug. Laura Lee didn't have to be a genius to figure out that Nita resented her presence.

Fascinated by the woman's cameo features and clothing, Laura Lee openly returned her stare. She heard only the key words of John's monologue about the Garcia family. They were former landowners, descendants of Spanish nobility. Political upheaval and the arrival of *Americanos* with gold to bribe officials with had brought about the fall of the Garcia family.

Laura Lee had noticed that while the other servants she'd glimpsed wore loose-fitting homespun clothing, Nita wore a white off-the-shoulder blouse and a skirt whose vibrant color rivaled the brilliant shadings of the Captain's feathers.

When she heard the warm, affectionate tone in John's voice as he spoke of Nita, Laura Lee wondered why he'd wanted her brought to the ranch. This raven-haired Spanish beauty obviously cared for him! Was the man blind not to notice?

"That'll be all, Nita," Seth said sternly. "Make certain Miz Laura Lee's rooms are prepared."

Ah, Laura Lee mused, her blue eyes twinkling with amusement as she watched Nita shoot Seth a haughty glare. For some unknown reason, Seth objected to the idea of an alliance between John and Nita.

Why?

And why hadn't Jack prepared her for the emotional intrigue that was obviously taking place here? Could it be that Jack was as unaware of Nita's affections as John apparently was? Or was she imagining things? Nita's loving attention might simply reflect devotion and gratitude. From what John was telling her, he seemed to treat the Garcias as friends rather than employees. It would be natural for Nita to dote on a man who had saved her family.

Deep in thought, she started when John touched her hand. Gracious, she hadn't even noticed that Seth had left them alone! What had John been saying? She hadn't the vaguest notion.

"I must be more tired than I realized," she said to excuse her rudeness. "My mind keeps wandering."

"I just said that I want you to be happy here. Jack assured me that he left Blythewood in capable hands. I know you'll be homesick for a while, but I'm hoping you'll adapt to your new way of life. Personally, I'm delighted to have you here." His broad smile faded as his eyes dropped to the polished arm of his wheelchair. "There's little hope of my returning to Heavenly Acres, so it's nice to have a piece of home brought to me."

"Jack told me about the accident. He feels guilty, responsible for what happened."

She returned the mint julep she'd been drinking to the table and gave John a steady look. This man had been Beau's best friend. Maybe he could replace the brother she had lost.

John leaned back in his chair, steepling his fingers over his flat stomach. He met her direct looks. For a moment he considered telling her his version of the accident, but now he could see how much she cared for Jack he couldn't bring himself to do it. He didn't want to lose her.

"Being tossed over the corral rail by an enraged bull was painless compared to being kicked in the teeth by my own brother." His eyes narrowed. "He told me he'd fallen in love with you."

She reached over and touched John's sleeve. "He told me he couldn't build his happiness on your misery. Between his guilt feelings and his honor, he's bound and determined to keep his promise to you. That's why I'm here when I should be with him."

"Blunt, aren't you?"

A Southern lady was supposed to blanket harsh truths with a thick layer of spun sugar, thought Laura Lee. "Did you expect fluttering eyelashes and a coy denial?" she asked. She smiled sadly. "Sorry, John, but I won't mislead you by sugarcoating how I feel or how Jack feels."

"You've changed from the sassy little pest who tagged after her brother into—"

"A woman who's in love with your brother," Laura Lee said quietly.

His hands dropped to the arms of the chair. "I'm crippled. That's why you won't give me a chance, isn't it?"

"No."

"I'll bet you could learn to love me if I could walk."

"John, you were Beau's best friend. You're Jack's only brother. Those are reasons enough for me to love you, but not the way you want to be loved."

"What makes you think I wouldn't settle for that?"

"Pride. It shows in the way you sit tall and won't let anyone push your chair around. Self-respect. Take a good look at yourself in the mirror, John. Are your clothes rumpled? Or too tight from overindulgence? You obviously care about your appearance, and you won't settle for a loveless marriage."

John grinned; his beguiling smile was a perfect replica of Jack's.

"Now you are sugarcoating the truth with flattery."

"Sincerity." Laura Lee returned his smile. "I want us to be friends, John."

With a curt nod, he glanced at his pocket watch and turned his chair toward the right wing of the house. "Nita!"

His raised voice disturbed Captain Bligh and brought an "Awwwk!" from the far side of the courtyard.

"I don't know about you," he said to Laura Lee, "but it's time for my siesta."

Laura Lee rose, wondering if she'd offended John by speaking with such directness. She watched as Nita emerged through a doorway and gracefully crossed to John's side. Leaning forward, she spoke to him in a voice too low for Laura Lee to hear. John frowned, then murmured something in response.

"Nita will take you to your rooms. Seth is waiting for me in mine. Ladies, if you'll excuse me?"

Laura Lee's blue eyes and Nita's brown eyes watched him propel his chair out of the room. Nita's curved lips tightened into a straight line as she looked at the petite intruder.

"He wants us to be friends," Nita said coolly.

Laura Lee heard the slight tremor in her voice. Animosity? Jealousy? She gathered that Nita would obey the quiet order John had issued, but it was clear that she didn't like submitting to her. She lowered her head to conceal her widening smile. John and Jack must be blind not to see how

Nita feels about John, she mused. Seth isn't, but he objects to it. What she had to do was open John's eyes and blindfold Seth.

But first she had to let Nita know she'd found an ally.

"I imagine John expressed his wishes because he doesn't want to be bothered by two bickering females disrupting his household."

Disdain for Laura Lee's mild assessment of what would take place between them had Nita lifting her aristocratic nose.

Smiling brightly, Laura Lee extended her hand. "Two sisters are expected to quarrel occasionally, though, aren't they?"

"Sisters?" Nita repeated slowly, thawing under the radiance of the other woman's grin. "How can that be?"

"Sisters-in-law. I'm in love with John's brother."

A husky laugh destroyed Nita's icy veneer. She took the offered hand and held it between her long, slender hands. "I was instructed to prepare your rooms. I guess I will have to have the jumping beans removed from beneath your bedsheets, eh?"

Chapter Fourteen

Nita's confession brought a genuine smile to Laura Lee's lips. "Beans that jump?"

"*Sí!* Nothing that would harm you. A *poco*... a little prank. You are not angry?"

Laura Lee shook her head. She followed Nita across the courtyard into a bedroom she assumed was part of the guest suite. "I've been known to pull little tricks myself."

"Do you like it? It's elegant, no?" Nita pirouetted around the room, running her fingers lightly over the polished walnut dresser. She stopped in front of the full-length mirror.

Her dark eyes met Laura Lee's blue eyes.

Both women measured their differences. Nita was tall and slender; Laura Lee was shorter, more rounded. Laura Lee's store-bought dress measured up poorly against the handstitched embroidery on Nita's blouse and skirt. Nita's hair was dark, shiny and well combed; Laura Lee's was fair, but trail dust had coated its natural luster.

"I had Pepe fill a tub in the other room," Nita said, breaking the silence. She turned Laura Lee around by the shoulders and began unbuttoning her dress. "While you freshen up, I'll remove the jumping beans, and then I'll help you wash your hair. I'll have you clean and fresh, *pronto*."

"I appreciate your kindness, Nita. I feel as though I could sleep for a week."

Three weeks had come and gone, and Laura Lee continued to feel drowsy. Every day the sun was high in the sky before she awoke. Afternoon siestas were never long enough. She tried politely to stay awake in the evening to be a friendly companion to John, but within an hour of eating dinner she'd be covering her mouth with her hand to hide her yawns.

Nita, bless her generous heart, would make clucking noises like a mother hen and shoo her off to bed.

Now, sitting in front of the dressing table combing her hair, Laura Lee wondered if she'd be able to cope with John's shifting moods—or her own, for that matter. The enthusiastic behavior he'd shown the day she'd arrived had been interspersed with long bouts of depression.

In the presence of others—Nita included—John acted thoroughly enamored with her, touching her hand, caressing her hair. Once he had winked and then blown a kiss in her direction. And yet, when they were alone, his zealous ardor turned to silent preoccupation.

In the past couple of days he'd adopted a strictly hands-off, don't-bother-me attitude toward her, in public and in private.

What troubled her most were the hours he locked himself in his study and refused to talk to anyone other than his trusted servant, Seth. When she'd tried to question Seth about John's brooding behavior, he'd excused those progressively lengthier periods of solitary confinement by calling them John's "dark spells."

Her own moods swayed between anxiety and contentment.

As she pulled a silver-handled brush through her hair, she realized that she had too much time on her hands, with nothing to fill the loneliness caused by Jack's absence. No responsibilities—John refused to share the ranches' bookkeeping chores. No routine chores—Nita and her mother supervised the kitchen help and the household cleaning. Nothing to keep her mind occupied, away from wild imaginary scenes with Jack.

Most days she couldn't sleep, couldn't eat, couldn't talk to anyone without constantly glancing around in the hope that Jack had broken his promise to give John a chance to win her affection.

And there were those paranoid moments, like now, while she was plaiting her hair in preparation for turning in for the night, when she could have sworn someone was watching her.

One by one she isolated and identified the night's sound: crickets . . . tree frogs . . . the ticking of a grandfather clock.

She tossed the brush on the dresser and crossed to the open window overlooking Jack's cabin. The fragrance of jasmine and gardenias sweetened the air. The yellow light from coal oil lanterns gleamed through the windows. She parted her lacy curtains and held them aside.

She'd considered the possibility that Jack was keeping watch over her, but she'd quickly discarded the idea as wishful thinking. He wasn't stalking the night, he wasn't prowling the house, he wasn't seeking entrance to her room. According to Seth, he wasn't within fifty miles of the ranch.

On those rare occasions when Jack inhabited his cabin, he kept his distance from the ranch house. She'd seen Seth carrying stacks of papers back and forth between John's office and Jack's cabin. The two brothers never socialized.

Her lips thinned as she dropped her arms to her side and let the curtains fall back into place. Tomorrow she'd talk to Jack, if she had to hog-tie him to get him to listen!

A light rapping on her door drew her attention.

"Yes?"

"It's me, John. Can I talk to you for a minute?"

Laura Lee gathered her cotton dressing gown tighter around her waist, loosened the knot and then retied it, tighter this time. She crossed to the door and opened it. Like herself, John was garbed in a nightshirt and robe.

"Can we go out into the courtyard? Everyone has retired to their quarters. We'll be alone."

Whatever he wanted to discuss, she thought, it must be important.

"Of course."

John abruptly turned his wheelchair around and moved out into the courtyard. The secret he'd been hiding for days could change everything. He waited impatiently for her to make herself comfortable in one of the chairs that stood there and then said, "Would it make a difference in how you feel about me if I could walk? Is that why you don't love me?"

"John..." She struggled to find a kind way to relieve his anxiety without raising his hopes. "You're like a brother to me. I do love you."

"But you don't have that special feeling a woman has for the man she marries, do you?"

Laura Lee raised her face to the star-filled sky, seeking wisdom. She didn't want to hurt John. He was a good man. She couldn't lie to him and let him build up false hopes.

"No, John, I don't."

He lifted her limp hand from the arm of her chair and brought it to his lips. "I thought I could make you love me. The harder I've tried, the more I've come to realize that I've got more of a chance of using these legs of mine than I have of winning your love."

"Love just happens, John. I didn't want to fall in love with Jack. I had good reason to hate him."

"Such as?"

She could feel his lips curve as they brushed against the back of her hand. "He was late arriving at Blythewood, which certainly complicated my life. He can be arrogant and dictatorial when he's crossed."

"He has his good traits, too. A man couldn't ask for a more loving brother. He could have come to the ranch house and flaunted his love for you in front of me, but he hasn't."

"No, he hasn't."

"There have been times when I wished he would. I've wanted to accuse him of betraying me." He lazily rubbed her knuckles with his thumb. "But deep down I know that neither of you has betrayed me. You fell in love, and I'm standing between you." His eyes dropped to his legs. His toe moved inside his slipper. " 'Sitting' would be more accurate."

Laura Lee didn't know how to reply to the dry remark. She was sorry John was crippled, but she felt sorrier for Jack, who felt responsible for his brother's being confined to a wheelchair. Then, too, she knew that John didn't want her pity. He wanted her to love him—and that was something that would never happen.

John sighed and returned her hand to the arm of her chair. "My being able to walk wouldn't make a difference, would it?"

"It would, but not the difference you want to hear. Jack would be rid of the guilt he feels if you could walk again. He'd be free to ask me to marry him."

"Is that what you want?"

A shooting star raced across the sky. Laura Lee closed her eyes and said, "With all my heart I wish we could all find love and happiness."

"When you wish on a star you aren't supposed to tell it, or it won't come true."

"Maybe it won't. Maybe Jack and I are star-crossed lovers who are never meant to be man and wife."

John knew how it felt to try and try and try again without success. Only when he'd reached the bottom of despair had he felt the first twinges of life in his toes. The yearning he heard in her voice almost made him blurt out his secret.

"Don't give up hope." He thumped his chest with his hand. "In here, I know everything is going to work out for the best."

Laura Lee barely heard his last words. She was so tired of fighting, of hoping, of wishing for the impossible. Tomorrow she'd give love one more try, but after that she'd give up. Fate had finally beaten her.

"Laura Lee?"

"Mmm?" She opened her heavy eyelids slowly.

"I'm not sorry that it didn't work out between us. If the closest I can come to Heavenly Acres is for you to be here as my sister-in-law, then so be it. I want you to talk to Jack first thing in the morning. In the meantime, I think you'd better get some sleep."

She smiled, not certain whether she'd really heard John give the permission that would free Jack from his self-imposed isolation or whether she'd fallen asleep and dreamed it. She got to her feet and brushed a sisterly kiss across John's cheek.

"G'night, John."

"G'night, Laura Lee. Sweet dreams."

He followed her to her room and then wheeled himself to his own room. The door closed behind his chair. He heard the key turn. He knew who'd been waiting for him.

"Nita?"

"Yes, John?"

"I'm getting a charley horse in my right leg. That's a good sign, isn't it?"

Her circular skirt billowed around her as she dropped to her knees in front of him. She parted his robe unceremoniously and raised his nightshirt. Her long black hair brushed against his bare leg as her strong fingers began massaging the clenched muscle.

"Do you think you'd better call Seth?"

"No." Nita smiled, fully aware of John's predicament. He wanted to keep his slow progress a secret from everyone in the household—Seth included—but he also wanted to protect her.

She'd discovered his secret quite by accident. She'd been crossing the courtyard late one night when she'd heard a groan coming from John's bedroom. Afraid he was having a nightmare, she'd quietly opened his door and found him stranded between his wheelchair and his dresser. Her gasp startled John. He turned, lost his balance and toppled to the floor. After she helped him to his feet, she convinced him that he needed her help.

He needs more than my helping him walk, she mused, her head raising. When she'd silently skirted the courtyard on her way from her room to his, she'd seen him talking to Laura Lee. He needed to have his male ego boosted.

With long, sure strokes, she continued massaging him until the hard muscle of his leg responded.

"Seth is jealous of anyone who gets close to you, other than Laura Lee. He'd ban me from your room. Is that what you want?"

John groaned as her red lips formed the last word. Her lips were unbelievably kissable. Where had he been while she'd turned into such a lovely woman? He'd seen her daily, and he'd never noticed! There had to be something wrong with him—worse than being crippled—for him not to have noticed the change.

"No. Don't call Seth."

Her hand moved to his knee. Her thumb circled the sensitive spot beside his kneecap. His eyes were as dark as her own; they blazed with his awareness of her. Nita felt like shouting with joy.

"The cramp is gone, *sí*?"

"Yes, Nita, it's gone." She was intoxicating him with the sweet fragrance of night jasmine as she rose. "Your hair smells good."

She could tell he hadn't meant to pay her the compliment by the way his hands gripped the wheels of his chair. Uncertain of what she should do, she waited, watching him move his chair to the side of the dresser.

"I gave Laura Lee her freedom tonight." He used the strength of his arms to lever himself out of his chair. "I've lived up to the Wynthrop end of the agreement. Jack can take care of her."

His eyes spoke volumes to Nita as he righted himself and gained his balance. She crossed to his side. He lifted his arm and lightly placed it around her shoulders.

"You won't be needing me take care of you much longer," she said quietly.

Steady on his feet now, he turned to Nita until she faced him.

"You've become a beautiful woman, Nita. I've always thought of you as . . ."

"A little sister." Her eyes dropped. Had she misread what she'd seen in his eyes?

"Look at me, Nita," he whispered. "Do I look like a big brother to you, too?"

Her head snapped up. "No."

"Tell me what you see."

"A strong, handsome man." The man I love, she silently added. Her lips puckered. She touched her fingertips to them and then to his. His full lower lip was trembling. Her fingers captured the moist heat of his breath as she curled her fingers into her palm.

"You care for me?"

She nodded. Only Laura Lee knew how much she cared for him. She loved him with all her heart and soul.

His lips curved as he slanted them to cover hers. He kissed her the way a gentleman kissed a lady for the first time. Sweetly, lips closed, barely touching her. He wanted more, but he contented himself with the soft sigh he heard as their lips parted.

"Slowly? One step at a time?" he whispered.

"For now," she agreed. Her dark eyes flared with promise. "It'll be another secret for us to share."

A string of tomorrows passed without Laura Lee's successfully cornering Jack. She'd been on the ranch two months without once "accidentally" bumping into him. John obviously wasn't the only person Jack was avoiding. The instant he sensed her nearness he seemed to vanish into thin air.

He'd even ignored John's repeated requests that he join them for evening meals.

Determined to speak to him, Laura Lee decided to foil his disappearing act by ambushing him. By spying on him from a distance—it was the closest she'd come to him—she'd learned his routine. He usually went to the barn alone once or twice a day—usually at daybreak and again at dusk—to feed Hellion. Between those feedings he was usually out of the immediate area. Most evenings he went to the bunkhouse or stayed in his cabin.

She had two choices: she could waylay him in his cabin or in the barn. She chose the more circumspect of the two—the barn.

Before dawn, dressed in a crimson split-skirt riding habit John had given her to "lift her spirits," she scurried across the wide expanse of grass between the house and the barn. The stable hands usually arrived around seven, after Jack had been there.

Like a soldier on a reconnaissance mission, she stealthily mapped out the dimly lit interior of the barn—twenty stalls, ten on each side, hayloft up the ladder, door at the far end leading to blacksmith's quarters, flanked by tack rooms filled with feed, saddles, bridles, lead ropes and animal medicines.

She decided the best place to hide was the empty stall across from Hellion's. Her head bobbed around as she slid the creaky gate open. Several hungry horses popped their heads over the gates of their stalls, whinnying in anticipation of their morning ration of feed.

"Shh! You'll be fed later!"

She had just stepped inside the stall when she heard Jack call from outside. "Who's there?"

Laura Lee sniffed. The stall she occupied was empty, but it hadn't been cleaned. She groaned and glanced down at her new boots. Wonderful. He'll never know it's me when I sneak up on him smelling like road apples!

"G'morning, Hellion." Jack splashed the pail of water he'd carried from the pump outside into the stallion's corner trough. "Yep, I know it's just you and me. I guess I'm a big skittery, huh, big fella?"

Laura Lee watched avidly as he opened the gate of Hellion's stall. For a split second the dawn's rays coming through the barn's door struck him full in the face. He squinted, raised his arm to block the light, then disappeared inside the stall.

Her heartbeat accelerated. He looked as if he hadn't slept a wink since Galveston, either!

"I'm worried, big fella. Damn worried. John's notes say she's been sleeping around the clock. Have I done the right thing?" He paused, then answered himself. "Well, I'm glad you believe in me, anyway. Nobody else does."

And I thought *I* was going daft, she mused, grinning. I talk to the Captain, but I sure as blazes don't answer for him.

"Let's see that front hoof of yours. Hmm." Jack faced Hellion, holding one of the horse's forelegs across his knee. A peculiar prickling sensation spread goose bumps on his neck. He dropped Hellion's foreleg, untied his bandanna and swiped at the back of his neck. "You're looking good."

"You look wonderful."

Jack spun around so fast it made him light-headed. His blood rushed as he stared at her, openmouthed. God, she was a sight for sore eyes!

"Hello, Laura Lee." He touched the brim of his Stetson. "You're looking good, too."

"Despite what you've heard? Seth must have told you that John isn't pushing to set a wedding date."

His Adam's apple bobbed up and down like a greenhorn on his first trail ride. "Yep." It suddenly occurred to him that something must have happened at the ranch house. He nodded in that direction. "Everything okay?"

"Fine."

She sounded miserable. He pushed the gate open and stepped close to her.

"You dont sound fine. What's causing those dark smudges under your eyes?"

"It isn't John keeping me up all night," she snapped, turning away from him. "I had to stay up all night so I could come out here at the crack of dawn to waylay you before you rode off into the sunrise! You can keep your flattery to yourself, thank you very kindly!"

Jack grinned. Jealousy had been gnawing at his guts for weeks. He'd figured that Laura Lee had lost interest in him, because otherwise she'd have found a way to see him before now. From the drop-dead glare she was giving him, it was a good thing he'd resisted the temptation to climb through her bedroom window. She'd have slapped his face silly for keeping his promise to John.

"You'll have to forgive me for my lack of graciousness. I spend more time conversing with Hellion than I do with a beautiful woman who's acting like an ill-tempered hoyden."

A warm tingle shot from her face to her toes, then ricocheted back.

She glanced over her shoulder. A lady was forgiving; a hoyden got even. In true hoyden fashion, she quipped, "I've seen saddlebags smaller than the bags under your eyes. While I'm standing at my window staring at your cabin, what are you doing?"

"Sleeping. Some of us can't nap the day away."

"Liar! No one can nap in this heat. I swear, I could fry an egg between my sheets."

Jack chuckled. It was cruel to be gladdened by the knowledge that she was losing sleep over him, but his shoulders felt as though she'd lifted a hundred-pound load of worry from them. He wanted to pull her into his arms and hug the daylights out of her.

"What's causing your sleepless nights?" she asked boldly.

You! he thought. He pushed his hat back from his forehead, mopped his brow with his sleeve, then pulled the hat low on his brow again. The attempt to hide his expression failed. She was much shorter than him, so she just stepped closer and tilted her head back. "Work."

"You're gone a lot."

"Uh-huh." When his thoughts of her reached the unbearable stage, he lit out like a scalded dog. Hell, he'd ridden to Galveston seeking relief in another woman's arms. That misguided impulse had left his face bright red the entire way back to the ranch. He'd thanked his lucky stars none of his men had tagged along with him. "I, uh, made a quick trip to Galveston."

Without thinking, she blurted out, "Oh, Jack. I wish you'd taken me with you." His pained expression made her add hastily, "Are Alden and the girls still there?"

"They've opened another saloon." He felt as though she'd taken her foot out of her mouth and shoved it into his. Their saloon was where he'd tried to find consolation. "Named it the Golden Parrot."

"Tell me about it!"

Groaning inwardly, crossing his ankles and leaning back against Hellion's stall, he said, "Not much to tell, other than that they miss you and the Captain. One of the girls made a huge stuffed bird that's supposed to look like a parrot. A customer nicknamed it the Blue Buzzard."

Her smile made his stomach do a flip-flop.

"Sounds as though they miss the Captain the most, huh?"

"You wouldn't say that if you'd heard the hundreds of questions I had to answer about your welfare." He rubbed his stubbly whiskers and wished he'd shaved. "Over Alden's opposition, Cactus Flower did offer to pay a small fortune for the Captain if you'd want to sell him."

"Never!"

"That's what I told them. Captain Bligh's squawking saved our skin the night of the fire."

Her face flamed hotly. She remembered what they had been doing the night of the fire.

Hellion nickered, then nudged Jack's shoulder, pushing him against her. He grabbed her arms to steady her.

"Sorry. Hellion's manners are worse than mine," he said. His legs were wobbling beneath him; he wondered if he could keep *his* balance.

"Don't be," she breathed.

And then they were wrapped in each other's arms, kissing openmouthed, obsessed with desire after weeks of denial.

Tearing her mouth from his, panting, Laura Lee begged, "Tell me, Jack. Say it. Say it now!"

"I love you. I can't let John have you."

She peppered kisses along his jaw as a reward for the admission.

"The past two months have been hell. My imagination has been driving me crazy!" His mouth covered hers desperately.

Wild, hot, wet kisses, with tongues meeting, retreating, delving deeper and deeper. Her nails scored his shoulders, back and ribs, leaving tracks on his shirt. She couldn't get close enough. He trembled beneath her hands; she quaked in response to his kisses.

"You're always on my mind," she whispered. "I listen for noises at night and I hope and pray that it's you coming to me. Once or twice I've seen you silhouetted at your window and I've wanted to run to you . . . to feel your arms wrap around me . . . keeping me safe. Oh, Jack, I've been so lonely without you!"

"Me too."

She was shaking like a leaf in a windstorm. Jack lifted her in his arms and carried her to the rear of the barn, where two bales of hay were stacked. He sat down and settled her on his lap, with one arm around her waist and the other holding her head against his chest.

"You've kept your promise to your brother. Haven't you tormented both of us too long with your guilt feelings?"

"I can't help blaming myself. I'm the one who refused to listen to John when he wanted to go back to Heavenly Acres . . . when he was *able* to go back. Now, thanks to me, he can't go anywhere. I swear to God, at the time I thought I was doing the right thing. The South isn't the way John remembers it."

"I know, Jack. Your brother is idealistic. . . .part of the Old South's aristocracy. It isn't the same. It never will be."

"I thought I was doing the best thing for both of you." He held her so tight he heard her back pop. Immediately he loosened his grip. "I'm beginning to think I did both of you a disservice. When I left you in Galveston and came back here I told John that I loved you...that you belonged with me. But when he said I hadn't given him a chance those old guilt feelings surfaced. You represent everything John lost when he moved to Texas. I had to give him a chance. Was I wrong?"

"Yes!" She hiccuped; family honor was as important to her as it was to Jack. "No."

He muffled her next hiccup against his shirtfront. "I do love you. John sent me a note saying he wanted to talk. I've been scared to death it would be bad news—that you'd fallen in love with him. I think it's time, love, for the three of us to have a heart-to-heart talk, don't you?"

Her attack of hiccups ended as quickly as it had begun. "Yes, please." She fiddled with the buttons on the front of his shirt, wondering if she should tell him about Nita's feelings for John. Although Nita had refused to confide completely in her, Laura Lee suspected that something was going on between them right under Seth's nose. "Jack, I don't think you have to worry about us being together making John unhappy."

His eyes lit with amusement. "You haven't been playing one of your cake tricks on him, have you?"

Grinning, Laura Lee ran her finger over the curve of his mustache. "No. I'm completely reformed."

He kissed her, ever so tenderly. He wanted to linger, to continue kissing her until the rest of the world gave up on them and spun off on its own. She made him feel strong enough to create a new world just for the two of them.

Reluctantly he ended the kiss. "Let's go, before the stableboy arrives."

"Where?" She crossed her fingers, hoping he was planning on taking her to his cabin.

"To the ranch house, to have a family discussion."

"Now?"

"No," he said drolly, flexing his biceps. "I'll turn back the clock, and we'll have this family tête-á-tête two months ago."

Vaguely she remembered wanting to reach out and stop the hands of the clock at the bank. She was as uneasy now as she had been then. Something was amiss, but she couldn't put her finger on it.

"Maybe we should wait."

"Procrastination won't cure the problem . . . it complicates it." He hugged her, then helped her to her feet and stood beside her, brushing the straw from the seat of his pants. "This won't be difficult."

Laura Lee flung her arms around his waist to calm her uneasiness. He combed his fingers through his hair to soothe his own nerves. He moved her off his lap, draped his arm over her shoulder and started walking toward the house. "John's had a fair chance. Now it's my turn."

Neither of them hurried. He matched his long stride to her short steps.

"Maybe you should start coming to the house for supper. That way he'll see us together and have time to adjust to the idea of us loving each other."

"Give him time to adjust? That's what Father kept saying about him living in Texas. We've been here years. He didn't adjust. He'll never adjust. John clings to the past—or, more precisely, to how things should have been." Jack shook his head in exasperation. "I love you. That hasn't changed, and it won't change, whether he adjusts to the idea or not."

His fingers lightly dropped from her shoulder to her waist as he opened the wrought-iron gate at the back of the courtyard. Laura Lee brushed a kiss along his jaw.

"A kiss for good luck," she whispered.

"We'll make our own luck."

Their eyes were on each other as they entered the courtyard.

"Well now, lookee who's here," a nasal voice wheezed. There was the sound of a gun cocking. "Lovebirds. I reckon it's bird season around here, huh?"

Chapter Fifteen

Laura Lee froze. Her terrified eyes took in the scene in the courtyard in one frightened glance. John sat frozen in his wheelchair, the stranger's six-shooter pointed squarely at his chest. Nita was cowering beside his chair. The rest of the Garcias stood with their hands over their heads, facing the stucco wall. The Captain twitched his wings; his yellow feet fidgeted on the perch.

"Whazza matter, girlie? Don't yer recognize my pretty face? We goes back a long ways."

The stranger pushed his sombrero off his head. The wooden bead beneath his shaggy beard tightened on his throat momentarily, then slid to the center of the cord, allowing the wide-brimmed hat to rest in the center of his back. The red scar that puckered the assailant's bushy eyebrow and one nostril immediately identified him.

"You're the man who was at the gambling table," Laura Lee croaked. Her tongue, like all the other muscles in her body, was stiff with alarm. Her mouth felt drier than a desert wind.

"That's right, girlie. Zeke Callum, at yore service. I reckon I did ya a big favor when I torched your saloon. Otherwise you'd jest be one more saloon gal." His empty hand gestured, indicating the courtyard. "Ya got yerself fixed up damned fancy here, don't ya? Yessiree, jest like back in Louisiana, only better."

Jack sidestepped around Laura Lee.

"Jest get back, mister," Callum said, poking the muzzle of his gun against John's chest. The wheelchair rolled back several inches, and Zeke stopped it with his boot. "I ain't foolin'. Don't matter t' me whether the cripple lives or dies. Prob'ly better off dead."

Scowling, his mouth set in a straight line, Jack studied the man's eyes. Zeke would kill in cold blood and laugh afterward, he decided. He'd have to bide his time and wait for the right moment. He couldn't risk John's life to save Laura Lee. Not yet. God help him, he hoped he didn't have to make that choice.

Zeke's smallish eyes shifted around the courtyard. He swiftly moved the gun to his empty hand, then jerked the wheelchair until it faced Jack and Laura Lee. "Now you jest git on over here, lady. . . real slow and easy like. Now! Or I'll blow his head off. Jest 'cause I missed back on the boat doesn't mean I'll miss this time."

Nita gasped audibly. "Don't hurt him, please," she begged. Her black eyes swung to Jack, appealing for help.

Laura Lee could feel Jack's breath slow and steady on her cheeks. His hand, at the base of her spine, nudged her forward. Knees locked, muscles tense, she started to pitch headfirst, but she recovered her balance by latching on to Jack's arm.

"Watch it, girlie. One false move 'n' I'll plug both of 'em—yer lover and his brother."

Zeke's sinister chuckle startled her mind from its stupor. He will. He'll shoot all of us without a qualm! Do something! Say something! Bargain with him! Find a damn loophole and string it around his scrawny neck!

"I'll give the money back that you lost. All of it. Just let me go to my room—"

"You ain't gettin' outa my sight, girlie. I been trackin' you like a hound dog on a 'possum trail ever since I got outa Andersonville."

The South's prisoner of war camp? She'd heard the conditions were deplorable there, but she didn't have anything to do with that. Why would he leave there and follow her?

Jack edged slightly in front of her. His eyes silently cautioned John not to move a muscle as his mind worked furiously to link what the man holding the gun had revealed with the other misfortunes that had plagued Laura Lee. Why would a bluebelly, a former prisoner of war, want to harm Laura Lee? He'd admitted to having taken a potshot at them on the boat. He must have followed them from there, to New Orleans, to Galveston. Laura Lee must have been right about someone dogging their tracks in New Orleans. Zeke had also admitted to being the arsonist who had set the Golden Parrot on fire. The cowardly son of a bitch must have been sneaking around the ranch, too. But why?

His black eyes skirted back to the gunman. Somehow he couldn't convince himself that this low-down sidewinder was in this by himself. Was he on Luke Reynolds's payroll?

Keep him talking, Jack thought. Get his finger off that goddamn trigger.

"Whatever Luke Reynolds paid you, I'll double it," he offered placidly.

"I don't know no Luke Reynolds. You ain't gonna pay me nothing, cowboy. She's the one who's gonna pay." His eyes leveled on Laura Lee's breasts. "I'm gonna finish what I started back in that barn. Don't ya figger I earned it?"

He aimed his gun at Laura Lee and stepped three paces toward them. With one finger he slowly traced his scar. "Her kinfolk ruint my face, jest 'cause I wuz funnin' with her. No woman kin look at me now without screamin' her head off."

Laura Lee recoiled as she identified Zeke Callum. She hadn't known his name then. He'd worn a sweat-soaked Yankee-blue uniform. He'd been unshaven but beardless.

Her worst nightmare had become reality—he was the Yankee soldier who'd tried to rape her! Black memories she'd locked behind the iron gates of her memory slipped insidiously into her consciousness, forcing her to relive bits and pieces of the horror. Her eyes glazed.

She heard the sharp crack of guns being fired; she smelled the stale sweat and whiskey breath mingling with the smoke coming from the mansion at Heavenly Acres; she felt this man's fingers clawing at her throat, choking her. She heard high-pitched wails of terror ripping from her chest as she scratched and kicked to free herself. And then his hands raised over his head.

Silence.

A hideous shriek of rage and pain.

Crimson blood. At first she thought the blood must be her own. Her scream became thin and reedy. Blackness threatened to engulf her. As her eyes rolled, she saw the blade of Tad's knife slice across his face for the second time.

"Oh, yer gonna pay, missy," Zeke Callum promised. "I kin tell ya remember. I'm gonna take care of you, and then I'm goin' after the boy. I coulda kilt him first, but he's easy pickings. Yer the one I'm gonna have my way with . . . and then I'm gonna kill ya . . . real slow." The tip of his gun waved to bring her closer. "You jest move on over here, away from the cowboy."

Out of the corner of his eye Jack saw the coloring in her face drain until she was a deathly white. A lesser woman would have fainted; Laura Lee didn't flinch, not even when the man's hand reached for her. Her eyes grew larger and larger, but she stood her ground, her chin raised defiantly.

"You'll never make it off this ranch alive," Jack said. He was thinking fast. He had to get his body between Laura Lee and Zeke Callum. The thought of that man touching so much as a hair on her head made him see red. "I'll muster a hundred ranch hands. You'll be dead within the hour."

The threat was enough to stop Zeke's hand from grabbing Laura Lee. He squinted up at Jack, his lips rising in a grotesque facsimile of a smile. "Then I reckon the only smart thing to do is kill the whole rotten bunch of you."

The raspy laugh that accompanied his threat turned Laura Lee's blood to ice. Butchering one woman or shooting a dozen men . . . it made no difference to Zeke.

"No," she whispered, moving toward the gunman. "You let them live. I'll help you tie them up so they can't come after us. Then I'll go with you. I'll do anything you want me to do."

Zeke gave a squeal of glee. "I knowed under those prim ruffles you was a genuine slut, jest like all them other Southern women who begged me to take 'em."

Laura Lee tried to keep herself from wondering how many other defenseless women he'd raped. She was the one who'd escaped, who'd left his face scarred. Revenge. He wanted revenge, and he'd slyly plotted and schemed to get it.

He held out his dirty palm.

Jack rolled to the balls of his feet. Zeke would undoubtedly shoot him, but he'd choke the life out of him before he died.

Laura Lee lifted her hand from her side.

Zeke's dirt-stained hand and Laura Lee's slender fingers were scant inches apart when all hell broke loose.

The Captain shrieked, "Stick 'em up, landlubber! Awwwk!"

John heaved out of his wheelchair, propelling his body with his muscular arms toward the would-be killer's shoulders.

"Back off!" The barrel of Zeke's gun swung from Laura Lee to the bird's cage and then around to John.

Nita flung her body between the pistol and John, screaming, "No!" They both tumbled to the ground.

A shot rang out just as Jack kicked the weapon from the man's hand. Laura Lee bent at the waist, rushed forward and rammed her shoulder into Zeke's stomach.

Zeke jackknifed at the middle, fastened his arm across her back and twisted his wiry body as they pitched backward. Laura Lee screamed as her elbows and shoulders took the brunt of the fall. His head slammed beneath her chin; her teeth snapped together and her neck whipped backward. Her hair tangled in the web of his fingers on one hand; his other hand clutched her throat. His thumb dug into her windpipe.

"I'm gonna throttle ya, bitch!"

The door to the house exploded open and Seth barreled through it, moving like an enraged bull.

Startled, Zeke looked around, and in that instant Jack dived for him, locked his arm across his scrawny chest and rolled his body off Laura Lee, but Zeke's fingers were balled in her curly hair, snatching, dragging her at arm's length.

One blow on the mouth from Jack's doubled fist made his eyes bulge, his lip split and his body stiffen as though he'd been struck by lightning. The heels of his boots raised four inches off the ground, then thudded heavily downward. His eyelids fluttered and shut.

"Get up, you son of a bitch!" Jack roared, wanting to tear him apart with his bare hands.

His clenched fingers wadded the front yoke of Zeke's shirt and jerked him upright. The would-be killer was unconscious; his head lolled lifelessly from one side to the other. Jack drew back his arm, ready to smash his face in if he so much as flickered an eyelash.

He wanted an excuse to kill him, and he wanted it bad.

Seth hooked his forearm into the crook of Jack's arm. "He doesn't look like he'll cause much more trouble, Mist' Jack. You can get off him. You won't get any satisfaction out of killing a man that can't fight back."

Jack was forced to agree. "We'll see what the sheriff has to say about arson and attempted murder," he said.

John was standing, looking a little sheepish, but there was also an air of repressed triumph about him.

"Nita, would you get my canes? I think our secret is out," he said huskily. A woman didn't step between a loaded gun and a man unless she felt more than kind regards. His fingers gently brushed the residue of tears from her cheeks. His hand dropped from her waist; he swatted her gently. To hell with taking one step at a time; he felt as though he could run faster than Hellion. "Hurry, love."

Laura Lee sat up and rubbed the sore spot on her chin. Suddenly her mouth fell open. "You—you're standing! Walking!"

"I'll be damned," Seth whispered, awed. His eyes widened in amazement. "Mist' John, you're out of your wheelchair. Merciful God, thank you, thank you."

"Thank Nita, Seth. I wouldn't have made it to my feet without her."

A broad smile split Jack's face. Inner joy made his black eyes shine like polished onyx as he extended his hand toward Laura Lee. "I thought the amazed expression on my face would warn Callum when I saw John rise from his wheelchair. Dammit, John, why didn't you tell us!"

A bit chagrined at having kept his recovery a secret, John pointed at the sprawled body and said, "Don't you think we'd better tie him up? You coldcocked him, but I don't think I'm up to him providing us with another surprise attack."

"I'll get some rope from the barn," Seth replied. "But you've got some mighty tall explaining to do when I get back, Mist' John." He slapped his thigh and chuckled with pleasure. "I got a feelin' this one is going to be better than Mist' Beau's catfish tale."

Nita reappeared with the two oak sticks that served as makeshift canes for John. There was no mistaking her pride in him, or the love flowing between the two of them as she handed the canes to him.

John slowly crossed to his brother. "You've always told me I need to stand on my own two feet and take a good look at what's going on around me," he said lightly as the tips of the canes scraped along the cobbled path. "I'd planned on telling you. I sent you a note, but you were too damn stubborn to listen to me this time, either."

Jack met his brother eye-to-eye for the first time in nearly a year. His arms opened. John's steps were slow, faltering, but he tossed one cane aside and flung his arm over his brother's shoulder.

It was the most beautiful sight Laura Lee had ever seen. Two giant-size men hugging each other, slapping each other's backs, tears coursing down their faces.

Smiling, Nita held her hand out to help Laura Lee to her feet. "Sisters?" she whispered. "I owe you everything. John never realized how much I loved him, or that he cared for me, until you arrived."

"What about that, big brother?" Jack asked, holding John at arm's length and grinning like a man who'd won the New Orleans lottery. "When you opened your eyes, did you see love shining from hers?"

"I've been a fool," John admitted, "but I'm going to make a bigger fool out of myself by falling flat on my face if I don't sit down immediately."

Jack started to wrap his arm around his brother's waist.

"Uh-uh, little brother," John protested mildly. "I can make it on my own."

"Yeah!" Jack was beaming. He twirled the tip of his mustache mischievously. "I'll just bet you can."

While the four of them gathered around the table, Seth returned and bundled Zeke Callum up securely, saying, "Now don't you-all be concerned about this here skunk. I'm going to throw him in the stable and set a couple of men to guard him. Then I'll ride to get the sheriff for you, Mist' John."

Jack sought Laura Lee's hand beneath the table and squeezed her fingers. Now he knew what she'd meant when she'd said they didn't have to build their happiness on John's misery. She must have known about Nita and John.

"While you're recovering from the shock of me walking, I want to set the record straight about what happened that day in the corral. I'm sick of you feeling guilty," John said. The stern look he gave Jack made it clear that he would brook no argument. He settled back in his chair. "It's ironic how the accident happened. I remember that day as though it were yesterday. I'd spent the morning staring at my painting of Heavenly Acres. I went to the corral to tell you that I was fed up with ranch life. I wanted to go home."

His eyes moved to Laura Lee, searching for understanding. "Jack's the rancher. I'm a planter."

"But—"

"Shut up, Jack." He softened the order with a smile. "That day wasn't the first time you wouldn't listen to me. Once you get something into your head there's no changing your mind."

Laura Lee couldn't resist poking Jack in the ribs and grinning. Under her breath she muttered, "And you say I'm the one who's stubborn!"

"You?" John snorted. "I'm surprised he'd notice. This isn't the first time I've tried to tell him what happened that day, either. That day I'd decided to clean his ears out with a stick of dynamite if I had to. But let me get on with it. There I was, sitting on the top rail of the corral fence, shouting and screaming at Jack while he prepared to brand a bull. The bull was in the next pen. The ranch hand who was at the chute between the two pens must have thought I was yelling at him. He lifted the gate just as I jumped off the fence. I landed on the side of my foot and twisted my ankle. I was half hobbling, half stumbling back to the rail when I felt myself being lifted and pitched toward the rails like a rag doll."

His hand moved to his side, where the scar from the bull's horns was. "I was so damn mad at Jack I thought someone had shot me. Maybe what I heard was Jack firing his pistol at the bull. The next thing I knew I was in bed, flat on my back, feeling dead from the waist down."

"How it happened is inconsequential," Jack said. "You did save me from the bull."

"Unintentionally. It was my own clumsiness, not bravery, that made me a cripple." He reached across the table and picked up Laura Lee's hand. "I don't regret using his guilt feelings to persuade him to fetch you. The day you arrived I had a long talk with myself. I decided I'd walk again just to prove to you I wasn't a lesser man than Jack."

John released Laura Lee's hand and put his hand over Nita's. "I'm going back to Louisiana, under my own power, with or without Jack's blessing. I think you'd like it there, too."

"Well, I'll be damned." All four of them turned toward the back gate, where Seth was standing. "You aren't going to marry Miz Shannon?"

"No, Seth, I'm going to marry Jack. Don't you think one Wynthrop is plenty?"

A wide grin split his face. "We're going home, Mist' John? Back to Heavenly Acres?"

Aware of Seth's possessiveness toward him, John silently sought permission from Nita with his dark eyes. Magnanimously she nodded her consent.

"Since you're so determined to leave Texas, I guess I'll have to consider taking this pint-size hoyden off your hands," Jack teased. Immediately he jumped back from the table so that she couldn't kick his shins. Then he sneaked around and whispered something delightfully wicked in her ear.

Blushing, Laura Lee lightly pinched his arm for making such an outrageous suggestion. "Scoundrel!"

John tossed his head back and gave a loud hoot of laughter. "She'd got you pegged, little brother. I'd say you're a perfect pair—a scoundrel and a hoyden. What do you think, Nita?"

She cast a secretive smile at Laura Lee. "Didn't you win the Golden Parrot on the lucky turn of a card?"

"Yes," Laura Lee replied. "A full house beat two pair."

"I'd say your luck is running true to form, then. Only this time I think it's Jack who has the wild card that will decide who wins."

Laura Lee stared quizzically at Nita; she didn't have the vaguest idea of what she'd meant by her comment. Before she could open her mouth to question her, Jack pushed his chair and scooped her into his arms. Hooting with laughter, he whirled her around and around until they were both dizzy.

"Stop!" she gasped, feeling light-headed and slightly nauseated.

"Why don't you show her your cabin?" John suggested, winking at Nita. "I'm certain you'll be able to explain Laura Lee's winning hand to her."

Jack didn't need further encouragement or an excuse to carry her away from the ranch house. "Don't let anybody come looking for us. My future wife and I are going to be busy. Very, very busy!"

"Doing what?" she asked, waving at John and Nita, then curling her arms around his shoulders as her heart joyfully sang, Wife! Mrs. Jacob Bertram Wynthrop! His wife!

"Discussing the terms of the new Shannon-Wynthrop agreement. I want everything official, in writing—signed, sealed and delivered."

"No loopholes?" She nipped his earlobe with her sharp teeth.

"Uh-uh." It was more a groan than a reply.

"You mean 'uh-oh.'" Out of the corner of her eye she'd caught sight of several ranch hands crossing toward them. "We're about to have company. You'd better put me down."

Jack hissed one of the Captain's favorite phrases under his breath. "Can't they saddle-break those broncos without me? Quit squirming. I can't put you down. You and your skirt are the only things keeping me from blushing like some greenhorn who's eating dust after he's been thrown."

"Hey, bossman!" Slim, the ranch foreman, shouted. "You're headed in the wrong direction! You're needed up at the corral!"

"I need you more than they do," Laura Lee whispered.

"How come you're carryin' Miss Laura Lee? Seth said there'd been a ruckus up at the big house. She ain't hurt, is she?"

"Yes," she answered as Jack replied, "No."

"I mean no," she corrected as Jack said, "Yes."

He chuckled; she blushed.

Slim shoved his straw hat back on his head and gave them a bewildered look. "Which is it? Yes or no? Do I need to get the missus to fix her up?"

"Yes, she's got a few scrapes, but it's nothing I can't handle," Jack replied, frowning momentarily. After the hint Nita had given him, he was worried about Laura Lee's insides. She could be hurting and not know it. "You men go ahead. I'll be up at the corral later. If not, carry on without me."

He strode right past them while Laura Lee laughed softly and whispered. "Much, much later."

"Uh, Laura Lee, you aren't having stomach cramps or anything, are you?"

"No. Why?"

"That piece of cattle dung flattened you. No nausea?"

"Stop worrying, Jack." She'd never admit it, but she loved having him fussing over her. She particularly loved the feel of his hands splayed across her rib cage. "No broken ribs. No cracked skull. Believe me, once you kicked his gun out of his hand—"

"Which reminds me." His face grew stern. "The next time I disarm a man, you step back and let me knock him down. With you ramming him in the gut, I couldn't get a clear swing at him. He'd almost snatched you bald before I could sort through the tangle of legs and arms to get a grip on him. From here on out, *I'll* do your fighting for you."

"You're mighty bossy for a man who plans on negotiating a new pact."

"You may not like some of the new rules around here." Spurs jingling, he mounted the steps to the front porch of his cabin. "But, by damn, I'm going to enforce them for your own good."

Laura Lee grinned. "I've been known to be a mite stubborn when somebody lays down rules that I have to abide by." She reached back and opened the door. "You can put me down."

"Rule one—a man carries his bride over the threshold. It's traditional."

She locked her fingers behind his head and nodded, only too happy to be agreeable.

Jack kissed the tip of her nose and carried her inside, straight to his unmade bed. "You're sure you aren't feeling any aches and pains?"

"A few aches," she replied honestly, "but, like you told your men—nothing that you can't handle." She winked up at him when he gently placed her head on his pillow and removed his hand from beneath her knees. Tenaciously she held on to his shoulders. "I'm not certain I should negotiate from this . . . weakened position. You wouldn't take advantage of me, would you?"

"If you're asking whether or not I'm going to make love to you..." His black eyes danced with merriment when she slid one hand down to the buttons on his shirt and nimbly unfastened them.

"Yeah, I am."

"Want to hear what my father used to say when Mother asked him ridiculous questions?"

She nodded, tugging his shirt off his shoulders. "I imagine, since he was a true Southern gentleman, he'd say something terribly romantic."

"Well, he had been in Texas a few years," Jack said. In one lithe movement he stood, pivoted and pulled her booted foot between his knees. He felt her brace the sole of her other boot on his backside. He tugged; she pushed.

"I love hearing the sweet things a man says to the woman he loves. What'd he say?"

Jack tossed one boot on the wooden planks. She put her other boot between his knees and placed her stocking-clad foot on his rump.

He really wasn't in a safe position to be provoking her, but he couldn't resist.

"Is a bull's butt beef?"

Laura Lee reacted instantly by rocking forward, bracing herself on her elbows for leverage and kicking his tail end. "Scoundrel!"

Propelled forward, he dropped the boot, howling with laughter. "I've been deserving that for a long time. You did warn me about sticking my head in the sand and what you'd do to the part of my anatomy waving in the wind. I thought I might as well get it over with. Feel better?"

"Immensely."

"Now for the next time."

Jack crossed to his rolltop desk, occasionally glancing over his shoulder to keep an eye on her. She'd turned provocatively on her side, her body curved toward him, and began lazily unbuttoning her blouse.

"Are you certain you want to draw up an agreement now?" she crooned. "Actions do speak louder than words."

Reactions, Jack silently amended. His involuntary response to her being languidly stretched on his bed, purring like a kitten, was a major threat to his sterling intentions. The buttons of his trousers burrowed into his rigid flesh.

It took a strong man's determination to focus his attention on the document he'd been reading and re-reading ever since he'd returned to the ranch. He dipped his pen in the inkwell and scrawled his signature on the paper. He wanted everything perfectly legal after all this confusion. He pursed his lips and blew hard to ensure that the ink had dried before rolling it up.

Modesty had Laura Lee slipping beneath the sheet to make quick work of shedding her clothing. In broad daylight it seemed almost . . . well, indecent.

He turned around and slowly approached her. "I hope your reading rate has improved since I asked you to read your father's agreement," he said in a tight voice. "You don't have to read the whole thing. Just the bottom line."

The teasing light had gone out of his eyes, despite his bantering tone. She knew the rolled sheet of paper he held out to her was vitally important. She took it, held it for a moment, then slowly unrolled it.

Tears welled in her eyes from an inner spring of happiness. She looked up at him, her heart swelling in her chest with love for this dear, dear man.

He dropped to his knees beside the bed. "It's a wedding license. I got it while we were in Galveston. I knew I had to give John a chance, but deep in my heart I knew you were the only woman I'd ever want to wed. Will you marry me?"

Smiling, her chin wobbling with emotion, she placed the marriage license on the small table beside the bed. She held her arms up to him, saying, "Jacob Bertram Wynthrop, you're the right Wynthrop for me."

"Oh, Laura Lee, Laura Lee..." His hands framed her face. "Don't cry, love. I never meant to hurt you. I thought I'd die when Zeke Callum pointed his gun in our direction and you stepped in front of me."

"I know. I looked over my shoulder and couldn't tell who was going to throttle me first—you or him." Her smile strengthened; she bracketed his face with her hands. The muslin sheet fell to her waist unnoticed. "I couldn't let him hurt you any more than Nita could let him hurt John. I guess that's part of what love is...."

"And this is part of loving one another, too." His hand moved to cover her stomach. "You're going to have my baby."

"Lots of babies," Laura Lee promised, warmed through and through by the thought of filling the ranch house with blond-headed, black-eyed sons who had the same gentle arrogance as their father. "Maybe five or six."

Jack shook his head. "One child. I'd say about seven, maybe seven and a half, months from now."

"It takes nine months," she lovingly corrected him, her fingers lightly tweaking his mustache. "You can't boss Mother Nature around. She takes her own sweet time."

Jack gently pushed her shoulders into the pillow and leaned over her. "Remember Nita's comment about your winning the Golden Parrot with a *full* house. And do you remember her saying something about me having the wild card this time?"

"Yeah, but you had me twirling around in your arms before I could ask her what she meant." She locked her arms around his neck and pulled his head closer. "Do we have to talk about them . . . now?"

"We are talking about us . . . you . . . me . . . and the baby you're carrying here." His hand had remained firmly on the rounded swell of her abdomen. "You must have gotten pregnant that night at the Golden Parrot."

"Oh!" Her face flamed at the thought of her own ignorance.

"Oh," Jack repeated. Wondering what was going on in that pretty little head of hers, he asked, "Hasn't anyone talked to you about being with child?"

"Doc Wainwright talked to me about a man and a woman making babies...sticks and circles and itching and scratching, but . . ."

Silently her mind ticked off the scant bits of information Cactus Flower had given her. Her eyes widened; her face turned as red as the inside of a watermelon. She hadn't had her bothersome monthly flow. She'd been too preoccupied with Jack to miss it!

"Thank goodness Doc Wainwright didn't get that far. He delivers babies throughout the parish, but he'd probably have told you he found them under a baby bush!"

"A baby!" She'd barely heard what Jack had been saying. "Oh, Jack! How wonderful! We're going to have a baby! I'm going to be a mother in—" her mathematical ability came to her aid "—December!"

Pleased that she was excited about having his child, Jack said, "I can't think of a better Christmas present."

"I love you, I love you, I love you," she told him, tightening the circle of love her arms made around his neck. Another thought occurred to her, a thought that made her loosen her arms and push him back. "Is it okay to make love?"

Jack chuckled, nuzzling her slender neck. "I thought you'd never ask. Yes, sweet love. It's more than okay. Kiss me?"

Aware that she was completely undressed and that Jack wasn't, she murmured against his lips, "What about your boots?"

"My boots?"

"Umm. Those leather things on your feet that have spurs on them? B-O-O-T-S."

He painted her lips with his. "The hoyden not only is a genius at arithmetic and reading . . . she can spell, too. Not to mention . . ."

"Boots. Belt. Britches," she said, listing the only barriers between them and ecstasy. "Should I take them off for you?"

The mere thought of her straddling his leg and tugging on his boot while he had his foot on that well-shaped derriere of hers was enough to propel him off the bed. They'd been intimate before, but he would never in this life be able to explain why he had to recover *before* they made love!

Content for the moment to lie in the center of his bed, smiling, as she watched him rip at his buttons, shuck down his pants, then hop from one foot to the other while wrestling with his boots, she let her hand trail over her stomach.

He'd taught her so many wonderful things, this wonderful man of hers. Before she'd been jerked from the saddle on the river road she'd never known such complete happiness. She fairly glowed from within.

This is love, she mused happily.

He turned around and came to her, strong and proud, as he had when they'd first made love. Nothing about him was strange or unfamiliar. When he lay down beside her she curved against him as though it were the most natural thing in the world to do.

"Someday, Mrs. Jack Wynthrop—" he sighed with pleasure against her temple "—after we've been married for thirty or forty years, I'll be able to get undressed without making a spectacle of myself."

His hand shimmied over the fingers resting on his jaw to her delicate wrist and on down to the sweet curve of her shoulder. He'd never known that desire and peace could inhabit the same body. His hand moved slowly down her rib cage to her waist.

"That's the same day I'll be sitting in the rocking chair with our grandchildren instead of waiting for you naked beneath the covers like a hussy."

One side of his mouth raised to form that heart-stopping smile of his. "Did I ever tell you why I never married?"

"Uh-uh. Why?"

"I liked willing, wanton women—notice I used the past tense. I mistakenly believed a Southern belle would be as prim and stiff as the petticoats she wore." His hand skittered over her hip. "You're tiny, but you're a whole lot of woman...with a thousand disguises that make you a never ending mystery. You can be innocent and ladylike or hot-tempered and a tiny bit bawdy. You're everything I dreamed of and felt certain didn't exist."

The tips of their noses touched, and still their eyes devoured each other.

"Did I tell you that your eyes remind me of Texas bluebonnets?"

Her hips arched closer to him. Her fingers brushed his sun-bleached sideburns. "No," she whispered, her breath mingling with his. "Yours are so black, like the centers of black-eyed Susans."

"Wildflowers, both of them. They bloom where other flowers can't survive."

"Neither of us is exactly faint of heart," she whispered dryly, smiling as her lips met his and her eyes closed.

His kiss tasted sweeter than sugarcane. It tasted of love and happiness and the promise of a glorious future. Greedily she savored the long-denied flavor.

He touched her breasts, weighing them in his hands, wondering if they'd change in the coming months as she grew heavy with his child. Something stirred inside him at the knowledge that he'd be with her each night to watch those changes.

She murmured his name as his wet tongue laved the tip, then suckled, tongued, then suckled again. She rocked against him, clinging, immersed in the pleasurable sensations.

I love you, Jack, she silently screamed. There were no reasons to hold back her heart's glad tidings.

"I love you, Jack! I'll never regret anything as long as I'm with you."

He trembled, as much from what she'd said as from her hand as it curled around him, stroking his flesh, loving him without innocence or inhibition. Unable to withstand another moment of the exquisite torment, he moved toward her.

He entered her slowly, with great reverence, as though she were sacred to him.

She drew him deep within her womanly heat. No longer a girl, only a woman, she rhythmically circled her hips to the beat of each thrust. The beat of her heart kept time, going faster and faster and faster, until it seemed to burst, engulfing her in the wondrous knowledge that he was hers completely.

She held his head between her breasts and smiled. She knew that for them there would be no endings, only beginnings.

Epilogue

"Can you see him?" Fairly dancing on tiptoe, Laura Lee bobbed and weaved to see around the others waiting for the steamer's passengers to disembark. She waved her ruffled silk parasol at the curly-headed boy dashing along the ship's railing. "There he is! Tad!"

Amusement tilted Jack's mustache. His wife of four months was a wellspring of joy to him. He pointed to a man with a youngster perched on his shoulders. "Want me to give you a boost?"

"No! He's coming! Tad! Over here!"

Unable to resist teasing her, Jack faked a groan as he lifted her onto a small wooden crate, bringing her face level with his. "Maybe he doesn't recognize you."

Laura Lee held on to the crown of her straw hat, which was decorated with magnolias, and glanced down at her pink dress. Her waistline had expanded by a fraction of an inch, but hardly enough to make her unrecognizable.

One glance at the merriment centered in her husband's black eyes had her giggling with delight. Most men wanted their pregnant wives cloistered until they gave birth. Jack, the proud papa-to-be, wanted everyone to notice. She belonged to him, and he wanted everyone to know it.

"Watch out, brother," John warned, grinning and clapping his brother on the back. "That new parasol you bought her is going to look like an Indian arrow shot through the crown of your new Stetson."

Caught up in the gaiety and the excitement, Nita asked, "Is that him? The boy running down the gangplank?"

"Sis!"

"Help me down, Jack!"

"Uh-uh." His arm held her in place. "I know what happens when two speeding locomotives crash head-on." He lifted his hat and waved it in a high arc. "Tad!"

Annoyed by his overprotectiveness, she repeated the first words she'd said the night they'd met. "Put me down!"

He clung to her waist as tenaciously as he had when he'd been astride his horse. "I'm saving you from harm."

"About like the way I saved you?" John asked him. "Let her go."

"I'm letting you go," Jack retorted. "That's my quota of letting go for one day."

Laura Lee squirmed impatiently. She draped her arm across her husband's shoulders and watched her brother make a beeline straight for them. Her heart felt as though it would burst with happiness.

How lucky could one woman be? she wondered. Having Tad, Jack and, in the near future, a baby was better than being dealt a royal flush!

Tad ran full tilt until his arms wrapped around Jack's legs and his head rammed against Jack's flat stomach. He's growing fast, Jack thought, wrapping his arms around the boy's shoulders and giving him a swift hug.

"Thanks for letting me come live with you!" Tad beamed with pleasure up at his sister. "My gosh, sis! You've grown a foot!"

"Jack told me I would," she quipped, sliding down Jack's side, bending forward and opening her arms. She remembered how it embarrassed Tad to have his sister hugging him in public and reconciled herself to holding him at arm's length. "Let me look at you."

Tad threw his arms around her neck and gave her a mighty hug. "I missed you something awful, sis. Blythewood was boring after you left."

"I missed you, too, sweetheart." Her arms circled him and drew him tightly against her breasts. She couldn't stem the tears of happiness brimming in her eyes. "I'm so glad you're here."

Jack watched the touching reunion, then turned his eyes toward John. "I'll miss you, big brother."

"The same here, Jack."

"Are you sure you don't want to stay at the ranch?"

Shaking his head, John replied dryly, "You don't give up easily, do you?"

"No," Jack admitted. Chuckling, he added, "But this time it won't take a crazy bull and a wheelchair to make me change my mind. Any man who can get back on his feet in less than two months has the stamina to rebuild Heavenly Acres."

John gathered his bride to his side. "I've got somebody to lean on in case of emergency. Don't worry, little brother, I'm going home . . . where I belong."

"Yeah, but I hate to think of you fighting my battles." Jack worried about the underhanded tricks the banker might pull on his brother. "I should have gone back and taken care of Luke Reynolds once and for all."

Stepping back from his sister's arms, Tad jerked on Jack's hand. "Luke Reynolds is missing."

"Missing?" Laura Lee repeated. "You mean missing like Beau?"

Tad nodded his head. "Uh-huh."

Stunned, Laura Lee asked, "What happened to him?"

"Doc Wainwright was at the general store saying something about . . . poetry . . . poet . . ."

"Poetic justice?" Jack supplied.

"Yeah! That's it. Doc said it was poetic justice for a man who'd chased the almighty dollar all his life to drown diving in the Mississippi while searching for a sunken boat carrying a Yankee gold shipment. They never did find his body, so he's missing, huh?"

Laura Lee nodded. "What about Betsy Mae?"

"She's running the bank. Doc says she's there late every night counting her money."

"And Brandy?" Laura Lee asked, anxious to catch up on all the news. "She wrote and said there was a special man in her life. She was *very* mysterious."

Tad grinned. "Mr. Glidden. He's real nice, sis. But talk about mysterious. He says he's got an invention that's gonna revol . . . revolution . . ."

"Revolutionalize?"

"Yeah, sis, that's the word. He's gonna revolutionize the whole West."

Jack grinned. "What's he invented? A new breed of cattle?"

"He won't talk about it, cause he says some ranchers aren't gonna like it. But Brandy thinks he's wonderful, even if he is from up North." He grabbed Jack by the hand. "What's the secret present you promised in your letter? Do I get it now?"

"Mind your manners, Tad," Laura Lee said affectionately. "It's waiting for you back at the buggy."

His head snapped around; his feet were already itching to move. "Can we go? Huh? Can we?"

Chuckling, Jack scooped him up and placed him squarely on his shoulders. "I don't want you running off and getting lost. Why don't you see if you can spot the carriage from up here?"

"They all look alike!" Tad complained.

"Don't you see the one with an old friend of yours on the front seat?" Laughing at her brother's impatience, she pointed to the left down the cobblestone street. "Look that way."

"Oh! Wow! You brought Captain Bligh!"

"Yes," Laura Lee answered. "And I taught him to say something special."

"Put me down! Please! I won't get lost! I promise!"

As Jack hoisted him off his shoulders and set him on the ground, Laura Lee watched them both. Pride and joy shone in her eyes. She snuggled her hand in the crook of Jack's arm.

"You two go ahead," John said, raising the gold-handled cane that Jack had given him as a farewell gift. "We'll be right behind you."

Arm in arm, a happy smile on her face and a cocky grin on his, Laura Lee and Jack followed Tad.

"Awwwk!"

"Oh, my gosh!" Tad stood with his mouth hanging open, staring at the palomino gelding tied behind the carriage. An orange saddle, decorated with sterling silver and just his size, was perched on the horse's back. Over the saddle horn was draped a small replica of Jack's holster that contained a handcarved wooden pistol. "Is it for me?"

"Yep," Jack drawled, like a true Texan. "But I'd better formally introduce you. Hold your hand out in front of his foreleg, would you? Meet your new owner, Tad Shannon."

Obediently the horse raised its hoof as though it were shaking hand.

"Wow! Did you name him?"

"I thought I'd leave that privilege up to you."

Tad put the horse's foreleg down; his brow puckered. "He needs a real good name, huh?"

Jack unhooked the holster from the saddle horn while Laura Lee retrieved Captain Bligh, who'd started to raise a ruckus.

"Awwwk. Preeetty lady."

Tad's frown vanished. He gave his new horse one more thoughtful look, then skipped over to his sister's side. "Hiya, Captain."

"Come on, Captain, that's not what I taught you to say," Laura Lee chided.

The parrot whistled shrilly. Then, clear as the summer day overhead, he said, "Happy family! Happy family! Awwwk! I love you!"

"That's it!" Tad shouted, his voice full of glee, as he wrapped his arms around Jack and his sister. "I'm naming my horse Happy...'cause that's how I feel. Aw, Captain! You're the smartest bird in the whole wide world! I've never been happier."

Laura Lee hugged her brother and smiled as she gazed up at her husband. "I couldn't have said it better myself. Happy family. I love you."

The Captain spread his wings, snapped his beak, looked straight at Tad...and winked.

* * * * *

Harlequin Historicals®

PASSPORT TO ROMANCE SWEEPSTAKES RULES

1 **HOW TO ENTER:** To enter, you must be the age of majority and complete the official entry form, or print your name, address, telephone number and age on a plain piece of paper and mail to: Passport to Romance, P.O Box 9056, Buffalo, NY 14269-9056. No mechanically reproduced entries accepted.
2. All entries must be received by the CONTEST CLOSING DATE, DECEMBER 31, 1990 TO BE ELIGIBLE.
3. **THE PRIZES:** There will be ten (10) Grand Prizes awarded, each consisting of a choice of a trip for two people from the following list·
   i) London, England (approximate retail value $5,050 U.S.)
   ii) England, Wales and Scotland (approximate retail value $6,400 U.S.)
   iii) Carribean Cruise (approximate retail value $7,300 U.S.)
   iv) Hawaii (approximate retail value $9,550 U.S.)
   v) Greek Island Cruise in the Mediterranean (approximate retail value $12,250 U.S.)
   vi) France (approximate retail value $7,300 U.S.)
4. Any winner may choose to receive any trip or a cash alternative prize of $5,000.00 U.S. in lieu of the trip.
5. **GENERAL RULES:** Odds of winning depend on number of entries received.
6. A random draw will be made by Nielsen Promotion Services, an independent judging organization, on January 29, 1991, in Buffalo, NY, at 11.30 a.m. from all eligible entries received on or before the Contest Closing Date.
7 Any Canadian entrants who are selected must correctly answer a time-limited, mathematical skill-testing question in order to win.
8. Full contest rules may be obtained by sending a stamped, self-addressed envelope to: "Passport to Romance Rules Request", P O Box 9998, Saint John, New Brunswick, Canada E2L 4N4.
9 Quebec residents may submit any litigation respecting the conduct and awarding of a prize in this contest to the Régie des loteries et courses du Québec.
10. Payment of taxes other than air and hotel taxes is the sole responsibility of the winner.
11 Void where prohibited by law

COUPON BOOKLET OFFER TERMS

To receive your Free travel-savings coupon booklets, complete the mail-in Offer Certificate on the preceeding page, including the necessary number of proofs-of-purchase, and mail to: Passport to Romance, P.O. Box 9057, Buffalo, NY 14269-9057 The coupon booklets include savings on travel-related products such as car rentals, hotels, cruises, flowers and restaurants. Some restrictions apply The offer is available in the United States and Canada. Requests must be postmarked by January 25, 1991 Only proofs-of-purchase from specially marked "Passport to Romance" Harlequin® or Silhouette® books will be accepted. The offer certificate must accompany your request and may not be reproduced in any manner. Offer void where prohibited or restricted by law LIMIT FOUR COUPON BOOKLETS PER NAME, FAMILY, GROUP, ORGANIZATION OR ADDRESS. Please allow up to 8 weeks after receipt of order for shipment. Enter quickly as quantities are limited. Unfulfilled mail-in offer requests will receive free Harlequin® or Silhouette® books (not previously available in retail stores), in quantities equal to the number of proofs-of-purchase required for Levels One to Four, as applicable.

PR-SWPS

OFFICIAL SWEEPSTAKES ENTRY FORM

Complete and return this Entry Form immediately—the more Entry Forms you submit, the better your chances of winning!

- Entry Forms must be received by **December 31, 1990**
- A random draw will take place on **January 29, 1991**
- Trip must be taken by **December 31, 1991**

3-HH-2-SW

YES, I want to win a PASSPORT TO ROMANCE vacation for two! I understand the prize includes round-trip air fare, accommodation and a daily spending allowance.

Name____________________

Address____________________

City__________ State__________ Zip__________

Telephone Number__________ Age______

Return entries to: **PASSPORT TO ROMANCE**, P.O Box 9056, Buffalo, NY 14269-9056

COUPON BOOKLET/OFFER CERTIFICATE

Item	LEVEL ONE Booklet 1	LEVEL TWO Booklet 1 & 2	LEVEL THREE Booklet 1, 2 & 3	LEVEL FOUR Booklet 1, 2, 3 & 4
Booklet 1 = $100+	$100+	$100+	$100+	$100+
Booklet 2 = $200+		$200+	$200+	$200+
Booklet 3 = $300+			$300+	$300+
Booklet 4 = $400+				$400+
Approximate Total Value of Savings	$100+	$300+	$600+	$1,000+
# of Proofs of Purchase Required	4	6	12	18
Check One	____	____	____	____

Name____________________

Address____________________

City__________ State__________ Zip__________

Return Offer Certificates to: **PASSPORT TO ROMANCE**, P.O. Box 9057, Buffalo, NY 14269-9057

Requests must be postmarked by **January 25, 1991**

ONE PROOF OF PURCHASE

3-HH-2

To collect your free coupon booklet you must include the necessary number of proofs-of-purchase with a properly completed Offer Certificate

See previous page for details